GW00726038

A Lasting Impression

One Boy's Wartime in the Country

Michael Dundrow

The Book Castle

First published 1981 by New Horizons

This edition – revised, reset and illustrated
with drawings and photographs –
first published November 1988
by
The Book Castle
12, Church Street
Dunstable
Bedfordshire, LU5 4RU

Reprinted 1989 (twice)
Reprinted 1990

© Michael Dundrow 1988

With thanks to Margaret Dundrow for her line drawings
and village sketchmap.
Photographs belong to the author and to Guy Henley,
Eric Holmes and Doug Swain whose kind co-operation
is gratefully acknowledged.

ISBN 1 871199 00 X

Printed and bound by Antony Rowe Ltd., Chippenham

All rights reserved

**Cover designed from a specially commissioned painting
by Joan Schneider**

CONTENTS

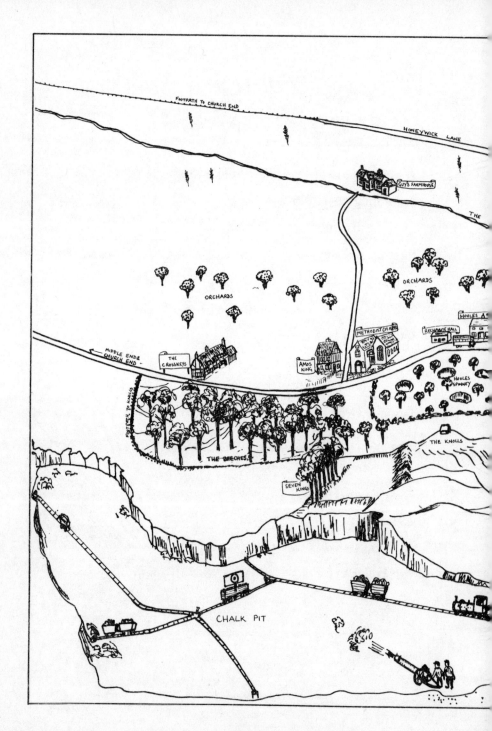

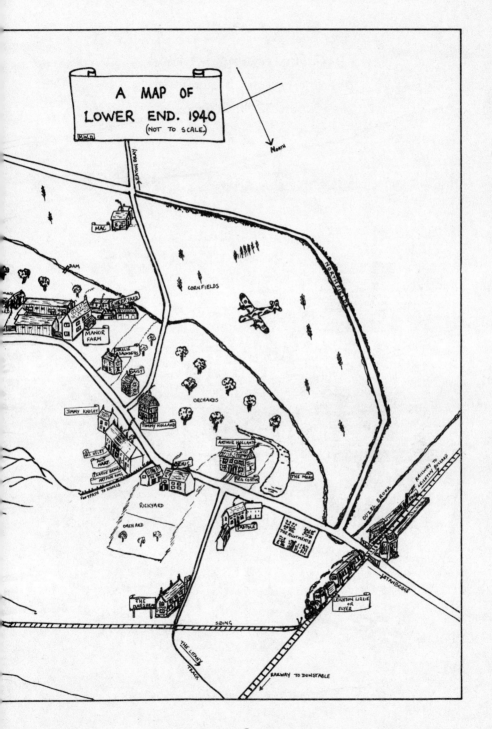

A MAP OF LOWER END. 1940 (NOT TO SCALE)

NORTH

EATON BRAY

MAC

DAM

VINEYARD

CORNFIELDS

NORTHALL RD

MANOR FARM

DOLLIE SAUNDERS

DAISY

JIMMY KNIGHT

TOMMY HOLLAND

ORCHARDS

MRS HELEY AUNTY MARY

ARTHUR HOLLAND

GEORGE BARBER ARTHUR KING

FOOTPATH TO KNOLLS

GRID

REG COSTIN

THE MOAT

RAILWAY TO LEIGHTON BUZZARD

OUTL. BROOK

RICKYARD

ORCHARD

MASPOLE

THE ALLOTMENTS

STANBRIDGE

THE MARSHES

SIDING

THE LITANY TRACK

LEIGHTON LIZZIE OR FLYER

RAILWAY TO DUNSTABLE

To all my Totternhoe friends,
past and present, I affectionately
dedicate these pages.

Designed by Milford Graphics for the jacket of the first edition

Chapter I

Stumbling into Eden

The bus squealed to a halt in a cloud of chalky dust. "Lower End," called the conductress looking meaningfully in our direction. We rose, my mother, my five-year-old sister and myself, hastily grabbed our assortment of battered luggage and scrambled off, almost emptying the great double decker. The bus pulled away, rounded the corner and disappeared down a long gentle slope among a forest of plum trees. Above our heads the laden branches leaned low over a roadside iron fence, each one weighty with fruit that was powdered with the lightest bloom of summer blue.

We stood on the pavement with sun baked cows' droppings at our feet and peered around at the strange new rural world we had entered. Eyes and ears brought up exclusively on the blackened brick and incessant clamour of London's East End felt somehow ill at ease in all that green and empty silence as the comforting sound of the bus died away. Nothing stirred on the dusty road. We seemed to be the only living creatures in that lush and drowsy landscape. There was nobody to meet us though we were expected and we had no idea which way to go. My mother looked again at the address she had on a crumpled paper. Suddenly from a gateway some way ahead, where cottages peeped through trees, there was a loud shout and my two cousins Aud and Doug came shooting out. "Phew, sorry we're late!" gasped Aud as they rushed up. "Girls," grumbled Doug, "I told her I could hear the bus coming but would she hurry?"

So we arrived in the village and reached our destination, a tiny mid-terraced cottage at the top of a long, gently inclined path flanked by gooseberry and blackcurrant bushes. Here, deep in rural Bedfordshire my aunt would endeavour to give us sanctuary from the ceaseless bombing of London. It was 1940 and I was just twelve and we had endured all the terror we could take, we had to get out. This was a year after the start of the war and the official mass evacuation of children from London. Most of these evacuees had returned home, so quiet had that first year been, but now that bombs were raining from the sky night and day there was a mad rush to get away on an unofficial, go-where-you-could basis. A Cockney family with few relatives beyond the sound of Bow Bells, we were very lucky in having my aunt to run to. They were Londoners like us and had been evacuated to the village but they had hung on during all that quiet first period – the phoney war.

Whilst my aunt sat with my mother over the first of many cups of tea in that cosy, cluttered, low-ceilinged room, my cousins whisked me off to see the village sights. Olive, my sister, was conveniently left at home as likely to be bothersome. Aud was about my age and Doug a few years younger; we knew each other well from before the war, got along fine and were more like friends than mere family. Back down onto the dusty road again we three wandered and this time there was activity. A farm cart piled high with bristling sheaves was rattling along at a smart pace pulled by a sweating mare, which in turn was led by a scruffy, cheerful boy of about my age. The load swayed as it went by us, the near wheel clipped the grass verge, and the top brushed against the overhanging trees leaving a trail of golden straws in the branches.

"You'll have it off, you idiot!" yelled Doug to the boy, who just grinned back in reply.

"Who's he?" I asked.

"Works for Costins," said Doug, adding mysteriously, "He's a Church Ender."

"Oh," I said, no wiser.

We walked along, chewing straws, nothing else of interest visible on the road, only a cottage or two here and there and another big orchard, its trees too, heavy with plums, leaning at all angles above lush grass.

"What's it like here?" I asked with a clear hint of big city condescension in my tone.

"Not bad," said Doug in similar vein.

"It's smashing, Mick," said Aud earnestly. "You wait and see. Much better than London isn't it Doug?"

"Well," said Doug kicking a stone, "depends."

We walked on. The road a hundred yards ahead forked in front of a crescent of council houses. It felt odd walking in the road with no pavement available, only a wide uncut grass verge. Grass so far, had been for me something strictly for keeping off in parks. I remember looking around at the few cottages, the masses of trees, the hedges and the orchards and the empty road with the same bemused air of wonderment that I would at some enchanted fairyland to which I had miraculously been spirited away. And with the same disbelief. It was all so different from my crowded streets, brick and mortar canyons, jostling pavements, traffic chaos and ceaseless noise. It was all unreal this peaceful, green and virtually deserted village. It was all some trick, a spell that surely must soon be broken. I'd wake up in a minute in the middle of a boisterous game of street football with a tin can for ball.

8

Honest, Mick," Aud was saying with enthusiasm, "you're going to love this place. I know it somehow. Let's go up on the Knolls first. We have some great fun up there don't we Doug?"

"Yeah," said Doug, catching her enthusiasm and abandoning his diffidence. "It's smashing for chasing. We have two sides and you have to track down the other side and there's lots of places to hide. Aud, I wonder if Mick can fight Eric Holmes?"

"Yes, easy," laughed Aud loyally.

I accepted this compliment without comment, squaring my shoulders at the imagined foe and seeing him already as a pathetic, cringing heap with blackened eye and bloody nose.

We turned up a little lane alongside an ancient black, tarred barn on top of which sat a line of swallows twittering about their imminent departure south. Immense banks of nettles bristled menacingly alongside the barn and grass and wayside plants grew in rampant frenzy.

"Hey Mick, did you know, nettles won't sting this month?" asked Aud standing in front of a few thousand of them.

"Oh, don't they?" I said, surprised. Even I knew about nettles.

"No," butted in Doug. "Look." He grasped a nettle leaf between thumb and finger. "No sting, see."

"Try it," invited Aud, "they really don't sting this month, honest."

I stretched out a fearful hand to a plant and brushed a leaf tentatively, drawing back like lightning on making contact but not before I was well and truly stung on the fingers. "Ouch!" I looked round reproachfully at my cousins. They were laughing their heads off. "They don't sting this month," repeated Aud deliberately, "but they do sting you. Get it?"

I got it. "You wait, I'll get you for that," I threatened darkly, more hurt by being fooled than by being stung.

"Look, here's a dock leaf!" exclaimed Doug. Rub that on, it'll stop the stinging. No, it's all right I swear. Cross my heart and hope to die. I'll show you my secret way of touching nettles," he went on by way of consolation and he again pinched a leaf firmly between thumb and forefinger. "Doesn't sting, see." I took the information in for future use but declined to practice, not wishing to tempt those vicious country plants into more attacks, and went on rubbing the dock leaf on the mass of little white spots stinging away on my fingers.

Soon the lane, rutted and running upwards between high hedges, showed the solid white of chalk beneath. We turned off through a gap in the hedge and I found myself staring at a broad grassy slope that rose gently before us. Some way above and beyond reared the white streaked slopes of a steep hill rising like the ramparts of some solid fortress to a broad flat summit. All this had been invisible from the road though I had been aware of rising ground behind my aunt's cottage.

We crossed the lower slopes, darting about like prowling tigers in the yellow grass which stood shoulder high and which was dotted here and there with hawthorn bushes. Large anthills generously topped with rabbits' droppings lurked to trip the unwary. Next in our upward progress we came to a mass of deep pits and high mounds stretching away in all directions where the grass was short, the soil thin and patches of chalk were visible everywhere. It was rather like a shell-torn battlefield softened by time and nature. Pathways wound around and between these hills and hollows where more small hawthorn bushes were dotted about and I didn't need telling that this was the tracking ground where all the fun was to be had.

"See what I mean Mick?" said Aud with a proprietary sweep of her arm.

It was a truly amazing place, the result perhaps of long forgotten quarrying, or, as some said, of archaeological excavation, though what could have been sought was a mystery. Aud and Doug threaded their way tortuously through this hilly maze, pointing out their favourite features with the casual air of ownership. I took in the scene with rapid glances here and there, giving little away, acting as if such marvels were my everyday lot in the East End.

We sampled some of the hills and pits and found them pretty good. A few yards, a curving path, and you'd exchanged one world for another and who could tell what you might encounter around each new bend? A short sharp climb and you were a mountaineer atop your own peak. A quick rush and slither and you were on your way to the centre of the earth. I was cautious at first as if running over grass might be dangerous or difficult, but my feet and legs knew at once they had been made for such work. It was exhilarating that first taste of those strange hills, it whetted the appetite for more, an appetite that once roused never became jaded but remained as keen and fresh as on that first day's encounter.

Having crossed this turbulent area we came to the foot of the huge chalk rampart that rose steeply before us, sheer up to the sky it seemed to me. We started up and it was like climbing the side wall of the world. My left hand touched the solid earth as I climbed bent over, my right stretched out towards the far horizon. As we climbed we looked down on a thick mantle of beech trees that hid the lower slopes further round the hill.

But it was into the distance that my eyes probed with greatest interest as I stopped for breath half way up. The village was invisible below the hill but stretching out beyond its borders lay a broad, flat vale carpeted with harvest fields, green meadows and the dark patchwork of orchards with greenhouses shimmering in sunlight like golden lakes and the whole vale set with clustering villages unnamed as yet for me. I was looking down on a vast tapestry of intricate design whose fringes were the bold chalk escarpment that rose some miles away to rival our own chalk hill, and a further off line of wooded hills that melted into the hazy blue distance. I had never in my life seen so far in a single glance. Surely the greater part of England lay down there before my eyes. I narrowed those eyes to slits and searched but couldn't quite make out the sea.

When we got to the very top I saw there was a small pimple of a knoll capping

Totternhoe Knolls "The Sledging Pit". Our slightly less renowned version of the famous Cresta Run.

View from the Knolls as it is today.
There was only the odd small tree and bush on those lower slopes, now densely covered, and of course the elms are all gone from the hedgerows.

the great rampart in the centre and on top of that sat a dugout, timber framed, sandbagged and steel-roofed.

"It belongs to the Home Guard," said Aud, "but they're not often here."

We raced over and occupied it after raking the inside with a few bursts of machine gun fire through the wall slits and lobbing in a cluster of chalk grenades for good measure. With the wind through those lookout slits watering my eyes I suddenly knew what it felt like to be an Alexander or a Napoleon in my command post high above the battle, deploying my troops on the plain below and controlling the battle in masterly style. It was certainly a magnificent observation post and if the German panzers had come rolling in from any point of the compass the local Home Guard would have had a grandstand view. That dugout was to play a vital role in our many campaigns across those hills and if we had thought about it I suppose we would have been very grateful to the Home Guard for providing it for us and for leaving us more or less undisturbed in our tenancy.

As we went on Aud explained that this wasn't the first time this high chalk hill had been prepared for defence. Just below the top knoll on the far side was a large rectangular and perfectly flat field that fell away steeply at the edge in most places, the site so it was said of an ancient castle. The whole great chalk hill itself I learnt later was properly called Castle Hill, though everyone called it just The Knolls; when or if a castle stood there and who occupied it I never discovered but there was a great ditch across one end of the flat field where the ground, instead of falling sharply away slopes more gently and would have needed some defence. Also seven magnificent beech trees standing in a row above the ditch were called the Seven Kings, perhaps after some pre-historic local chieftains whose memory lived long in folklore. In the months and years ahead whenever we crossed that field at dusk with the wind rustling the beeches and combing the long grass, it was easy to see those rough hilltop ancestors armed to the teeth, patrolling their pallisades peering about ferociously for enemies.

We only went as far as the top knoll that first day. I felt as though I was on the roof of the world. As far round the immediate vicinity as I could see there were woods and slopes, thickets and stretches of open grassland to explore. The wind blew freely and the views were limitless. It was heady stuff to one who had left teeming London only hours before. Though knowing nothing outside the East End I felt sure I had chanced upon a very special place, here was atmosphere, character, adventure. No room for city type boredom now.

"Come on we'd better get back," said Aud reluctantly, "it must be tea-time."

We went down the steep slope at breakneck speed, hurtling over the ankle-breaking surface like gazelles before running out onto the level and plunging once more into the maze of little hills. By the time we got down onto the road I suppose I had been in the village about an hour yet already I felt at home. Without thinking about it I was immediately at one with the spirit of the place and seemed to come not as a stranger, but as one rediscovering a familiar scene of long ago.

Back in the cottage once again there wasn't much exploration to be done. It was just a two-up two-down place, the sort of dwelling that farm workers had for generations reared large families in. Down was mostly a largish living room with a beam across it that an average man had to duck to avoid, the same with the stable doorway. Walls thick enough for a small fortress, low ceilings and small windows made it cosy and attractive. A tiny kitchen was tacked on the back whilst upstairs consisted of two small bedrooms where all six of us were somehow going to have to be packed in to sleep.

That first evening far from London there was no risk of the three refugees feeling homesick with Aunt Marj in command. She was so jolly and cheerful that the small cottage glowed with good humour and we sat down to a lively tea of jokes and jelly and cake. After tea we had a lively sing song around the old harmonium with Aunt Marj playing and the rest of us bawling raucously. Then there was a knock on the door and Mrs Brooks popped in from next door to borrow a cupful of sugar. "It's baking a cake I am for Charlie's tea," she exclaimed in her sing song Welsh accent. The sugar was willingly loaned and we were all introduced, as was Mrs Brooks' young daughter Joyce peeping over the lower half of the stable door.

Later, as dusk fell, Aud and Doug took me out for a last walk. Bats wheeled above us in the silence of the empty road, on the western horizon slatey blue clouds were piled in gold fringed heaps. Behind the blacked out windows of the cottages that we passed sat the unknown children and adults who were soon to become my friends and the pillars supporting my new life in the village, but my thoughts on that first nightfall were of the strange quietness, the deep dark shadows of tree and barn and the fluttering bats that ushered in my first night in the country.

Chapter II

Uncle Alf's Initiative

When I woke next morning it was to find the room flooded with light from the sun glaring through the tiny white-painted window. The whitewashed ceiling, white woodwork and door made the room vibrate with a light that was so clean and pure it was almost tangible. I was at the bottom of a double bed next to Olive, feet pointing towards the head where Aud and Doug were still asleep, four of us in the one bed. I could hear voices from the tiny kitchen downstairs. My mother and Aunt Marj were up and must have tiptoed through our room to descend the twisting stairs that led down from the corner. I had actually slept the whole night through for the first time in weeks.

I rubbed the sleep from my eyes and yawned, stretched and kicked someone at the other end of the bed. Doug grunted and tossed about. I craned my neck up to see if he was awake but he was doing his best to retain a hold on sleep. I relaxed and let my eyes wander around. The room was so small that the double bed almost filled it. It was tight against the wall on one side with just a narrow space the other side near the stairs. The floorboards dipped and rose in a gentle swell and the ceiling undulated in sympathy a little way above my upstretched arm. I wondered how far I could stretch my feet. Yes, I might just reach the pillow at the far end if I slid down a bit. I tried it again.

"Phew!" cried Aud, "what's that stink! Hey, cut it out," and she sat bolt upright, grabbed her pillow and brought it down with a great thump on my head.

I giggled. "Right," I yelled and snatched my pillow, sat up and lashed out at Aud, missed and hit Doug. He groaned and buried himself deeper in the bedclothes.

Aud got in a smart whack on me, then the bed convulsed as we sprang to our knees to get more force into blows which fell like thunder drops.

"Oi, pack it in," grumbled Doug sitting up at last, all attempt at sleep abandoned.

"Aw, shut up!" snapped Aud pushing her pillow hard into his face and taking a massive blow from me as she did so.

"Right, you've asked for it," growled Doug with grim determination. For the next two or three minutes it was bedlam with three flailing pillows, feathers flying like a snowstorm, heaving and swaying bodies, shrieks, grunts and protesting bed springs. Olive woke up and lay on her back watching, quite unperturbed by the mayhem around her.

"What are you up to up there?" came Aunt Marj's voice echoing from downstairs. "You'll have the ceiling down if you go on like that."

"We subsided, sated with battle, faces in pillows to stifle the laughter. Aunt Marj's step was on the stairs. "I'm surprised at you two," she accused Aud and Doug, "you should know better."

"Aud pointed at me in mock fury. "What about him?" she said, "he started it."

But her mother had already turned to go back downstairs. "It's not fair," said Aud, "visitors never get the blame." In another moment or two we got up in fine fettle for another fun-packed day.

We were as snug as rats in a barley rick in that little cottage. Its cosy intimacy suited us children down to the ground. For one thing there was no bathroom so we got away with minimal washing, a highly desirable state of affairs for any boy and one that I had natural leanings towards. Then, they were so good hearted, Aud and Doug, so boisterous and lively, so ready for fun, we got on unbelievably well, sharing our lives wholeheartedly and unreservedly as only children can. We seemed continually to set each other off on an interminable round of laughter and mild mischief and fun of every description, for all of which we had an insatiable appetite.

It would have been heaven to have gone on living like that but it must have been quite otherwise for our mothers. It wasn't the age-old trouble of two women not being able to share the same kitchen, the sisters were on too good terms for that. It was more the fact that you could hardly turn round in the kitchen anyway. Convenient perhaps for a family of two or three but difficult when you double that number. Four lively and untidy children in that small space created chaos or would have done if Aunt Marj hadn't taken a firm but good humoured line with us. Luckily the weather was fine, day after day of sunshine, so we spent a great deal of time out of doors.

Then after a few days my Uncle Alf came down for some leave from the Metropolitan Police and things became really congested. One large policeman practically filled the cottage on his own, the other six of us had to slip by where we could. Quite obviously things couldn't go on like that for long, though we children weren't pressing for change, indeed we weren't aware that there was a problem, we were too busy enjoying ourselves. Neither could we go back to London. That was impossible for even there in the village we saw the nightly flashes from far over the horizon and heard the occasional distant rumble, fainter than a dying thunderstorm, but unmistakeable as the audible and visible evidence of London's continuing agony.

The adults tolerated the situation for a few more days whilst we were out enjoying the end of the school holidays and I was getting acquainted with the village. But Uncle Alf was never one for letting the grass grow under his feet, he was always quick in speech and action, impatient of delay, as befitted his job as driver in the Flying Squad. So in a short time after his arrival he had decided what needed to be done and immediately had a word here and a word there with friends he had made in the village and as if by magic came up with a solution.

One morning after breakfast he came bustling in from the kitchen narrowly missing knocking his head on the low beam. "Here, clear out you lot," he said to Aud and Doug and bundled them out of the door into the sunshine, "I want to have a word with Mick, man to man."

"Not fair," grumbled Aud, "why can't we stay?"

He came back, closed the kitchen door on my mother and Aunt Marj and sat down.

"Look here, Mick," he said, "you know you can't stay here much longer don't you? We'd love to keep you but it's just too crowded, you can see that for yourself. No room to swing a cat. Well, just by a bit of luck I know of a farm up the road that's looking for an evacuee. They want a boy because a boy's more useful on a farm, I suppose. Olive's a bit too young to go there as well I'm afraid. How would you like to give it a try? Save having to go further away wouldn't it? And a farm too, it's a chance in a lifetime, you'll have a wonderful time. It's only a couple of minutes from here, Costin's it is at Manor Farm. I can take you up there now and you can see what it's like. What do you say, shall we give it a go?"

There was a banging and a rapping on the door. "Can we come in now?" they were yelling from outside.

"Oh, Gawd blimey, all right, all right, I suppose you'd better come in," said Uncle Alf unfastening the door in mock annoyance. "Well, don't tell me you weren't listening at the keyhole," he grinned.

I was trying to take in what I'd just heard and decide what I thought about it. It was such an unexpected move, it fell on my ears like a bombshell so I don't suppose I looked as thrilled as he'd hoped I'd be at the prospect of living on a farm. Farms meant nothing to me, leaving the cottage did. I had a moment of panic as I realised I would have to leave my mother and sister and would be entirely on my own among strangers. But of course I was twelve and was being spoken to man to man; I had to take it on the chin and keep a stiff upper lip.

So I said nothing as I acquiesced but all the same as we started out along the road I was praying real earnest little prayers to God to rescue me from this threat of separation. "Please, please God don't let it happen. I'll be good, honest I will for ever."

"No, you can't come," said Uncle Alf firmly to Aud and Doug. "Do you think they want the whole tribe trailing along there?"

16

Whilst we were talking to the farmer and his wife I kept hoping against hope that nothing would come of it. I had eyes for nothing on that visit, just a longing for the business to end so I could get back to the security of the cottage. I did become aware, however, that against these people's determined patriotism my hopes were as nothing. They had already decided before they saw me that it was their duty to have an evacuee; it was all over before it began. I suppose my only hope lay in going berserk, acting like a hooligan and picking up a chair and hurling through the window. So as I listened with sinking heart the matter was agreed, I would come back the next day to stay.

On the way back Uncle Alf was beaming. "You're a lucky lad Mick," he said. Then with a glance at my glum features he added with a twinkle in his eye, "You don't know how lucky you are. You just wait and see."

The remainder of that last day with my cousins was savoured as if it were my last on earth. Wherever we went, whatever we did, however much I enjoyed myself, I couldn't entirely forget it was as on the eve of execution.

We wandered down to the bus stop seat where we found Aud's close friend Betty Austin and her younger sisters Mary and Doris, all with long glowing red hair. They met there on the seat because they were billetted in different houses and Betty had to keep an eye on the two younger ones. I had got to know nearly all the children in the few days I had been there and I'd already got used to Betty's serious conversations with Aud. Actually she had already shaken my confidence to its foundations when she remarked in the general stream of conversation on my second day there, "I think boys who don't wear underpants are very unhygienic." This is a class of opinion I'd never heard expressed before. I just turned away hot under the collar wondering if she somehow knew that I'd never worn underpants in my life.

There was nothing trivial in Betty's earnest talk with Aud; unlike us boys' brisk comments on each other and anything that took our fancy, they settled down on the seat to a deep discussion oblivious of everything else. I heard mention of missionaries and India and starvation, so Doug and I wandered over the road where through the hedge we could see Jimmy Knight in his garden doing some digging. He leaned on his spade and grinned at us but said he couldn't come out because he'd got ever so much digging to do before his dad came home. A serious boy was Jimmy. So we wandered back over the road to where a bullace tree trailed a branch loaded with ripe yellowish plums over the fence almost to the ground. We helped ourselves and as Joan Smith and Emmy Holland walked by they joined us. Joan was a Londoner about my age, living in Emmy's house. Joan was anything but serious, very much a tomboy, dark haired, lean and angular featured and within a minute I was giving her a 'piggy back' so that she could pick the bullaces higher up. We were laughing and staggering about and Emmy tried to give Doug a lift up because she was bigger and much fatter than him and we all collided and collapsed in a heap and lay there on the grass eating our juicy plums and spitting the stones high in the air.

Mrs Heley, my aunt's neighbour on the other side from the sing song, borrowing Brooks, was a kindly faced widow in her sixties, dressed in black, her silver-grey hair in a tight bun and as we came up the path home she was out at her front door calling to us. She wondered whether we could help her by picking some of the apples off her big old russet tree that stood in the lawn in front of her house. We didn't need asking twice but immediately set to with careless enthusiasm, climbing the short trunk into the stout lower branches like chimpanzees on a spree and tossing down the apples into the grass. Mrs Heley soon put a stop to that. "Put them carefully into these baskets," she said kindly but firmly, "they won't keep five minutes if you bruise them."

We soon piled high the baskets with the greeny-brown, gold flecked fruit, taking bites out of our own chosen specimens the while, and were then despatched to the other end of the terrace with a basketful for Mrs Heley's father who was the owner of the whole terrace. Arthur King was a white haired and bewhiskered patriarch of over ninety, still upright and firm on his feet. He was also superintendent of the Sunday School, a lay preacher and a pillar of the Methodist Chapel. As he walked back with us to the apple tree he asked us questions about ourselves and wondered whether London children liked living in the village and smiled with pleasure when we said we loved it. I wondered if he'd ever been to London. It was probably a den of iniquity to him. Like an ancient oak among saplings he seemed a relic of deep rural innocence. Already middle aged when Queen Victoria died he'd gone on quietly growing his beans and shallots, collecting his few shillings rent each week and piously walking along to chapel every Sunday. "Such a lot of strangers about here nowadays," he piped looking around vaguely, "not like it used to be," and three of those strangers followed his eyes around as if searching for hordes of invading townees. We stood by the apple tree rooted by the fascination of great age. I'm sure we half expected some God-like act from him, changing perhaps those dull, sharp tasting russets into sweet, shiny red and mouth watering apples. He looked old enough and wise enough for God.

My mother and Aunt Marj came out into the sunshine to join us. A young woman came striding up the path, it was Olive Heley come to visit her mother-in-law, the owner of the many bruised russets. I was soon to discover that Olive was a lively and earnest Sunday School teacher recently returned from her honeymoon. So the mixture of generations stood by the old tree as the evening sun turned the windows to golden mirrors and bathed the deep red bricks in its warm rays. You could not imagine a more peaceful scene just forty miles or so from Londoners preparing for another night of terror.

Later on Aud and Doug and I wandered down to Eric's place to see what he was doing. Eric, a village lad, was fast becoming my best friend apart from my cousins. He was dark haired, about my age and size and I wasn't sure I could beat him in a fight in spite of Aud's opinion, nor he me, so naturally we were drawn to each other, together we were a tough unit. Eric lived on an ideal one man farm, most Englishman's dream, or at least most city dwellers' dream. A few acres out near Eaton Bray put down to cereals, a few acres of potatoes alongside, a small orchard of plum and apple trees behind the house with another wheat field beyond that and a nice old farm house with a few barns around the yard, all run by Eric's dad plus Eric when he wasn't at school. His

Eric still lives in this lovely old brick house where I first met him nearly 40 years ago.

Eric's house today, practically unchanged in 40 years.

dad had been a blacksmith in the local quarry. He was now the epitome of the happy farmer. Silver haired, twinkling blue eyes in a brown leather face, slow and pithy of speech, puffing contentedly at his pipe he went about his leisurely way, subservient to none.

Eric was mowing the grass verge in front of his house when we got there. Gyp, his fourteen-year-old dog, lay in the gateway. We stopped by the red painted corrugated iron fence watching Eric and stroking his dog. We were very impressed when Eric stopped and leaned on his mower handle to tell us that really Gyp was about eighty. There was some formula he trotted out for converting dog years into human years and I looked with new respect at the venerable hound sleeping in the sunshine just as an old man dozes on a bench.

I had never pushed a lawn mower before, lawns being rather uncommon around our Poplar streets, and Eric was kind enough to let me have a go at his when I asked him. He lounged against the fence watching me with a critical eye as Aud and Doug surveyed the scene gloomily. I felt mighty proud as I whirred by grinning idiotically at the spectators. It was only a rough piece of grass luckily for I hadn't quite got the idea that the strips had to be parallel. I continued for some time without any competition from Aud and Doug until Eric suddenly took the mower again when his mother looked out between the curtains.

I told him I was going up to Costin's to live the next day.

"She's my Aunt Em," he said, "my mum and her are sisters."

This bit of news made me feel better about going to the farm. If Mrs Costin was Eric's aunt perhaps she would be all right. If they were all connected and I was Eric's friend it would be bound to help matters.

The mowing finished, we all climbed over the gate into the yard where a few chickens were scratching about in the dust. Eric went round the back of the house to put the mower away and when he reappeared he was carrying a long, stout bow and a couple of arrows with chicken feather flights. "That's a nice looking bow said Doug admiringly, "can I have a shot?"

"Yep, in a minute," said Eric, pleased at the praise but not showing it. We walked on up past the new ricks of wheat and out into the orchard. Eric pressed on the bow and tightened the string through a notch in the top. Doug's shot soared satisfyingly above the plum trees and thudded into the ground startling the mare grazing by the hedge. We all had some shooting practice after that, gravely passing the bow from hand to hand and ambitiously firing at apples on fence posts. It was a pretty good feeling loosing off arrows even though they tended to go everywhere except towards the target. Funny that! Errol Flynn had made it look so easy in 'Robin Hood'! None of us came anywhere near hitting an apple so we decided the arrows were less than perfect and scoured the hedges looking for some good straight sticks. I wanted some of my own for the bow I had then and there determined to make. "Look for ash," said Eric, "they make good arrows."

We looked, I at least not having the faintest idea what ash looked like. But

Betty Austin with 14-year-old Gyp the dog with Eric in his orchard.

A corner of Eric's rickyard behind the house.

Eric said we found some and he cut a few off with his penknife.

The shadows were lengthening as we wandered back down, thoughtfully peeling the bark off our arrows as we went and occasionally trying to hit a bat as they gyrated silently around us. We left Eric, then the three of us trudged slowly along the darkening road to spend our last night together at the cottage. I don't remember being sad, after all I would still have all these friends and perhaps I was dimly aware that although I might not know an ash tree from a beech or elm, I was beginning to enjoy the things you could do in the country and I wanted to experience some more. I was likely to do that with a vengeance on a farm so perhaps it would be worth a try.

When we went up to bed we had another very satisfying pillow fight, laying into each other solidly. We'd learnt to stifle the howls and shrieks and roared with only muffled laughter as we battered each other mercilessly. None of our antics could awaken Olive, she'd got used to sleeping through the blitz. Aunt Marj turned a deaf ear to it all knowing it was to be our last. We fell exhausted to sleep.

Chapter III

First Day at the Farm

The next morning my transfer from cottage to farm was a typically English, low key affair. At breakfast and afterwards it was just as if we were facing a normal day. The talk was about everything but the big subject that was my preoccupation. Even Aud and Doug seemed not quite their usual uninhibited selves, perhaps they'd been got at not to rock the boat. Later as the time drew near the event had to be faced up to and there were some encouraging remarks designed to relieve my growing gloom as we sat about paralysed out of our normal activity.

"You'll only be a little way up the road after all."

"All the children will want to come up to play with you on the farm."

"Aud and Doug wish they were moving onto a farm, they're quite jealous. Leave us like a shot they would if they could have your chance."

I wanly acknowledged these ritual consolations.

My mother had packed up my belongings, I wasn't burdened with much, and at mid-morning my uncle suggested we walk along to the farm. I was resigned to the fact that I would have to go but now that the time was at hand I was beginning to feel a bit sick inside at the thought of those strangers waiting for me.

"You off now then Mick?" said Aunt Marj brightly. "Pop back and tell us what it's like later on won't you?"

My mother said little. She tried to be cheerful but her anxious eyes betrayed the turmoil beneath the surface. When we left London I don't suppose she had realised it would involve us in splitting up.

"You two coming as well?" asked Uncle Alf of Aud and Doug who were hovering curiously, sniffing the undercurrents.

So the three of them accompanied me along the sunlit road past the bus stop where we had arrived in the village only a week or so before, then on to the farm and down the sloping yard to the front door which stood open. In response to my uncle's call Mrs Costin came out smiling a welcome.

"Come in all of you," she said. Then looking at me she said, "I'm really pleased you've come," with such friendliness that was like oil poured on my troubled sea.

"No, we won't come in thanks," said Uncle Alf. "See you later Mick," and he gave me a huge reassuring wink, grabbed Aud and Doug's arm and marched them up the slope and away.

I followed Mrs Costin into the front kitchen, which though I had been in briefly the day before, I now saw as for the first time. I had noticed nothing then so fervently was I hoping against hope that I wouldn't have to come.

"Well Mick," she said seriously, "you are very welcome here. We are all pleased to have you and I want you to look on this house as your home from now on."

She smiled as she said, "Well, that's my speechmaking done."

Her clear blue eyes sparkled in a ruddy countenance which glowed with sincerity and good humour. She was shortish and comfortably-built and must have been about sixty then. Her hair was silvery-grey, short and crisply wavy. "I know it's going to seem strange at first," she went on, "but you'll soon get used to us. I've got a feeling we're going to get on well."

I knew immediately with that unerring instinct of childhood that I had in Mrs Costin an ally and a kindred spirit. For some reason she liked me and would be on my side. I also knew that I liked her and could trust her completely.

"Well, come upstairs first to take your things up," she said, "and I'll show you around a bit on the way." We went through a door into the next room two steps up from the front kitchen. "This is the dining room," said Mrs Costin and we stopped a moment. I looked around seeing something different about this room from any other I had ever seen. My eyes rested on a magnificent solid oak dining table in the centre of the room, standing on a deep piled carpet and with many elegant matching chairs around it. I glanced around at a great dresser in the corner of the room in the same oak with a huge mirror as its back and on whose shelf were displayed many pieces of gleaming silver tableware. Along one wall was a large modern fireplace with tiled and panelled surround flanked by two deep, floral patterned armchairs. A comfortable chesterfield filled the large semi-circular bay window which gave the room a feeling of spaciousness and light. A grandfather clock stood beside the chair slowly and strongly ticking away the silent hours.

All this splendour caused me little reaction save a slight unease, a flickered acknowledgement that here was a different world. I said nothing, made no comparisons with the cottage or my own home, such comparisons were not yet part of my life. Farmhouses were beyond my experience of course and anything could presumably be expected from them in the same way that you would

There's not been much outward change in this recent view of the fine old farmhouse which was my wartime home.

Aunt Marj sitting with Mrs Costin in the garden at Manor Farm 1940.

expect another planet to be different. True, the clock was fascinating, I'd never seen one as big as that before. I reckoned I might be able to hide inside it. The rest I dismissed as no concern of mine. Mrs Costin's dismissive matter of factness too, made light of mere furniture. "Needs a good dusting," she said and we moved on.

On the far side of the room was the door to the staircase and just beyond this was another room. Mrs Costin pushed open the door and we glanced in. "This is the drawing room," she said and my impression was of a dim jungle clearing due to the drawn curtains, a large potted palm and the dark polished furniture. "Fred doesn't like the sunlight getting at his piano," Mrs Costin explained, indicating the darkly shining monster with its curved back raised in the semi-gloom. I just had time to notice an interesting glass fronted cabinet with little china ornaments in before the door closed.

We went on upstairs. "You'll be sharing a bed with my youngest son Bob," she said as we arrived at the end of a long corridor after passing several rooms. "Fred my eldest son sleeps here too, it's a big room," she added. It was indeed a large room, especially after the cottage, high ceilinged and with plenty of free space around the two wide double beds. I was most interested in the washstand in the corner with its china pitchers decorated in blue and with ewers and bucket beneath. "What can all that be about?" I wondered. My few clothes were soon swallowed up in one of the two enormous wardrobes and chests of drawers.

On the way down we stopped at the end of the corridor and Mrs Costin pushed open a door. We mounted a step and looked in. "That's the spare bedroom," she said. I saw a huge, sumptuous four poster bed and had a fleeting view of comfortable chairs and deep piled rugs and once again a marble topped washstand with its elegantly decorated jugs and washbowls. "We don't use it very often now," she said as we went on down the stairs, "but it all has to be kept clean," she concluded with a sigh.

Downstairs again in the front kitchen Mrs Costin left me to my own devices. "I'm afraid I've got to get on," she said with a glance at the clock on the wall. "There'll be three hungry men coming in soon and won't there just be trouble if dinner's not ready! You can look around outside if you like, I don't think there's anyone about, they're all down the field this morning." She bustled off down the passageway towards the back of the house somewhere.

I walked into the yard and looked out on my strange new world. Blacktarred barns and mossy tiled cowsheds formed three sides of a large quadrangle of which the house formed the fourth side, its sloping yard separated by a fence from the main farm yard. On the far side of the square from the house was a wide gap between cowsheds which gave access to further sheds, the rickyard beyond and a way onto the road.

It seemed enormous to me that first morning. Eric's little farmyard was dwarfed by this. I walked across the yard and around the huge dunghill where a multitude of hens were scratching under the fussy guardianship of a magnificent cockerel. I poked my head into a few doorways and surveyed the mostly incomprehensible contents of cavernous barns in the semi-gloom and saw the rows of empty stalls in the cowsheds. I didn't feel sufficiently at ease to explore thoroughly, it was almost as if I was trespassing, so I scouted around briefly, walking out to the rickyard and around the six or seven new ricks that filled it, seeing things but understanding practically nothing.

Below the barns and rickyard, beyond a huge fan of churned, baked mud outside the gate was the orchard where dense rows of plum trees stretched away to a distant hedge. Several horses and cows grazed beneath the trees and chickens pecked and scratched busily in the grass. I leaned on the orchard gate and looked around. "How far did this farm's land stretch?" I wondered. Fancy one man owning all this!" I dreamed of how it would feel to own whole fields, sheds, cows, machines.

I looked up out of my daydreams. I was going to have to live amongst all these barns and orchards and cowstalls. How would I fit in I wondered. I felt nervous and lonely and wished I had someone of my own age with me. What was it going to be like on my own? Not much fun on your own, I grumbled feeling sorry for myself. There would be plenty of room though. Perhaps too much. Space, one's own private space, was something I had always had a strict minimum of. In Poplar we shared houses, stairs, passageways, yards and gardens, toilet even, with other families as did everybody else I knew. I lived cheek-by-jowl with untold masses of other people, crowds everywhere. And now? I looked out over the orchard and onto fields beyond and to the side and I couldn't see another house nor another person. I was going to be able to walk anywhere I wanted, all over the fields, in the barns, everywhere, just as if I owned the place. Or was I? I wasn't sure what to think. I'd have to wait until I met the others, the ones I hadn't seen yet, to know if I was going to like it or not. If they didn't like me I might be in for a rough time. I would know the minute we met.

I remember looking around the yard and feeling critical of the great beds of nettles growing over rusting and rotting implements lying about. I didn't realise that the only spaces I was used to were carefully tended parks where nettles were almost unknown. Nor, of course did I then appreciate that farmers weren't country gentlemen with a show house and ornamental grounds to run, but hardworking businessmen with more to worry about than making their yards look pretty.

I turned and wandered back across the silent and deserted yard and indoors again. It came as no surprise to learn that there was no bathroom in the house and no flush lavatory. I wasn't used to the former and it was only the lack of the latter that bothered me, though I'd quickly got used to the bucket at the cottage. Mrs Costin directed me along the garden path to the last of a series of little outhouses where there was just a wooden seat at two levels with circles cut in them and lids to cover a deep, draughty and evil smelling pit. After that first occasion it took me several days before I could bring myself to use it again. I preferred, like a wild animal, the grassy undergrowth of the hillside that soared just across the road.

Some minutes later there was a clatter of hooves on the road outside and into the yard drove three men in a pony and trap. This was it. I braced myself for the encounter. Their boots rang on the stone floor as they crashed into the back kitchen where I was watching Mrs Costin preparing to dish up. They all greeted me jovially and in a rush of good humoured banter. Mr Costin, lean and weather beaten, about sixty five, wearing a waistcoat, collar and tie, relaxed his stern features as he smiled and said indicating me that they'd be all right now that they had a new man on the farm.

"Ow's our Cockney sparrer?" enquired Fred in my supposed accent. He was broad shouldered, tanned, with dark wavy hair and his face puckered into a friendly smile.

Bob, the youngest, slim and fine boned with features much resembling his father, warned me with a grin that he kicked like a mule in bed. "Have you put him a chamber pot his side mother?" Bob asked. "He's not sharing mine I hope."

"Go on with you," said Mrs Costin smiling encouragingly at me, "he'll have his own."

"I hope so," said Fred. "You'll need a gozunder 'cos it's an awful long way out to the lavatory if you get taken short in the middle of the night."

"Do you think you could talk about something else?" said Mrs Costin. "What a subject the very first time you meet the poor boy. Whatever will he think of us?"

"Oh, mother, he's used to us, aren't you Mick?" exclaimed Fred. "You ought to hear the things that uncle of his says and gets up to. Chamber pots have got nothing on it," and Fred chortled at some particularly juicy reminiscence.

I was revelling in this, delighted and relieved to start off so warmly as we all went along the passage to the front kitchen carrying dishes of meat and vegetables. I knew straightaway that somehow I'd had the incredible luck of falling in with a cheerful, jovial family who would accept me as one of them.

I was given my place at the big cloth covered table, next to Fred at the bookcase end, a place I kept for my entire stay until it felt like my own property.

Mr Costin soon carved the small piece of rationed meat which looked lost on the large meat dish, Mrs Costin served out the vegetables and we fell to. As the talk swung about from subject to subject, local gossip mostly, I was left to acclimatise myself in peace for which I was thankful. As everything in the room was new to me I had big eyes for all of it. This was the room where we lived most of the time, where over the next four years I spent countless hours with the family, the one that I came to know intimately and whose tiniest details remain etched in my memory decades on.

Opposite where I was sitting was a huge fireplace with its blackleaded grate and oven at one side. This oven, unlike the one in the back kitchen did no cooking and was only used for drying out logs. There was a large old clock on the wall like those I'd come across in big shops. Its large white, Roman numeralled face, its loud ticking and short swinging brass pendulum were fascinating. Once a week it was ceremonially rewound with a big key by Mr Costin, no one else ever touched it. A highly polished radiogramme stood beneath the clock and was the most modern thing in the room. Behind me was a huge highbacked dresser whose shelves were lined with dozens of plates and dishes of various sizes, never used, and which I later learned were willow pattern. On its wide top were several old copper and pewter tea urns and the upright two piece telephone stood there too. Spacious cupboards underneath were filled with children's toys and games peacefully resting, waiting for the awakening touch of grandchildren. A large roll top bureau stood against one wall with a large etching of Constable's Hay Wain above it. A treadle sewing machine was in the window by the door where there was also a bundle of walking sticks partly concealing the long barrels of a twelve bore shotgun. A gleaming copper warming pan hung on the wall by the dining room door. It was all homely but uncluttered, neat and comfortable and welcoming at the same time.

Mrs Costin brought in a large steamed pudding stuffed with dates, a dish of custard and one of rice and with it came in a new era for me of ample meals, good solid English farmhouse cooking that opened a city boy's eyes wide with greed and wonder. I consumed a huge portion and had to decline the offer of more, but I was promised I could finish the pudding off for tea or supper if I wished. "You can't have the rice though, Fred likes to finish that off at tea-time, nor the custard, Mr Costin likes that later on." In such ways I quickly learned the intimate details of my new family's life and took my place in the pecking order.

At one o'clock Mr Costin switched on the wireless, left it on to hear the main points of the news whilst he checked his big gold pocket watch, then abruptly switched off declaring it was time they were getting back to work. Fred asked me if I would like to come ploughing with him and I said I would. I hadn't anything special to do that afternoon and ploughing might be interesting. We piled into the pony trap and clattered off through the village and didn't I just feel proud as we passed my cousin's cottage. I hoped they saw me on my first ever ride. The pony trotted at a good pace, her shoes drumming a loud staccato on the road, giving the impression of even greater speed. I already felt half a farmer.

I spent most of the afternoon sitting on the tractor's broad mudguard as we crawled endlessly up and down the broad acres of stubble. Behind us the silvery ploughshares humped rich brown soil caressingly into ruler straight lines on which at a discreet distance the inland legion of wheeling, mewing gulls competed with glossy black rooks for anything that moved. It was fascinating, hypnotic, watching the ragged stubble curving over effortlessly in a graceful brown bow wave. Only a fortnight before it would have been unthinkable that I from the teeming anthills of the East End should be out in the middle of a huge lonely field riding on a tractor as we ploughed the land. Yet I sat there as if I had been doing it for years and never once expressed the least surprise at what I was experiencing for the first time.

Ploughing is an incredibly monotonous job. Travelling up and down, up and down the field interminably, keeping the front offside wheel down in the previous furrow, yanking on the chain at the end of each strip to bring the ploughshares up out of the soil whilst the turn was made on the headland then letting them slip back in as the new strip was begun. All day long, hour after hour, day after day Fred did that job, sometimes in shirtsleeves, more often in topcoat against the rough weather for there was no cab on tractors then. He must have had plenty of time for thought as he covered something like a couple of hundred acres each season. He did it all by himself as indeed he drove the tractor for everything it did about the farm. Perhaps ploughing satisfied some part of Fred's nature that craved for solitude but I doubt it. It was more likely a case of enduring what he had to in the line of duty. For Fred loved company, loved to be with people where the warmth of his personality could be felt as an active force by those around him.

The whole open spread of the Knolls lay before us about half a mile away, rising through slopes that were fast becoming familiar, the distance ironing out the maze of little hills but the upper slopes clear cut in the afternoon sunshine.

Fred spoke but little, it was so noisy that you had to shout as the old Fordson roared unceasingly, its hot exhaust blowing back in my face, the field ahead dancing in the heatwaves. When after a couple of hours or so Fred stopped to tip some more paraffin into the tractor I decided I'd had enough of my noisy and not too comfortable position so I left him to walk back up the road to the village between the high, untrimmed hedges. Gradually as I walked the Knolls came into greater prominence and I had an awareness of it as a sentry standing guard over the village. The road mounted a slight shelf above the valley floor and the houses began. As I walked past I looked cheerfully up at my aunt's cottage where the day before had been like an eve of execution but as I couldn't see anyone about I went on towards the farm feeling quite independent.

I found the cowsheds full of cows, dozens of them, mostly reddish-brown and white, shuffling their feet, heads down in the manger quietly eating their ration of cattle cake, rattling the chains around their necks as they tossed their heads at the ever present flies. Arthur the cowman was bustling about attending to his charges' needs. A quick active man, short and stockily built, he smiled quizzically at me when I first met him, said something rapidly in a thick local accent which I didn't grasp at all then went on with his work, humming gently to himself as he washed the cows' hindquarters before starting milking.

Then into the yard came the pony and trap again with Mr Costin, Bob, Fred and another man, Reg, the third farming brother. He was tall and strong looking with an open friendly regard from his steady blue eyes. He came across the yard to inspect the newcomer and with his first few cheerful words of greeting I knew that I had found another lifelong friend. A bond of trust and affection sprang fully formed into being and was never broken.

The afternoon milking began. I was all eyes of course at this new experience which was obviously an important part of the farm's life. Fred saw to the collecting up of the milk in large metal buckets, carrying them over to the farmhouse porch where an electric motor pumped water from the well directly outside the front door. This well which never dried up in the years I was there, supplied the water for cooling the milk. It also went through to the tap in the back kitchen where we occasionally had the odd worm swimming in a glass of water.

The others on the three-legged stools set on with the milking by hand, a job which had to be done every day of the year whatever other work was in hand, whether in the middle of harvest or at threshing time. This was the one job on the farm which could never be put off till later. In those first few minutes, standing close watching what was going on, I was suddenly squirted and thoroughly soaked with jets of milk by Bob and Reg, caught in a liquid crossfire. There were howls of laughter all round, they were going to enjoy having a boy about the place to tease, especially one as raw as I was.

I stood idly about watching the milking at a safe distance after that and listening to the loud tune that the jets made in the empty bucket gradually quietening and lowering in pitch as the bottom became covered, then there was just a steady hiss and froth for many minutes until the day's supply ran out.

"How would you like a job then Mick?" asked Mr Costin who couldn't abide anyone, least of all boys, standing around idle.

"All right," I answered, wondering what I was letting myself in for.

"Go and fetch a basket from indoors in the dairy and go round the place and collect up the eggs," he said. That sounded a nice, harmless sort of job that any idiot could do, even me.

So I did, with a bit of advice about the sort of locations to search. I found my way around all the large number of barns and sheds and picked up a great number of eggs under mangers, behind corn bins, in disused carts and around the rickyard. It took me a long time that first day but I enjoyed it. It was a job I did for most of my days on the farm and I soon became expert at it, nosing out all the likely laying places though the hens usually gave themselves away cackling as they came away from the nest, they are not the most intelligent of creatures. Sometimes however, a hen outdid me in cunning and proudly brought forth her brood of tiny chicks from some dense bramble patch or stand of nettles behind the sheds.

That first time I came back across the yard after a long and thorough search, flushed with success and proud that I was playing a part in the running of things even on my first day.

"Let's have a look at how many you've got then," called Fred from under the cowshed.

I showed him the basket with about three dozen eggs. "Mm," he said, "not too bad. Are you sure that's all you can find, did you look everywhere?"

I felt a bit deflated at that but said I'd had a thorough search but might have missed a few not being used to the job.

"Perhaps they're beginning to drop off," said Fred, "I've noticed they've been going down a bit lately. What those hens need is a good run round. That would make them lay. It's a pity I haven't got the time to do it."

"A run round?" I repeated doubtfully.

"Yes, they don't get enough exercise. If someone could give them a real good run round, make 'em sweat, they'd come back on to lay marvellously, wouldn't they Bob?"

"Oh, yes," said Bob, "it makes a world of difference. There's nothing hens like better than a good run round."

I ruminated on this for a moment or two, then seeing clearly where my duty lay I set the basket of eggs down carefully and began chasing the hens in the yard that were up till then scratching contentedly. I felt a bit of an idiot as I clapped my hands and lurched towards the first one but in no time at all I was deeply involved and the air was filled with furious squawking, flying feathers, cackling and flapping of wings as I harried dozens of them unmercifully around the yard determined to raise egg production to unprecedented levels. They ran like made, protesting loudly, from the crazy boy who never gave them a moment's peace but pursued them frenetically around and around the great dunghill. I glanced round at the cowsheds in the midst of my exertions, anticipating approval and encouragement but saw everybody falling about with helpless laughter, all milking brought to a halt as they regarded the hiliarious spectacle. Even the cows turned their big brown eyes on the scene, wide with astonishment.

I stopped in my tracks, a wry smile on my face as I realised I'd been tricked. They'd put one over on a Cockney lad and weren't they all just pleased with themselves!

"What have you stopped for Mick?" called Fred, momentarily gaining control of his hysterics, "you were doing so well."

I screwed up my face in disgust and slowly approached my tormentors.

That was, however, the first and last time I was caught out in spite of several further attempts. I was to hear of victims in the district who had been sent to buy a pint of pigeon's milk or a tin of elbow grease or to the blacksmith's for a set of leather shoes for the horse. The peak of excellence in this game lay in the ability to keep the poor fool going from errand to errand and one blacksmith sent on his leather shoe customer to the hardware shop for a rubber file to finish off the shoes. The stories were endless about what poor ignorant townies had been fooled into doing by knowing country folk. They were the reverse of the 'country yokel' stories loved by city dwellers. So on my first day at the farm I picked up my basket of eggs and went indoors wiser than when I started out.

When the milking was over we sat down to a magnificent tea of bread, spread with home made butter and home made greengage jam. There was a whole big plateful and never did bread and butter taste so delicious. The jam, taken from a proper dish with a spoon, not knifed out of the jar, had an irresistible flavour. Saccharin tablets, like miniature depth charges, fizzed in our tea for the sugar ration couldn't stand up to the many strains upon it.

Reg came in for a few minutes' chat and a cup of tea before he went back down to his own home. "Well, we seem to have survived our first day with an evacuee," he said grinning in my direction.

"I'm worried about surviving my first night," said Bob, "he might think he's still giving his hens a good run round."

Fred spluttered in his teacup at the recollection and Mrs Costin tut-tutted, "What a lot you've come into Mick. Still, how would you like to finish off that date pudding?"

"Yes please," I said with enthusiasm.

"What cold!" exclaimed Mr Costin. "You must have a cast iron stomach. It'd kill me I reckon."

It was all the same to me, I could eat almost anything. I occasionally, especially in later years, had a slight twinge of concern about this omniverous ability when I heard other sensitive palates expressing their loathing of this or that, to me, delectable dish. "Cold bread and butter pudding! How could you! Ugh." Surely I ought to cultivate greater sensibility, I told myself, it was obviously necessary to any pretensions of refinement. But there was nothing to be done, I just unselectively liked and devoured practically everything that came my way. It was a minor ability that I found useful when, later on, I went to live in France for some while.

The phone rang and as Fred answered it there was complete hush. It was one of the unwritten laws in action, no one talked in the room whilst the phone was being used. If they did so much as dare to whisper there was invariably a hand clapped over the mouthpiece and a dramatic "Shush, I can't hear a thing!" So with active ears and idle tongues from the rest of us Fred's telephone voice immediately became more posh and he pronounced his words with great care and precision, his Bedfordshire accent disappeared completely as the words dropped out one by one all neatly parcelled and trimmed off.

"That was Betty Dollimore," he said as he replaced the receiver, "she won't be able to sing at Harvest Festival."

"Oh, what a shame," said Mrs Costin. "Who else can you get?"

"I don't know, it's getting a bit late now, but I reckon I'll ask Alf Swain, Mick's uncle. He's got a really fine voice. If he can get time off I think he'll do it for us." I felt a warm glow of family pride, it helped redress the balance of things a bit.

I finished off the cold date pudding and had a good sized chunk of the huge fruit cake that sat in the middle of the table. It wasn't till later that I realised that cake must have been in my honour because dried fruit was as scarce as gold dust. Everyone tucked in with murmurs of appreciation.

"Are you on duty tonight Reg?" Mrs Costin asked. Along with Arthur who lived next door to him, Reg was a warden in the A.R.P. He had a tin helmet, a special sort of gas mask and a stirrup pump which he kept in a bucket by his back door in case the village should be set ablaze by incendiary bombs. They went on regular patrol around Lower End to make sure nobody was breaking the blackout regulations.

Reg nodded. "I didn't tell you what happened last Tuesday did I? he asked. "Well, laugh, I nearly died. Arthur and I were out at about ten o'clock round near the Duke's Head when we saw this torch flashing about. It was in that field just past the Council houses so we went over to the gate to see what it was all about. You'd be surprised at who it was. A certain married lady, or female shall we say, and a gentleman who wasn't her husband out in the middle of this field. I'll tell you later who it was. I could hear them talking and make them out in the torchlight. They didn't know we were there. I just called out, "Put that light out please," and walked away. That's somebody who won't be able to look me in the eye next time I see them I'll be bound."

Tea finished, Bob set about sprucing himself up to go up to Dunstable on his bike for the evening to see his girlfriend. Fred went out to do some gardening. He and his mother as I was to discover, were the only ones interested in gardening and I think Fred did it mainly because someone had to keep the garden tidy. It was Mrs Costin who loved to tend the flowers whenever she had the time which wasn't very often. I can't remember Mr Costin or Bob ever taking a hand at anything in the garden, nor to my shame did I ever offer to help or do anything more than wander around admiring the profusion of plants in well ordered beds and borders. For farmers the garden was a good one, an attractive rectangle behind the house that you could look out onto from the kitchen which stuck out behind at right angles to the end of the house. Mrs Costin once apologised for the attractiveness of the garden saying that most good farmers were poor gardeners and hoped it didn't mean they were poor farmers. There were flower borders around the lawn, a long raised bed against the fence by the road, a large pear tree and a Victoria plum tree against the house wall and a good vegetable plot at the back which Arthur used to be sent in to deal with when there was an odd slack day on the farm, a good move because if anyone knew his vegetables it was Arthur who regularly carried off prizes for his allotment produce at the village shows.

Right at the back by the thick hedge of tall evergreens, planted to keep the neighbours' prying eyes at bay, all sorts of interesting and to me unusual plants grew. Just about all plants were unusual to me in those days, save perhaps marigolds and poppies which not even the impoverished soil, cats and atrocious conditions of our little plot in Poplar could keep down. I remember at the farm clumps of Solomon's seal, whose strange name set me wondering as I gazed at their long stems of hanging white bells. Periwinkles rambled about freely among luxurious growth, littering the ground with their mauve-blue crosses. Lily-of-the-Valley I discovered there and first sniffed greedily at their powerful scent and of all things I was told one pretty, lacey pink flower that sprang from a fleshy rosette was called London Pride. Odd sort of plant for my city to be proud of I thought. Surely there must be something much grander that would be more suitable.

Fred had an aviary of budgerigars at the end of the path. On a summer's day their quick flashes of green and blue as they darted between the branches placed inside and their loud chattering, added an exotic touch to that corner of the garden. In winter the snow was blown through the wire mesh and the birds huddled miserably together in the glacial draughts, their breed memories perhaps making them long for the burning Australian sun. Sadly the budgies dwindled away to nothing as it became increasingly difficult then impossible to get any seed for them.

With the early evening dispersal to assorted activities I wandered off down the road to my aunt's cottage to report on the first day. They could all tell from my relaxed, casual and unforthcoming manner of answering their questions that all was well. I totally accepted my new home in spite of the serious worries about what I was going to do for a lavatory. I didn't say anything about that to anyone, toying in my mind with the idea of coming back to the cottage whenever the need arose but suspecting its impractibility. Strangely, I felt no great desire to get back to the cottage in spite of the wonderful time I'd had there. So quickly do children adapt! I was pleased to see my mother and sister of course but in a taken for granted way, nothing desperate or emotional about it. A drastic change had indeed occurred from the morning's anxiety to the evening's calm. I pretended the former had never been. Uncle Alf had gone back to the blitz, his few days leave having ended.

Aud and Doug and I went out to play after a few minutes. We called for Eric and he asked me how I'd got on at the farm. "Not bad," I said, "who else can we get?" We soon rounded up the Zanninetti twins, Betty and Joan and Jimmy Knight and went up the Knolls tracking. One gang went off round the ranges of little hills and the other went in pursuit after a racing count to a hundred. It was good, hectic and breathless fun where we exercised our version of Red Indian skills of silent, invisible, snakelike slithering, of lying unobserved in a hollow while the enemy passed only feet away, or of powerful running on steep slopes to escape a determined foe. I'd learned quite a lot since I first came up on the Knolls but hadn't yet achieved complete familiarity. The knowledge of what lay around each bend, just how steep each slope was though unseen, where there was a hawthorn bush to hide behind, every little vital detail of the whole extensive terrain came with a little more time.

The shadows lengthened, twilight deepened into dusk and dew began to settle on the grass before we called it a day and came off the hills down to the deserted road. We split up and after calling in at the cottage to say goodnight to my mother and aunt, I went off back to the farm feeling more than ever that I belonged in the village now that I had my own independent existence, my own home and a good band of friends.

When I got indoors Mr Costin was sitting in his high-backed wooden chair reading the Express, Mrs Costin had a pile of socks on the table before her to darn. It was very quiet in the room, the large wall clock ticking away emphasised the silence, the shaded light shining on the green table cloth left the far corners of the room in shadow. I sat down in the old armchair beneath the warming pan on the wall and looked around getting the feel of the room, drinking in its atmosphere, sensing its vibrations. Mrs Costin gave me a few of Bob's old comics to look at and I sat reading and joining in now and again the little conversations that from time to time broke the stillness. They had sat there alone like that for years now as the children had grown and either married or spent their evenings out. Just the two of them with the circle of light playing on the broad table between them and the surrounding shadows gradually deepening. Now with me in the house they were being reminded of those days when their own children were young and about the place in the evening and perhaps they were not entirely displeased to feel the years rolled back and advancing age seemingly kept at bay.

Fred was out on duty as Special Constable. Not content with being a farmer, as demanding a job as you could have, and with strenuous determination finding time for music which raised existence into life for him, he even found time to play his policing role, an important part of the war effort and a time consuming one as well. But such was the national will for survival and so aware was everyone of the need for personal service that contributions such as Fred's were commonplace.

A little later he called in with his farmer friend from Church End, Ralph Archer on their patrol of the village. At nine o'clock the booming tones of Big Ben hushed Ralph's tale of how farmer Beale up at Church End had dealt with "they two Ministry chaps as came to see 'im 'bout 'is milk return" to their discomfort and the district's amusement. Whilst the announcer was sombrely detailing the death and destruction caused in London and many other cities in the most recent raids and various other overseas disasters, the table was laid and we all sat down to a supper of cold meat, cheese and cold potatoes, except Fred who, as always, had his bowl of bread and milk. Then the two Specials, well fortified against the night, resumed their patrol.

At half past nine Mrs Costin suggested it was about my bedtime. "We're none of us night owls here," she said smiling, "we have to get up too early for that I suppose."

"Time to go up Wooden Hill and down Sheet Alley as my father used to say," said Mr Costin.

Because of the blackout you couldn't switch lights on in each room as you went through so Mrs Costin came with me to the bedroom just to make sure I would be all right that first time. She drew the thick curtains at the window then switched on. "There you are," she said, "I daresay you'll sleep soundly tonight. Oh, and in the morning you can have a wash at the stand over there."

She paused with her hand on the doorknob. "Your first day here hasn't been too bad I hope Mick?" she enquired. I hope my smile conveyed more than the rather grudging "No" I came out with.

"I just know you're going to fit in well," she said. "Good night."

"Good night," I called as the door closed.

I had a pretty confident feeling about the future as I looked around this new bedroom with its solid, reassuring furniture. My earlier fears about not being welcomed by all the family had proved groundless. There was no room for a mistake in my impression, I knew in my bones when I was or wasn't liked and I had sensed no unfriendliness, nothing but an honest to goodness welcome for the stray Cockney lad come into their midst. No wonder I was light hearted as I leaped upon the bed which was high and huge but softly enveloping when I slid between the cool cotton sheets. I lay listening to the night sounds through the open window. I could hear the faint rustling of the breeze in the top of the tall elm by the corner of the rickyard and sometimes from downstairs came the indecipherable blur of voices. I wished I could hear what they were saying and wondered if any of it was about me. I was certainly thinking about them as I slipped easily to sleep.

Chapter IV

In and Out of School

No matter that Britain was fighting for its life, alone, back to the wall in its grimmest war situation for centuries with invasion expected any day as the German tiger prepared to leap the moat and have its supposedly defenceless victim by the throat. The gimlet eye of education batted not an eyelid as it sought out every reluctant pupil no matter how far the war had flung him and hauled him into a classroom to learn about Eskimos and to memorise the capes and bays of Australia.

So it was no wonder that a few days after my arrival at the farm and whilst the Few were fighting desperately for our lives in the skies above the fields of Kent and Sussex, Aud and Doug, the Austin sisters, Jimmy Knight, Joan Smith and a few others called for me after breakfast. With gas masks in boxes slung over our shoulders we walked up the hill and along the road to Middle End where the schools were situated. The village was in the unusual position of having two schools. One, the old red brick, high windowed building that had incarcerated generations of village children, the other and my destination, the nearby pebble dashed Memorial Hall where an evacuated North London primary school settled in when war broke out. Now with its numbers greatly depleted by many departures home during the phoney war, it was struggling on, taking in a few odds and ends of newcomers like myself, refugees from the bombing.

It was fortunate that the school's numbers were small for the Memorial Hall wasn't exactly ideal for use as an educational institution. It was a modern building though, put up a few years before the war, the pride of the village, perfect for whist drives and dances. In fact those usual social functions carried on. We had none of the heavy desks usual in a classroom but worked at green baize covered card tables somewhat unsteadily. We children weren't allowed to clomp across the fine wooden block floor in our great boots and shoes, we had to wear plimsolls or even go in bare feet. The Hall was freezing cold in winter when snow lay upon the ground. The small square electric heaters attached to the wall were impotent to warm the glacial currents that frolicked over the wide

38

expanse of floor numbing our feet and ankles. Tracing maps of Equatorial Africa did little to thaw frozen fingers, the only solution was to down pencils and plunge hands into pockets for a few minutes to stave off frost bite.

Miss Jones was the headmistress. She was probably in her mid-fifties, short, plump and proudly Welsh. She taught the older children, myself included, about a dozen in all. There was another class of younger children up on the stage with the curtains drawn across to stop us waving to each other and another group of still younger ones in the little kitchen at the back where they made the tea for the dances and whist drives. The top class with Miss Jones sat in a corner at the far end from the stage and I daresay we attempted to do the usual things that Junior schools did then and still do today. I confess I have few precise memories of what went on through the long hours of confinement there though I well recollect the exquisite agony of sitting poring over books when in fine warm weather the door and windows stood wide open, the breeze entering freely agitated the curtains and my restless spirit, the sunshine poured from the sky like liquid gold and I could hear the leaves in a row of elms just outside taunting me in my captivity.

She ruled us with a rod of iron did Miss Jones, but a rod usually encased in velvet and only occasionally withdrawn. Like most teachers she was of the sensible, no nonsense brigade, hearty and friendly enough in her spinsterish way. It was a way we did not comprehend, nor seek to, but suffered whilst we must then forgot the moment we were unleashed.

But on the whole I was happy enough at that makeshift school. Not that we ever considered the question of whether or not we were happy, things were the way they were and we just endured them or rejoiced in them. It never occurred to me that I was being deprived of a year of secondary education with Science and French and Woodwork. Instead we had country dancing, which I hated, on that lovely wooden floor. Miss Jones was also keen on folk songs and we learnt our share of these and soon learned to slip in our own whispered irreverences to 'Greensleeves' and 'The Ash Grove'. On fine afternoons we sometimes used to take our chairs outside under the elms, well away from the Elsan toilet by the far corner of the fence, and whilst the girls did sewing, sitting round in a circle, we boys used to read them tales of knightly adventure and stories of enchanted lands where fairy folk rubbed shoulders with well-bred boys and girls. Above all we read those ageless golden legends of Greece and Rome which although I didn't give them much thought then, are strangely enough among the few enduring school things I learnt which stuck in my mind after those hot and restless days of youth. We also learnt the Welsh National Anthem in Welsh. It might as well have been Chinese for all we bothered, for we soon learnt to rattle it off parrot fashion so often did we sing it. I'm sure it gave Miss Jones a thrill to think that she was spreading Welsh culture among the English youth but sadly for her it nearly all slid away into limbo as easily and naturally as water off a duck's back.

Now and again in spring and summer we walked up to the allotments behind the village school and dug and raked and generally tortured the soil of a little plot we had there. I don't recall that much ever grew there but then I don't suppose I connected our activities with the possibility of actually growing anything. For me at least a few more years had to pass before the burying of seed in soil and watching the tiny seedlings come shouldering their way up through the earth crumbs was to have the magical impact which, once felt, is possessed for ever.

In that little school we were free from eleven plus pressures, free from inspectors, exams and anxious parents. The days passed in a tolerable blur and I soon learned enough of those deep mysteries a boy ought to know about life from Joan in our long walks to and from school to more than make up for any lack of academic learning within the school walls themselves.

Sometimes whilst we were at school the air raid siren went. That sound, rising and falling in all its relentless evocation of impending doom, is still to me the most blood curdling sound on earth. Even now should I hear it in an old movie it transports me in terror to the days when death fell from the skies with its dying notes.

In the school, however, we were well drilled by Miss Jones. There was no rushing, no stampede. Having downed tools we filed through a little door in the side of the stage, down a few steps and sat beneath the boards amid the rubble and bits of wood that littered the floor, surrounded by bare bricks and with the rough joists and planks of the stage overhead. It wasn't exactly a secure place against bombs perhaps but we felt safe enough. It was the semi-gloom that did it. It was all very thrilling and we were bubbling with excitement as we sat on our benches listening and waiting for the explosions of war to engulf us. Any notion of school being wiped out is heaven to children; of course we knew that no harm would come to us, only to the teachers perhaps.

We never heard anything untoward however, save once some dronings in the sky which Jack Dempster pronounced to be Heinkels. "Silly boy," said Miss Jones with a withering glance. "I know, let's sing 'Land of my Fathers', that'll cheer us all up."

So the dark corners echoed to some half hearted efforts until we once again relapsed into a breathless anticipation of hostilities. At which point the all clear went and we emerged strangely into the quiet hall with its curtains flapping gently and the king looking down at us rather sternly across the dance floor.

Everybody in the two schools went home for lunch, there being no such institution as school meals then. One midday whilst we were at home the sirens started wailing. Nobody took any notice, any more than if a cow in the orchard started bellowing for its calf which had just been taken to market, they had long since learned to disregard such occurrences. But suddenly we heard a loud droning somewhere overhead and a few moments later came the dull thud of an explosion.

"Well," said Mrs Costin looking thunderstruck. She was standing, tablespoon upraised, having been serving herself with vegetables. All chewing stopped, knives and forks clattered onto plates, heads turned towards windows, ears cocked up. There was a moment's silence and absolute stillness round the table then everyone ran outside and gazed about though there was nothing to be seen or heard in the clear blue lunchtime sky.

"Could o' crashed I s'pose," said Bob gazing up hoping to see a parachute gently descending. He fancied rounding up a Jerry with his pitchfork.

"One of ours perhaps", ventured Mrs Costin.

"Course not woman, didn't you hear the warning?" said Mr Costin curtly.

"Twant no plane crashed at all," said Fred. "I heard that engine after the bang. Must have been a bomb."

So with continuing speculation as to what had happened we trailed back in and continued eating before our meat pie got cold. However, before it was time to go back to school, news had arrived in the village by bicycle and achieved almost instantaneous distribution, that an oil bomb had fallen in the fields somewhere out in a remote and uninhabited area between us and a neighbouring village.

"Probably trying for the railway line," decided Fred with his Special Constabulary authority, referring to the single track that took a few one coach trains each day between Dunstable and Leighton Buzzard.

By one of those rare but dazzling displays of empathy that children are capable of, we all congregated in the road outside Aud and Doug's cottage a few minutes later, and all with the firm intention of going to see that oil bomb hole. We were confidently defiant about school. "They won't mind," said Doug, "too bad if they do anyway."

Burghley School, all labelled up, heading out of London bound for Bedfordshire.

"Mum said she didn't mind if we went," said Aud, bending the truth a little to suit the mood, "so old Miss Jones can just go and whistle."

"Well, it's important I say," declared Betty, "it might not happen again in our lifetime. We've got a right to go."

"Come on, it's going to be fun," shouted Joan. "Let's get going."

No one protested, none defected, there were no faint hearts. In one eager, intent body we moved off down the road, five-year-olds clutching the hands of older siblings, all determined to see what a real live bomb crater looked like.

We must have been a couple of dozen I suppose, just about all the primary age children there were at our end of the village. Eric wasn't so lucky, he was up in Dunstable at the secondary school and wasn't he just consumed with envy when he got home at teatime and heard about our adventure! It didn't weigh with me at all that I had seen hundreds of bomb craters and been terrified and in mortal danger from the explosions that made them and had surveyed vast seas of destruction and seen the whole of the East India Docks a gigantic wall of flame. This oil bomb in a distant field was obviously different and had to be investigated, it was too obvious to merit comparison. For one thing I'd never heard of an oil bomb. But the species of bomb was immaterial, it was a bit of war action we were after and which drew us like a magnet.

Next morning, however, it was a bomb of a different sort that exploded among us with a terrific detonation. Miss Jones wasn't amused at our little escapade, she wasn't amused at all. Rockets flew in all directions, the air was acrid with her scornful, smouldering remarks. We were hauled up before her and given a thorough dressing down. We had taken time off school, without permission and unjustifiably in her view. And just to see a hole in the ground. We had recklessly jeopardised our future for a silly escapade. She had only had three in her class for the afternoon and she took that as a personal insult. Her Welsh fire fizzed and crackled and meekly we took it all.

I'm afraid I shall have to make a report about it," she said after the main force of the eruption was over. "It will have to go to the office." We wrinkled our noses and screwed up our eyes in an effort to picture the horror with which our wildness would be received by these unimaginable 'powers' in vast marble halls somewhere in the heart of Empire.

On the whole though we were unrepentant, among ourselves anyway. We felt it had been worth it. We had eventually tracked the crater down after much time spent walking through many fields. On the way there we were buzzing with excitement and anticipation and on the way back glowing with satisfaction spiced with just a dash of the fear of wrathful retribution. A couple of chaps hedging and ditching had stopped their work in response to our eager enquiries and come out into the road to get a good look at us, this miniature Hamelin band, piperless. "Waal," drawled one of them with a slow smile, "bomb is it yer looking fer? Where were it Tom?" and he half lifted his cap with one hand and scratched his balding head, still clutching his hook.

Tom took a long slow look at us before replying as if deciding whether he'd got any right discussing such weighty things with mere kids.

"Reckon it were 'bout 'arf way to Billi'ton," he grunted grudgingly at last, 'cross that way."

Thanking them we hurried on seeing the beginning of a likely track.

"Tes a fair ole step mind," warned the hook clutcher and they turned back, heads shaking sorrowfully, to tidying up the hedge.

When we finally got there the crater turned out to be a shallow hole about three yards wide in a ploughed field and we saw a bit of twisted metal and the ground around was blackened and the stuff on our fingers and in some cases clothes, looked and smelt like oil. True, no damage had been done, there was no blood nor bodies lying about and there wasn't a scrap of official concern over this savage attack upon our native soil, in fact there seemed nobody for miles across the flat empty fields. And if they had been aiming for the railway line they were rotten shots for there was no track to be seen anywhere near. But our imaginations more than made up for any deficiency in authentic horror. "We could have been playing just here," someone said.

"Yeah, could have been out blackberrying. Gosh, look at those big ones up there."

"And it could have fallen right in the middle of us."

"Would 'ave killed all you lot."

"Yeah, just think how sorry our mums and dads would 'ave been then."

There was a moment's silence whilst everyone savoured the delicious thrill of their own death and their parents' remorse for all the unjust punishments they had meted out to their offspring who were now among the angels.

Thus thoroughly cheered up we came home very pleased with ourselves having taken the whole afternoon for the outing. Miss Jones had, it is true, carried on a bit more than we thought she would, but fair enough that was what schoolteachers were for and we were willing to pay the price. And we secretly told ourselves that we would do the same again if need be. We also complained bitterly among ourselves that the village school had taken the matter very calmly, no explosions, no rantings, no recriminations.

Perhaps from that incident there grew in the mind of someone in the village that Miss Jones was an exceedingly odd fish and perhaps more than just odd. For one day not long after the oil bomb incident, the village suddenly hummed with great excitement and we almost moved into the official espionage annals of the war. It was after school one day that I was up in the bedroom changing into old clothes to go out to some particularly dirty game when Mrs Costin called up, "Mick, will you come down please, there's someone here to see you."

I came down and there in the sitting room with Mrs Costin were two men in raincoats holding trilby hats.

"Now Mick," said Mrs Costin. "These two gentlemen are policemen and they want to ask you a few questions. Sit down and try to answer as best you can."

In those few pregnant seconds before the inquisition started, my recent misdeeds were disgorged into my conscious mind in one huge undigested mass, dozens of cases of trespass, apple stealing, bottle smashing, truth frequently embellished and a morass of illwill wished on friend and foe alike. Take your choice, I was guilty and I knew it.

"Well son," said one of the men sitting down himself and trying to smile reassuringly, "it's about school I.want to ask you."

"School!" said my mind sweeping away the mass of evil, relieved yet astonished. Then, "Oh Lord," I thought, "so that's the trouble. Surely Miss Jones hasn't put the police onto us for skipping school for one measly afternoon.

I must have flushed guiltily for the other man butted in, "Now, it's nothing to worry about lad, you haven't done anything wrong." I hope my eyes didn't register the flashed thought, "Not that you've found out about yet perhaps."

"We want to ask you about your headmistress, Miss Jones," went on the first man. He paused, searching for the best way to enlist my co-operation. "Do you like her?" he came out with lamely. "Do you get on well with her? What do all the children think of her? Is she popular?"

I needed time to think about a question like that in these circumstances. I just looked back at them stupidly, scarcely able to believe my own ears. I suspected a trap and kept mum, fearing worse was to come.

He tried again. "We've heard that she has been saying what a good man Hitler is and how he has made Germany into a fine country and how she hopes the Germans will win the war and things like that. Can you remember Miss Jones saying that sort of thing? Perhaps it was part of a history lesson. It could be important so think carefully."

I was completely mystified at this although it was a more fruitful line than being asked whether I liked Miss Jones. But although I was eager not to disappoint these secret agents and to do my bit for Britain, I could only lamely admit that I knew nothing about such sayings by Miss Jones. I tried to remember what we had been doing in the way of history lately but not even though I frantically searched my memory for any likely scraps could I find anything that might condemn her as a spy. At that moment I would dearly like to have done so, not out of malice but to keep the ball rolling as it were, build up the excitement, get carried away by the thrill of it and see where it might lead. Of course we had all heard tales of the spies who guided the bombers in with flashing torches from the bottom of the garden on dark nights, but Miss Jones one of them?

The two gentlemen somewhat wearily thanked us both, swore us to absolute secrecy and went and with them departed any dawning hopes I may have had of involvement in the cloak and dagger world of counter espionage.

The affair was of course the big subject of conversation in the village immediately afterwards and Fred with his Specials' superior expertise in security matters opted for non-committal but vaguely disturbing opinions, intimating that though he couldn't let us into his own knowledge of the case yet, there could be profound implications for all of us and that it was all tied in with a vast network of spies who were working for our downfall, maybe from a back street in Dunstable or some abandoned building out in the fields somewhere.

Naturally for the next few days we regarded with suspicion any empty, isolated building around the village, especially if it was overgrown with ivy or had branches coming up through the roof where an aerial might be hoisted. A quick look round for the transmitter, a scratch with feet among the straw for concealed weapons, half bricks in our hands just in case, and Eric and I would cross another suspect off our list and have a quick practice at how we would have disposed of the cowering Boche in the corner.

The morning after the detectives' visit we observed Miss Jones with that degree of intensity that only young eyes are capable of. Whenever her eyes weren't on us, ours were on her, probing every crease and wrinkle, every hair and spot and occasional wart, trying to see if that pink Welsh skin concealed the grey hide of a German spy. Miss Jones however, showed not the slightest concern, appeared completely unruffled and at ease, taking us soberly through our usual routine and eventually conducting us in her national anthem with her usual fervour. We never did discover whether she was aware of the gossip about her, she never referred to it and the village, to its credit, was quick to have done with such malicious nonsense, started probably as a prank or by someone with an imagined grudge against her.

One day near the end of the school year Miss Jones took me and a girl classmate in her little green Austin seven up to Dunstable to visit a London school that was evacuated there. We were definitely too old for a junior school now and had to be found a secondary school somewhere, preferably one from London, for, horror of horrors, you couldn't trust local, country education. No, Londoners had to be taught in London schools, it was only right and proper. So off we went for an interview to this school in Dunstable, "Not just an ordinary elementary school," Miss Jones pointed out with pride, "but a Central School." Swept away for ever by the Butler Act of 1944, Central Schools played an honourable if brief role in English Secondary Education. By keeping boys till sixteen they provided an extra rung on the ladder of opportunity up which their pupils could clamber, higher than those in elementary schools where you left at fourteen but not so high as in the grammar schools where you could stay till eighteen.

We were shown around and had an interview with the headmaster who was very friendly though ancient, having stayed on well beyond the point of retirement to help with the problems of evacuation. Everything must have gone off successfully for our transfer was arranged for the autumn. So I left the little school in the Memorial Hall and instead caught the bus each morning for the three mile trip to town. The school lingered on a while but eventually the remaining children were transferred to the village school along with Miss Rhodes the teacher of the younger class. She married the vicar in due course and continued in the school long after the war was over. Miss Pepperall, the other teacher, moved to the Dunstable school with us. As for the Memorial Hall it returned exclusively to its Whist Drives, dances and the like which it doubtless continues with to this day unless the bingo revolution has swept the old pastimes away.

Miss Jones returned to London and out of my life for ever. Yet whenever I hear the fervent singing of 'Land of My Fathers' I still think of her and still mechanically repeat those words learned so many years ago in that Bedfordshire Memorial Hall; –'Gwlard, gwlard, pleidol ouvre in gwlard–'.

Chapter V

Village Games

I soon acquired another very good friend. Mac wasn't an evacuee but his family was new to the village and he lived in an isolated row of new houses on the Eaton Bray border. No other children lived there so Mac and his younger brother Nipper were always in the village playing, and Mac became one of our select band of brothers who did everything together.

Mac was the clown, the buffoon of our group. He was good natured and tolerant of the ragging that his far fetched tales and comical way of telling them provoked. We never did discover whether his father won the V.C. as Mac claimed, or whether he organised the camouflaging of Whipsnade's huge chalk lion as Mac assured us he had, or was a prime developer of radar, or radiolocation as it was called then, whose mysterious towers appeared in the fields at Dagnall allegedly at Mac's dad's behest. One thing was sure, we never set eyes on this illustrious dad. He was away on hush hush war missions Mac assured us, and was far too involved to take any leave. Which was a pity really for we conceived a picture of him as a combination of Tarzan and Einstein.

At the bottom of the orchard was an acre or so of low lying meadow that was almost permanently flooded. For a few weeks in early Spring the air around this pond was filled with the low harsh cacophony of amorous croaking and we would watch with an almost guilty fascination the clumps of frogs, one atop the other, crawling in ungainly fashion about the mud or squatting half submerged in water and tapioca-like spawn. The pond's margins were favoured by peewits for nesting sites. They wheeled and tumbled above our heads and dive bombed in a vain attempt to keep us away, then they would land and limp off dragging a wing, feigning injury to lure us away from their nests. But we were up to their tricks and several times brought to the kitchen handfuls of the dark olive-green eggs with black blotches to be used for cooking.

One rainy day Mac and I were prowling around the bottom barn. It was a gloomy, cavernous place save when in summer the big door high up in the end wall was swung open to let in the light and air. Then along with the sunlight the swallows would streak in to their nests high up in the tops of the timbers. Those old barns were inexhaustible treasure houses to inquisitive, questing boys. You never knew what you might find. Slid between the overlapping boards were the blades of old sickles and scythes of unimaginable antiquity, pock-marked with rust and with worm-eaten handles. We discovered a dusty yoke with chains still attached from which buckets were suspended, and pondered on when and by whom that was last used. Old horse brasses we found and old pieces of harness and all manner of odd shaped tools and implements, outmoded and laid to rest amid the dust and shadows.

Right at the back of the barn we came across a couple of ancient motor bikes covered in thick dust and cobwebs. They were minus their wheels and were rusty and looked as though they had been there for decades; I imagined them to have been Fred's and Reg's when they were young men obsessed with speed and noise. We brushed them off, dragged them out into a pool of light and leapt on to complete several circuits of the dirt track in neck and neck competition. Then having given an exhibition on the wall of death we turned our attention to the flat bottomed petrol tanks. Mac suggested that we take them off and use them as boats on the pond in the orchard.

I could see what he meant; they had that sleek streamlined look, the futuristic design that boats were bound to adopt sooner or later. There was a problem with a pipe or two jutting out at the bottom but we managed to bash those off and plug the holes, and the filler caps converted nicely to a revolutionary type of combined bridge and gunnery block. We soon completed the job and, as the rain had by then stopped, lost no time in launching them upon their maritime career. Thereafter Mac and I spent many an hour in wellingtons, propelling our craft with long sticks around the world's oceans. Graf Spee, Exeter, Scharnhorst, Hood, our naval campaigns, with clods of mud for missiles, made up in enthusiastic action for what they lacked in tactical finesse.

During a lull in naval activity one day Mac and I decided on a spot of land reclamation and set to work to dig a canal across the ten yards or so of meadow that separated the pond from a cattle drinking hole by the brook. The intention was to drain the pond with the vague notion of presenting Mr Costin with an acre or so of reclaimed grazing. This we felt would not be without significance in the national struggle for survival. After all, we reasoned, it had been done for the Fens so why shouldn't we do it for our marshland. As the piece of meadow between the pond and the drinking hole was a slight ridge we had a surprising amount of excavating to do with the old hand trowels we had 'borrowed'. We thought that three or four inches wide ought to be sufficient for our canal and as deep as necessary to get the water to flow. Every spare moment for several days was devoted to our great work. Tea over, Mac would be waiting outside and we'd slip off mysteriously to the orchard saying nothing about our driving ambition. Some of the other boys came to find out what we were up to and stayed to admire and to assist in the work.

Great was our excitement and sense of achievement as the first trickle of water ran along the entire ten yard length of the canal and emptied into the

Henley's mechanised fruit picking team prepares for action!

The lovely old farmhouse where Guy lived, and still lives, at the end of Chapel Lane.

drinking hole. We imagined it would be just like taking the plug out of the sink, there'd be a bit of a swish and a gurgle and then, hey presto! all the water would be gone. Not so unfortunately. Although the water did continue to flow for a while it never seemed to lower the level of the pond, to our great disappointment, and cattle always trampled all over it when we weren't there, reducing all our careful engineering to a mangled muddy mess. So eventually we gave it up and went back to our petrol tank flotilla, but all the activity together over the construction of the Mickmac canal cemented the relationship between us, and Mac and I were firm friends ever after. For some reason land drainage as a career never did appeal to me in later life, though Mac or his father may have excelled in it for all I know.

Dam building was always one of our periodic obsessions and the whole gang of us would suddenly decide we would like to see how deep a pool we could make in front of a dam – we dreamed of being able to swim in our own home-made pool. In that chalky land there wasn't a decent sized river for miles with pools that we could swim in so it was no surprise that on hot, listless summer days we would stare irritably at our trickle of a brook and dream of what might have been.

There and then at the bottom of the orchard we would begin to throw up a dam. Great handfuls of blue-grey clay would be scooped from the stream bed and built up over a core of the biggest stones we could find. The stream was only three or four feet wide and it ran beneath a tunnel of trees which sheltered us from any would-be interference, especially from Horace Henley's field which bordered the far bank. Closing the final gap in the dam was always the most hectic part of our water engineering, with the current racing through in all its concentrated force. But with sheer weight of numbers we always won and thereafter raced to raise the clay faster than the water rose, exulting as the bed on one side drained dry and the deepening pool spread upstream on the other side. We never raised the water to swimming depth though we certainly filled our wellingtons as we strode about like Gullivers in the Lilliputian sea.

For a while we had splendid visions of our altered landscape, Horace Henley's fields sunk beneath a vast lake where we would boat and swim to our hearts' content, and a desert downstream strewn with the skeletons of cattle as in an Arizona western. Then either our two foot high wall collapsed in spite of all our shouting and rushing madly about with handfuls of clay and sticks, and a miniature tidal wave swept all before it, or the water lapped over the top and sidled around the ends to form a temporary weir before final and inevitable disintegration.

We were never discouraged, we had sniffed briefly the heady scent of power over the elements and would soon be back for another try. It was also one of the few activities into which we could all throw our energies reasonably free from the fear of wrathful broadsides from some adult.

Behind the farmhouse and below the end of the bottom barn was the sheepyard, a relic of the days not so long past, when sheep had been kept on the farm as they were throughout the whole area. The Knolls undoubtedly had its flocks and its shepherds in past times, as did all the steep-sloped chalk hills in the district. Now there was never a sheep to be seen anywhere for miles around. The sheepyard consisted of low, open fronted sheds forming three sides of a square and having the high end of the main barns as its fourth side. A five-barred gate led into the orchard. This enclosure was our cricket ground.

Dusty, cramped, stony and uneven it may have been but it was a marvellous arena for practising and perfecting ball skills. Day after day we played there, endlessly catching, throwing and striking balls that came at all speeds and at all angles off the various surfaces and objects, until we had become as adept with a ball as our natural ability would allow. Bob used to join us in the evening quite often and Eric, Mac, Doug and I had hundreds of fierce games with him there. Bob was playing for the Minor Counties side at the time and he kept us on the go clouting the tennis ball around that confined cauldron with incredible strength and gusto.

A post of the shed was the wicket and we bowled from the barn end; the shed outer wall was our wicket keeper. The ball sizzled around that yard like a rocket and we soon learned to thump it with no mean force too. As the space was so confined, about ten yards square of open ground, you had to learn to field well and to duck quickly to stay alive. There was no running to score, each wall had its run value and a hit into the orchard was six and out. We bowled under arm and it was always a spinner's wicket. Bob could make the ball break both ways, from the leg and the off, and we weren't slow in emulating him and although we never achieved his prowess we learnt a lot and could make the ball leap and spurt about in the dust helped by the bumpy surface. The thing to do was to bowl so rapidly that the batsman never settled. Ours was no leisurely, gentlemanly game, we worked up a sweat running, fielding, ducking, shouting, until someone was out or the ball was temporarily lost under the pony trap or some piece of machinery left standing under the sheds.

When Bob wasn't there it was Eric and I that were kings; Mac never had quite the same instinctive skill with a ball, even his dad wasn't much good at cricket, he informed us, being Scots of course. Occasionally when smaller children came up we would graciously allow them to field for us, but they usually fled in terror when we started cracking the ball against the barn's wooden wall with a noise like a rifle shot.

Cricket in the yard was one of our great standbys and a firm favourite and we were not of course restricted to the official season, we were just as likely to open hostilities on a fine day in November or February as in July. A useful alternative to cricket was hot rice, where you had to throw the ball at the batsman and try to hit him below the knee. He could move about as he liked all over the yard. That was hectic fun if there was a group of you hurling the ball like a thunderbolt, bouncing it off walls, feinting then slipping it to another player who would hurl it in, hit the target, then rush and grab the bat, and on we would go again rushing about and shouting like lunatics.

Football was never a popular game with us. We were lacking in numbers for a decent game, there was no accepted pitch in Lower End, where slopes abounded, and one soon got fed up trudging twenty yards to fetch the ball each time someone kicked it past the goal. Football lacked the high speed and excitement of our brand of cricket where everyone was actively engaged all the time.

After our introduction to archery in the first days of my arrival in the village, we all became enthusiastic with the bow and arrow, though our achievements were never encouraging. Having made our bows with much discussion and co-operation, so that everyone had something reasonable that they could bend and twang, and having cut a few arrows each as straight as possible, the next thing was, what should we do for a target? Pieces of card or apples didn't satisfy us for long, we had our hunting instincts to obey. Rabbits were the obvious answer, nobody owned them, they moved and could be killed with impunity for they were everywhere in plague quantities. So as dusk fell our band of Bedfordshire Bowmen slipped like shadows through the orchard, stopping statuesque behind a tree at a signal, loaded bows at the ready as the bunnies went about their evening feed.

Of course, no self respecting rabbit was going to let itself be shot by mere boys but very occasionally out of contempt or utter weariness of our comic antics, one or two let us come within range, sitting up in the long grass to watch us. Excitedly we would take aim, the idea being that if we all fired together someone would be bound to hit the target. 'Fire' came the hissed command. The arrows thudded into the ground anything but simultaneously and over a spread of ten yards or so, long after their targets were well below ground, laughing or cursing as befitted their characters.

Perhaps our results would have been better if we'd had access to yew but there was none and local willow consisted only of a few pollarded specimens alongside the brook. These points weighed with us but we weren't fussy and were prepared to try any sort of strong straight stick. In spite of earnest endeavours we never became very proficient archers, perhaps the Crecy tradition was dead in us.

One day, however, Eric came along with an idea which added a new string to our bow and, although it was summer, temporarily ended cricket's innings. He had just an arrow and a piece of string and he demonstrated to Mac and me how to send that arrow an amazing distance with incredible ease. He had a knot at the end of the string which he wound once round the arrow below the cigarette card flights. Then he ran the string down to the arrow's point, gripped arrow and string there together and gave a powerful throw upwards and out. The arrow flew almost the entire width of the meadow alongside the orchard and thudded firmly into the ground a couple of hundred yards or more away. Eric gave us his "Well, what do you think of that then?" look.

Needless to say we were very impressed although we pointed out it was a method designed for distance not for accuracy. All right against the massed ranks of Germans advancing across the orchard but not much good against their marauding bands of snipers that we occasionally had to deal with. Soon enough, volleys of arrows were darkening the sky over the meadow and many

Ralph Holland the thatcher lived in a little cottage, now no more, next to Eric.

Bert Procter with Margaret Henley on the horse. The Knolls are in the background.

a competition we had to see who could hurl his arrow furthest. In spite of scores of near misses amongst the cows and hens dotted about none was actually transfixed, though several arrows thudded into Charlie Saunders' orchard next door where his pigs wandered freely; his goat was on a long tether and his many ducks and geese busied themselves in the long grass.

He was a friendly old chap, Charlie Saunders. He was retired and played at keeping all manner of stock on his acre or so of land. We used to see him striding down between the trees in his brown farmer's coat, capped and wellingtoned, giving his own peculiarly strident poultry call and broadcasting the seed from the bucket on his arm with great sweeps into the grass. Then all the ducks, geese and hens converged on him in a great cacophony of sound and he stood in the midst of that sea of feeding poultry like some modern St Francis.

Whilst playing cricket we very occasionally skied the ball behind the wicket over the low shed roof and into Charlie's place. So we'd wander round in a gang and he'd welcome us in, help us to find the ball and show us round. He kept dozens of guinea pigs, rats and rabbits of various hues in his sheds and it was rumoured that he sent them away for vivisection but he never mentioned that and we didn't. We stroked some of his rabbits, had our fingers nipped by his guinea pigs, scratched his sow's back and looked around a bit at everything of interest. His wife was a friendly soul too, she took Mary Austin in and kept her for a long time. Mrs Saunders didn't go out much, she was probably not in very good health. We used to see her outdoors polishing the brass name plate on the cottage gate, Ko-zi-Kot, but that was about as far as she went. Charlie would stride off to Chapel on his own on Sunday evenings in his smart blue suit and trilby hat.

One of the things that brought all the children of Lower End in a great band to play together was the freezing over of the Moat. Our castle on top of the Knolls may have been problematical, our Moat down below was undeniable, though it surrounded no fortress. It was a long pond, fed by no stream, many feet deep and about five or six yards wide, fringed with trees and bushes. It was lower down in the village by Fosse's rickyard. Reg's house was nearby and, when an Arctic spell came as it always did in those times, we watched the thickening ice each day, standing on the edge poking it with sticks and skimming stones across, until Reg pronounced it safe for us to venture on. The first year I was there the ice was so thick that Reg said he was sure he could have driven the tractor across it, that was a memorable winter for thick, long lying snow and ice. Thumbs up having been given, we all swooped down on the ice, slipping and sliding about in a great frenzy of activity. With a fearsome collection of hockey sticks torn from the surrounding jungle we flailed our way over the rink in the fondly imagined style of the Toronto Tigers.

All you needed to do was to divide the great mass of sliders into two roughly equal teams keeping as many of your own friends as possible on your side. For the start the players were in their own half of the ice but as soon as the solemn ritual of the 'bully off' was completed, everyone was everywhere and nobody knew who was on whose side. More players were usually on their backs than on their feet at any given moment. It didn't matter, we got on with the fun regardless of what happened to the chunk of stone we were meant to be hitting and little games within the game broke out whenever an idle moment occurred. The pair of moorhens who normally had this secluded stretch of water to themselves, now deprived of their natural element, fled in terror of our noisy games and skulked in the undergrowth at the far end of the Moat where it bent round and shallowed away to nothing, doubtless praying for an early thaw.

Many a time in winter I've woken to that peculiar white silence of the early morning that told me the instant I opened my eyes that snow, deep snow had fallen. Every sound in the yard was muffled, the rough clatter of buckets on stone was silenced, cows moved about as if in carpet slippers. I could hear Fred creaking over the snow in his gum boots and there was the absolute silence of no traffic on the road. I dressed in a rush, washed in icy water at the washstand even more speedily, slipped on a pair of wellingtons and went outside to be met by that tingling slap of freezing air on the face that is deep winter's frosty greeting.

Between the side of the house and the barns the snow didn't have a chance, it was a narrow wind funnel that permitted only a shallow covering, sullied already by the passage of feet. But up on the road it was a different story, the smooth curves of untouched drifts stretched away in a frozen tide swell where the tarmac had been and was no more. A line or two of broken snow showed where Reg and Arthur had trampled through up to their knees to do the milking but there wasn't a single blemish by wheels to be seen. No buses got through, no early morning traffic of any kind, and snowploughs being unheard of then the chances were that was how it would stay all day and perhaps the next with a bit of luck.

In the certain knowledge that there could be no school that day the Knolls drew me irresistibly. I knew I would have to climb up and sample the Arctic wildness of those heights though I managed to keep the actual setting out at bay, reserved for later, to be thought about with a secret excitement whilst we had breakfast. The grumblings and grim faces over the fried eggs showed how adults didn't have a boy's delight in deep snow. To them it meant added difficulties and delays, no morning mail, no paper, no milk lorry to collect the half dozen or so churns, to say nothing of the difficulty of movement for man and beast and the hardship of working outdoors in sub zero temperatures.

It was with a wild exultant joy that almost would not be contained that I eventually climbed the steep path opposite the house, so steep that the tussocks of grass showed still where the snow could not settle. No more snow was falling, the wind had dropped and the air was almost still under a heavy, leaden sky. Up on the top was a miniature tundra, a gleaming snowy waste with bushes shedding their white load from sheer weight in the slightest of breezes that now and then stirred the hoary old man's beard and rustled a little brown wispy grass on the side of sheltered hollows. Across the fresh unfrozen surface of the smooth snow the tracks of rabbits and the footprints of birds could easily be followed. A lone yellow hammer seemed to accompany me as it flitted silently between hawthorn bushes seeking some lingering berries.

I felt like a trapper in the Arctic living on his wits for survival in that total icy waste. The flat plain below was blanketed in white, familiar features sunk beneath a sea of snow. Telegraph poles alone showed the line of the road, hedges and trees stood out blackly and over everything hung a rare cloak of stillness in which the least sound carried for miles on the clear, frosty air . . . I wandered about here and there around the little hills, my tracks the only sign of human life in all that lost Siberian waste. One of my recurring daydreams was to live up there on the hills in some chalky cavern, to lie out on the grass of a summer's night and enjoy the dawn with birds and animals who would become my friends. But the harshness of winter froze out the daydreams and I didn't picture myself so close to Nature that day as I stamped around in snow near the tops of my wellingtons.

In those times of deep snow which never failed us each winter, another exciting communal activity emerged to occupy our leisure. Everyone who had a sledge or anything that could be sat on to slide over snow, even old tin tea trays, climbed up to the Knolls, chose a slope out of the scores of possible ones large and small, and for several hours each day transformed a corner of Bedfordshire into the ski slopes of Switzerland.

There was one devilishly steep-sided pit that was our special favourite and which gave the biggest thrills and spills of all. The angle of slope was well over 45° and once started from the top the descent was a breathless flash, a blur of motion. It must have been about forty feet or so to the bottom before the rise up the other side. Given good deep snow, one was fairly likely to stay upright and reach halfway up the far side triumphantly, but if there were grassy humps and tussocks showing through the snow then the descent was perilous and a spill at high speed likely. However, our tumbles never did us any harm, the snow was soft and cushioning and we just rolled over in it a few times then got up and brushed ourselves down. So in spite of my heart being in my mouth each time, I'd go down repeatedly, usually on the back of Eric's or Doug's sledge, for I, like many others, didn't have a sledge of my own but acted as crew to others, the double weight helping to keep the sledge in contact with the surface.

Our snowfights on the Knolls were pretty good affairs too. No sides, every man for himself and the air was thick with flying snow whenever a good crowd was up there sledging. How often have I felt that special tingling sensation in hands that have, so to speak, got their second wind from grasping snowballs and could go on for hours without feeling the cold and when the quality of snow was just right for firm solid missiles that wouldn't disintegrate half way but land good and hard on their target.

Sliding on the Moat and sledging on the Knolls were the two main events that brought all the children together and both those were winter events. In the other seasons we were never quite so united though we older boys and girls frequently came together to make a good sized gang. Apart from Eric and Mac there were only two other boys of about my age from our end of the village, Tadpole and Guy. Tadpole lived in the council houses and was a close friend of Guy, a farmer's son from below the Chapel. We occasionally all played

The young Guy Henley's first home by the bus stop in Lower End. Jimmy Knight lived next door.

together and were always good friends, but usually Guy and Tadpole kept to themselves and spent their time around Guy's farm. We went down to the farm now and again but were never really at home there as Tadpole was.

However, the threat of invasion, as in the adult world, united us as little else was able to. The Church End boys decided one day it would be fun to come down and beat us up and impose their sovereignty on the whole village. Theirs was the largest part of the village and was as distinct and different from Lower End as if they were two separate villages. Rather resembling a dog's bone in shape the village had a knob of population at each end and a long middle stretch to keep them apart. So although it was one parish, each end of the bone thought of itself as separate from and more important than the other. In particular our end, Lower End, the smaller and more sparsely peopled end, fiercely maintained its independence and identity from the larger, more powerful big brother at Church End.

The Church End boys outnumbered us by many and we quite naturally looked on them as the dreaded enemy. They issued their challenge, a stone fight on the Knolls – "If you don't come and fight us you're a lot of cissies and we'll come down and beat you up anyway" – stated the day and time, and laughed and joked at the thought of us putting up any resistance.

We had a meeting to discuss the crisis. The girls were ebullient, excessively optimistic and disparaging of the enemy; the boys were quiet and cautious, fearful of the opposition and critical of the girls.

"Who do they think they are?" asked Betty scornfully, "we'll show 'em."

"Oh yeah, all right for you to talk," said Mac.

"What's the matter," laughed Joan, "you're not scared are you?"

"Well, if he's not, I am," said Tadpole with a frank grin. "It's all right for you girls to be so cheerful, we'll have to do the fighting."

"We'll beat them," declared Aud decisively, "and we"ll help won't we girls?"

Eric and I remained taciturn, glum. I could picture some of those big Church Enders and I couldn't see a few girls being much help.

"Come on, show a bit of guts you lot," exhorted Betty.

We shuffled about uneasily.

"Are we going to fight them or are they going to call us cowards?" demanded Joan.

"No-one calls a Macdonald a coward," said Mac fiercely, then grinned sheepishly.

"Oh, all right," said Eric with some exasperation, "I s'pose we'll have to fight them."

"Don't show such keenness," said Betty venomously.

So in the age-old fashion we worked ourselves up into a frame of mind for war, there seemed no other honourable course open to us.

Three young men of Lower End down at Guy's.

The day came and we were ready. We had mustered almost the entire child population of our end and were up on the Knolls before the appointed time to take up a strong position. We knew our hills better than the Church Enders and we decided to defend the Spyglass, a high, steep-sided hill, not overlooked and with plenty of loose chalk lying about. It wasn't long before the enemy came swarming over the hills, not outnumbering us in fact, for some of them hadn't turned up, but they were bigger and older than us and they hadn't got the liability of girls or much younger boys.

The Church Enders left us in no doubt about what they thought of us. "Can't fight their own battles, got to have girls to fight for them."

"What a lot of heroes. Wait till we get at them."

"You'd better surrender straightaway, before we murder you."

We replied with our endlessly repeated refrain, "Church End, Church End, leave you in the lurch end," nonsensical, but intensely annoying to our adversaries.

These and many similar niceties having been exchanged the battle began in grim earnest. We were scared but defiant. Stones flew thick and fast but throwing downwards from the slopes of the Spyglass we had the advantage, and the Church Enders, lacking any tactical finesse and thinking to annihilate us quickly, came at us in a group, offering us an easy target. They also had the difficulty of throwing uphill whilst having to climb upwards at the same time. They couldn't just walk through our rain of missiles and to their surprise they had to split up, take what cover they could and keep at long range. The battle went on for ages, evenly balanced; everyone on our side fought heroically. We grew in confidence seeing them falter and with the knowledge that our pride was at stake. The smaller children found stones for the bigger ones so that we were able to keep up a continual barrage to such good effect that eventually the enemy drew back and gave us a breather. It was a miracle that no one had been seriously hurt, for quite sizeable chunks of hard chalk were being hurled furiously on both sides.

In the interval Betty and Aud, veritable Boadiceas exulting in the struggle, raised our already high morale to fever pitch by their earnest exhortations and we knew we couldn't be beaten as the Church Enders came again, circling the Spyglass probing for a better place to attack. But we had chosen our fortress well, it was equally steep all round. They collected piles of stones, filled their pockets and came at us in a determined body. It was touch and go several times.

"You might as well give in," yelled Elwin Witts as they charged.

"Go back home," we yelled back in defiance, "you're not wanted here."

"We'll teach you a lesson," threatened Johnny Janes as he hurled a stone.

"Rotten shot," we chorused, returning his stone with interest.

It looked for a while as though they might break through and reach the top of the Spyglass and we knew that would be the end of us, but we managed to hit several of them hard enough to deter them from a final rush and once again after a long struggle they withdrew to neighbouring slopes, baffled and humiliated. After that only sporadic and long range exchanges took place and at last to our delight the Church Enders went off, still issuing threats and insults but knowing they had failed to live up to their assumed mastery of the village. We had fought well, in keeping with the tradition of that place, and our defence of their old territory would not perhaps have displeased the shades of those earlier, pre-historic defenders of those hills.

Flushed with triumph we followed them down to the road where there took place several shoulder to shoulder, eyeball to eyeball confrontations between us boys; threats were freely exchanged and wills tested. But it was all bluff, the real battle was over. After a few minutes they suddenly became friendlier and admitted that we had put up a good show. There were smiles all round, the atmosphere became relaxed and our adversaries soon departed with honour and good humour restored. That was the last invasion we suffered and our victory did no end of good to our morale and welded evacuees and village children even more firmly into one friendly group.

Like all good gangs we had a den. Ours was a summer den, a treehouse in a maple oak a little way beyond the Moat. It wasn't exactly in a central position, we had to make a specific journey to get there, but we found it was just the occasional kind of lair that satisfied our needs and it was secret, known and used only by the older boys and girls. It was a rough affair of a few planks to make a platform about fifteen feet up, but sitting there amid summer's dense foliage gave us the true Tarzan feeling, reinforced by the rope we could lower for a quick descent if necessary.

We would wander along there sometimes on a fine evening, through Four Acre Meadow, skirting the tree-lined Moat and skimming a few stones along its surface, or if we were lucky, finding an old bottle that we could throw into the middle and bombard till a well aimed stone smashed it; we prided ourselves on our accurate stone throwing and the successful bottle smasher suddenly put on two inches in height. Sometimes we disturbed the resident pair of moorhens around their huge, twiggy nest built out a few feet from the shore on a bushy island. We never did more than look at the pale, blotched eggs but the rats weren't so particular, and there were seldom more than two or three chicks straining along the calm water after their parents when we came along to disturb them on our expeditions.

From the Moat we continued along the hedge past elms and hawthorn till we came to our tree whose branches were so blessed with footrests, convenient handholds and forks that it would have been a shame not to climb it. No use anyone telling us it was only fifteen feet off the ground, we felt we were up in the roof of the jungle as we perched around the planks and planned how we were going to improve the rudimentary house. We would give it walls of slender branches, thatch the roof, bring up cooking things and stools and make a proper ladder and. . . and. . . It made good talk but somehow it never got done and we were just as pleased with it the way it was anyhow.

Chapter VI

Down on the Farm

I hadn't wasted any time in settling in at the farm; I took to it straight away as if I had been waiting for years for just that opportunity. At twelve years old I was pliable, malleable material, used to a completely different life but not so set and embedded in that life that I couldn't adapt to any other. And of course, I had every incentive to learn new ways, new routines, to fit into a new kind of life and survive. Welcomed and encouraged quietly but kindly by all the family, I couldn't fail to realise that everyone wished to make a success of their evacuee. It is indeed no less than the truth to say that I was treated in every way as one of the family. No little corners of privilege were reserved to make me conscious of my outsider status. No great fuss·was made in front of visiting relations or friends, no curiosity value made of my presence, none of the apologetic, "and here's our East End evacuee," type of thing, I was just quietly involved in the general talk and activity, neither neglected nor made to perform, treated in fact like any other twelve year old son.

The fact that my new life fitted me like a glove meant of course that my old life fitted me less well. My foster family's acceptance of me as one of them meant that I was less firmly rooted in my own family and this was one of the inevitable sadnesses of evacuation in some cases.

My sister Olive had not been so fortunate as me in finding a home in the village. Practically everyone who was willing to have an evacuee had got one by then. I had just been extremely lucky to find a place at the farm which had somehow remained unfilled till then. So, soon after I went to the farm Olive had gone to a foster home in Dunstable and I used to go up on the bus to visit her every couple of weeks and take her sweets and things my mother sent in food parcels.

How I used to look forward to those little parcels! There was always a Mars bar each and various other goodies, my mother's sweet ration saved up and added to by our Gran who lived next door. Between parcels, in her weekly letter my mother stitched down a sixpenny piece onto the writing paper with white cotton. You could buy a lot with sixpence then when small bars of toffee cost a farthing.

Being so young Olive missed my mother a great deal; five is no age to be stranded amongst strangers. So much so that after less than a year, when things had become a little quieter and safer in the capital, she returned home much to her relief. My mother had gone back to London and to work soon after we were settled in our foster homes. How hard it was on mothers in those times, having to accept separation from their children. But in the majority of cases they did it with supreme unselfishness, putting their children's safety above all personal feeling.

By the autumn the Battle of Britain was over; the Germans no longer had mastery of the air above our islands as they threatened to have in those decisive summer days of 1940 when their planes came over in seemingly endless waves. I remember the general feeling of despair and anger amongst our neighbours in London as we stood looking up at the countless silver dots reflecting the afternoon sun as the Germans roared contemptuously in with no opposition, to drop their lethal loads of bombs on our defenceless heads. Now, after their drubbing at the hands of The Few, it was different, the enemy no longer risked mass daylight raids. The night raids were still bad but not so intense as they had once been and Londoners soon learned to live with them.

Soon after my arrival at the farm Daisy, Mrs Costin's married daughter, came to stay for a few weeks. She had something of her father's sharpness of features, there was a clean cut, no nonsense air about her. In the mould of the classic English countrywoman she was cool and sophisticated yet somehow almost horsey, down to earth and immensely practical. Eric, her husband, was with the British Expeditionary Force at Dunkirk. Those long summer weeks of 1940 were very tense, worrying and tearful ones for Daisy as she waited for news of Eric.

The bulletins on the wireless, though basically good in that so many of our soldiers were getting away in the armada of little craft that brought off that miracle rescue, were nevertheless confused. We knew there were a good many casualities as well as many taken prisoner. So Daisy had to be treated with kid gloves whilst uncertainty over Eric's fate lasted. There were several outbursts which I witnessed after some news item had been discussed and opinions aired about the Dunkirk affair less than tactfully in Daisy's hearing. But the day when she heard that Eric was safe and unharmed in England was a day of pure golden rhapsody and relief for Daisy. All the pent up emotion and anxiety of weeks was washed away in a flood of happy tears that she did not attempt to conceal, to be followed by laughter and great gaiety and an overwhelming longing to see him again. The normally staid and sober farmhouse was a seething den of excitement that day you may be sure.

She went away for a few days to meet Eric and to go with him on leave on a second honeymoon and from the moment of her return she was so lighthearted, cheerful and sunny natured that she heightened even more the atmosphere of joviality and good humour which normally prevailed at the farm.

Daisy was kind and good and hard working but having left the farm to get married and having seen how 'up to the minute' suburban women lived in Gerrard's Cross where Eric was a bank cashier, she had no patience with the laborious, old fashioned ways of her mother. In the back kitchen stood the old cooking range that had cooked the family meals for generations. Daisy would have none of it. Her mother had struggled with it all her married life, lighting the fire at six each morning, cooking over it all day, even in summer with the room like a furnace, then cleaning it all out in the evening, blackleading it to make the metalwork gleam richly with a dark velvety shine. Daisy, the new Daisy of Gerrard's Cross, wouldn't touch it and complained bitterly when her mother persevered with it.

"It's ridiculous, mother," she protested, "this range is donkey's years out of date, the whole thing needs scrapping before it kills you. It isn't as though you can't afford a modern stove, either gas or electricity. Anything would be better than that ancient monstrosity."

"Hmm?" replied her mother, shaking her head slightly as she did when weighing things up, "we'll see." She didn't say much more but it was the years of familiarity with the old range that spoke for her. How could she abandon such a loyal servant? And yet there was truth in what Daisy said, she had to admit it to herself. She wasn't getting any younger. The seeds of change began to sprout.

Long, long before the rise of feminism Daisy's incisively determined way of showing the men, who were supremely indifferent to how the house was run unless their comfort or convenience were jeopardised, that they were allowing their mother to kill herself with work while they stood by and did nothing about it, had its results. On washing days Mrs Costin used to carry a huge basketful of wet clothes across the sheepyard and out into the orchard where she hung them out to dry. But not if Daisy could do anything about it she didn't. "Couldn't one of you great men have helped mother with that washing basket?" she demanded when they were all indoors.

"Now how did we know it needed carrying out?" one of them replied, "we were up in the cowshed." Or down in the field it may have been.

"Mother," said Daisy with that mixture of humour and censure that she employed so well, "you'll kill yourself if you go on like that. You shouldn't be heaving heavy things about like that at your time of life when there's strapping great men here to do it for you."

"Oh well," said Mrs Costin in some embarrassment, "I wanted to get on with it."

"Get on with it!" echoed Daisy with a laugh as the men watched wide eyed, "the only getting on you'll do like that is into your grave. And if the washing doesn't get dry so what? I should have thought someone could have taken it out for you when they're about the place, it's more important than mucking out cowsheds."

Dressed reluctantly in Sunday best the author much to his disgust, hauled up to Dunstable to Smy's photographic studio.

Somehow or other that heavy basket of wet clothes always got carried out by male hands from then on. No one asked Daisy why she didn't carry the basket herself if she was so keen to ease her mother's burden. Fortunately her increasingly rotund appearance made such a remark inappropriate and even I had realised that another grandchild, and Daisy's first, was well on the way. It was eventually to turn out to be a little girl, Judith, the apple of her grand parents' eye.

Various modern amenities began to appear after that. The very first was the introduction of a new gas cooker and the abandoning of the old kitchen range. A gas light with an incandescent mantle cast its brilliant white light in the back kitchen and the oil lamp stood on the side bench tarnishing, its cheerful glow extinguished for ever.

To prevent starvation bringing the country to its knees, education was reluctantly persuaded to relax its iron grip a little so that farm children could help out at certain critical times such as the potato harvest. So I was delighted after I had been at the farm a couple of months to be allowed a week off school to help pick up the potatoes. This was the first big job I was to be involved in and I was looking forward to it immensely. I vaguely realised some work was involved but I thought of it mostly as a holiday and one made all the sweeter because the other children were at school except Eric who had potatoes to harvest with his dad. I didn't anticipate any great difficulty with the job, anyone could pick up a few potatoes I thought, it was child's play and not even a look over the scores of rows of potatoes, each row a good furlong in length, gave me any cause for disquiet at what might lie ahead. Nor did the fact that there was another similar-sized potato field around Northfield waiting for us. This was going to be an excellent opportunity to show them that they hadn't got a useless lodger but someone who could be a valuable help.

We were still having our meals, especially breakfast, in the back kitchen in the light of the oil lamp. We sat on benches at a rough deal table scrubbed grey-white till the grain stood up in ridges. On the first Monday of potato picking, it being washing day too, the copper in the corner was early alight warming the room, and wisps of steam were beginning to seep from under the wooden cover. The large old iron-framed mangle stood ready across the room for the action it would see later and the polished bricks of the floor rang as the men's steel-shod boots clashed across them as they came in from milking.

When we got down to the field in the cold grey of the November morning there was a gang of about eight rough, tough looking women, middle aged mostly who'd come to do the picking. With scarves around their heads, wearing old mackintoshes and wellington boots, they may not have been a pretty sight and their language was often scorching, but couldn't they work!

Fred drove the tractor with the spinner behind that scooped the potatoes out of their ridges and scattered them in a wide row behind. Reg and Bob were both dealing with the sacks, tying them, loading them on the trailer when full and putting out new ones. I had to take a bucket and join the gang of women.

The start was unpretentious, like some obscure cross country race. We stood about by the ends of the rows, buckets on arms, waiting whilst last minute adjustments were made to the tackle. Then with a roar the tractor was away and in seconds earth and potatoes were flying up to land in a broad swathe behind like the brown wake of a land cruiser. With a surge we all swarmed over the course and the hare and tortoise race was on, only in this version the tortoise never overtook the hare even when it paused for a long sleep out of pity for its pathetic pursuers.

I was amazed and horrified at the speed with which those women picked up potatoes. There had been a frost overnight and my fingers were soon numb with cold but those women, wearing mittens, went on at an amazing rate regardless of the cold, bent double as they darted about over the soil like eager terriers, potatoes drumming into pails in a continuous tattoo.

It wasn't long before I discovered the real bugbear of potato picking – backache. By mid morning with my fingers regaining a semblance of sensation and when I'd lost count of how many millions of times I had emptied my bucket, my back felt as though it would snap in two with the continuous bending over. The inclination was to stand up and stretch and arch the back luxuriously for minutes on end to find relief from the insistent aching that attacked as soon as I bent down. But of course that picked up no potatoes. And those women sailed right on as if they weren't bothered at all. And I don't suppose they were for they were well used to the work; going round as a gang to all the farms in the district they soon became indestructible.

By dinner time the ache was unbelievable, red hot daggers were being fiendishly twisted in my back. All my fine notions about being an essential member of the farm team, a super help from the city, vanished as the frost in warm sun and I longed to tie up bags with Reg or walk around inspecting like Mr Costin or sit on the tractor's broad mudguard with Fred as I had done at ploughing, anything so long as I didn't have to keep bending, bending over, fingers to the earth, picking up potatoes. But there was no little sinecure for me, no escape from the agony, no honourable way out. I began to appreciate the length of these rows. Interminably they stretched ahead, on and on into purgatory; and the hours stretched ahead whilst the women were grubbing about, their india rubber spines bent double over potatoes in a broad track that stretched away for ever.

I did survive the first day, I don't quite know how, having been as if stretched on an inquisitorial rack and pulled and pulled until the spinal joints parted. All the others realised very well what I was going through and made their concern and sympathy evident by many cold comfort remarks and horrific anecdotes.

So I discovered that a day in the field could be long, arduous, tedious and without the least touch of the romantic. Thank goodness I could at least go at a slightly easier pace than the women for I wasn't on their piece rate of pay. They hardly relaxed for a moment till midday then they just perched on sacks and ate their sandwiches before setting off again quickly to make up some of the leeway between the spinner and themselves. They had no further rest until finishing time at five o'clock. Whereas we did go back to the house to a hot meal in comfort at midday where there was the pleasure of sitting in a chair to ease tortured flesh, never so much appreciated till then. And though I was driven on again by all the industriousness around me, I didn't work half as hard as those formidable women. Fred casually remarked that there wasn't a man alive that could keep up with them so at least I felt a little less guilty at my own inability to keep up with them.

All in all it was a pretty grim experience that first day's potato picking, no fun at all, no other young company and not much in the way of light hearted interludes. It brought me face to face with the harsh reality of farm work.

When I went off to play with my friends in the evening I was hard put to it to sound convincing that it had been a wonderful day's holiday from school. At that moment I would willingly have returned to my desk for the rest of the week, the rigours of facing Miss Jones were as nothing to the agony of facing massed potatoes, but luckily I kept all that to myself. I was off to bed early that night and can still recall the exquisite sensuous delight of stretching out flat on my back on the soft mattress with caressingly cool sheets, the aches and pains langorously declining to a delicious state of wellbeing where sleep stole swiftly in.

The next day was one of near equal agony and I saw little pleasure in a beautiful though frosty morning. It was worse if anything for I knew from the outset how slowly the long hours would drag away, how potatoes would stretch away to infinity and my back be submitted to pitiless torture. But having survived the first day there seemed no good reason not to survive the second and so it passed in barely acceptable agony. Gradually though, as day followed day, the desperation I had felt at first melted away, I found I had survived my initiation.

I also discovered by the end of the week what it was like to be exposed to bad weather with no hope of escape. Several times a cold November rain fell as we worked. Everything went on as though it were midsummer. The ladies in their macs and wellingtons were completely weather proof and moreover weren't willing to miss a minute's earning time even if they did get a soaking. The men sometimes used to form a hessian sack into a cape and hood and carry on in the cold rain. It was the same with a cold wind, it just had to be endured though it often seemed to pass right through the human frame and froze the marrow in my bones, and my fingers lost all feeling so that I just had to stop work, blow into my hands and stamp about. Sometimes it got so bad we were nearly all stamping, swinging our arms about and slapping our sides like a group of animated scarecrows. There just was no escape from the elements in the middle of an open field with work to be done.

By the end of the week backache had diminished to negligible proportions. I could afford to be dismissive and light hearted about the job when anyone enquired anxiously how I was bearing up to all the bending. "Oh that," I'd say, "it's not so bad really." My spine too had become rubberised, my hands rough and calloused as befitted a veteran of the potato field. It was an experience better to look back on than to undergo but one which I endured for several more potato seasons to come.

Although I wasn't paid for working I received an excellent reward for my labours soon after the week's work was done and I was back at school leaving the women to manage as well as they could without me. On the Saturday morning Mr Costin asked me to come outside for a moment and there leaning against the fence was a bike — old, a little battered but a fully going concern, sturdy and with a fair remnant of gleaming chrome. It was the sort of vehicle that wouldn't mind a boy's boisterous treatment, not one of your slick, smooth painted, 'crime to scratch' models, but one that had obviously been around a bit, seen the rough side of life and knew how to look after itself.

"It's yours, Mick," he said. "That's to make all the backache worthwhile. Aren't you going to try it?"

My very first bike! I saw it as in a dream. I'd had no inkling, no word had been breathed. It came mysteriously and whence it came I never knew.

With a mumbled word of thanks I went over to it and placed my hands reverently on saddle and handle bar. Mrs Costin was evidently in on the secret for she came out in the porch to see the presentation. Fred came over from the milking sheds and Reg just then came riding into the yard on his bike. Their smiles at my evident pleasure loosened my tongue and I proclaimed, "It's smashing."

"Smashing, is it?" laughed Reg. "I hope that's just what it won't be."

"Not a bad old grid by the look of it," said Fred and that's what it became known as from then on, the grid. And what a boon it was to me! I wheeled it carefully up onto the road, sat on and tried it for saddle height — it wasn't far out. Then I pushed off and went for my first ride along the road. I'd had rides on other boys' bikes and could handle one all right. I liked the feel of this one straight away, there was something solid and strong about it, nothing fancy or fussy. I sensed reliability throughout its frame.

Nobody said anything about road safety. There were never any accidents with bikes involving cars in the village, there weren't enough cars to make a problem. Mr Costin had a big elderly black Morris with the temperature guage on the bonnet, which he drove sedately to market, but none of his sons had cars and petrol rationing was so tight that the Morris was used only occasionally. As far as I remember that was the only car in Lower End at the time, certainly none of my friends' dads owned a car or ever had, the general level of aspirations was still very modest.

Practically everybody in the village had a bike, however. Both Eric and Mac possessed one and now that I had joined them my world suddenly expanded. The whole flat vale stretched out for miles ready for an investigation which up till then had been impossible. Now when I went down to Eric's I jumped on my bike. I rode out to Mac's house and met his mother for the first time and found her a very sympathetic soul who told me how glad she was her boys had found good friends because with her husband away on war work she was afraid of bad influences getting to work on them.

I had a thousand uses for a bike besides the sheer fun of riding it up and down the road showing off with the others as we rode long distances 'no hands'. Wherever work was being done in the fields I could get there by bike, the farthest fields were a good half hour's walk from the house. I'd ride across the meadows, down little cow paths to fetch the cows up for milking and in the evenings ride out to some far flung field of stubble to shut in the hens that were doing the ancient gleaners' work.

For the first few weeks I cleaned the grid's ageing chrome on Saturday mornings, standing it upside down in the sheepyard to get at the wheel hubs and chain area more easily. I got to know it in every little intimate detail. Every nut, every moving part, everything that needed adjustment or oiling became so familiar that I felt a complete oneness with that machine such as I have experienced with no other. Maintenance was little problem, I enjoyed mending the occasional puncture providing it wasn't far from home. I used to borrow old spoons from the kitchen for use as tyre levers, but very little went wrong with that bike in all the years it served me.

There was just one hill in the immediate neighbourhood that used to force us off our bikes to push them ignominiously to the top. That was Lancot Hill between Church End and Dunstable. It often used to defeat the buses in winter-time too when there was a coating of ice or snow on the road. We had many a day's holiday because the bus couldn't get up, and sometimes down, Lancot Hill. It was our greatest two wheeled ambition to cycle all the way up that particular mountain but we needed several more years' growing before we could conquer it and even then our victory was at the cost of near exhaustion with the effort. But coming down, head low over the handlebars, the rush of wind closing our eyes to slits, the bike frame quivering with speed, that was an experience worth having.

On the same day that he gave me the bike, a few minutes later in fact when I'd returned from my baptismal ride and proudly stood the grid against the fence so that I could see it from indoors, Mr Costin took out the gold watch which he always wore in his waistcoat pocket, the gold chain draped across his chest. "Look at this," he said and put the heavy watch in my hand. I admired the exquisitely designed face and solid chunkiness of the gold case. He went on in a lingering, unusually soft and nostalgic tone of voice, "My father said he'd give me a gold watch and chain when I could go to plough on my own with a pair of horses." He paused. "I got this half hunter when I was twelve," he concluded and the pride that had lasted from that far off day was still evident in his voice and expression as he slipped the watch back into his pocket.

"As old as me," I thought, and was glad I hadn't made too much fuss over my paltry bit of backache.

Chapter VII

Alarms and Explosions

As far as enemy activity was concerned, especially in the later years of the war, we would go far for months or even a year without being visibly or audibly aware that a war was on. The village was, however, only forty miles from London, not the four hundred that it often seemed as though it could have been. So in the early days especially we would hear the air raid warning go when German aircraft were droning their way to or from the capital, maybe not even passing within many miles of the village. Later, the finger on the warning button thought twice before disturbing our sleep or our daytime activities and as the raids gradually decreased in frequency over the years we were left longer and longer in peace. With air raid sirens it was a bit as it is with church bells. With the wind in the right direction we heard Leighton's siren wailing forth faintly but unmistakably from the four miles across the plain. A different wind might bring us Dunstable's warning wafting across the chalk hills, with several other points towards Whipsnade and Ivinghoe joining in at a greater distance according to the wind direction.

I suppose that the number of actual war incidents in the village could be counted on the fingers of one hand. The great oil bomb attack already recounted was the first such incident and after it we were air raid veterans ready for anything the Germans could throw at us. That is to say the others were now veterans, I had been a veteran from the start. It was surprising though how quickly I had put those horrific experiences from me. I didn't wake in the night screaming from nightmares. Those stupendous raids did not seem to have left any permanent scarring. Thankfully that is the way it is with most children, and in any case I hadn't actually been blown up or injured in any way, nor was our house damaged apart from windows, though it was blown to bits later on, fortunately whilst no one was there, though my Grandmother next door was injured and so badly shaken up that she never really recovered and died not long afterwards.

71

In the village the second great war incident happened not very long after the first and was to me much more exciting. It was a Saturday morning and it was muck spreading time and I was helping. The winter's day was briskly fine, an ideal day for moving mountains, and an early attack had been mounted on the mountainous dunghill in the yard, steaming away like a slumbering volcano. Fred and Arthur in the yard had loaded the cart. Heavy work it was, dislodging the tightly compressed manure. A forkful of dung hung like a ton weight on the hands, a weight that had to be flung up high onto the cart. My job was to take the cart down to the field and bring back the one that was meanwhile being unloaded. The loaded cart was heavy enough to make Dolly, the youngest mare, heave and pant up the rough slope out of the yard and onto the road. It wasn't the pleasantest of jobs maybe, muck cart, but the nose soon accustoms itself to the smell which with well rotted manure as that was, is peculiarly sweet and far from unpleasant. It was anyway, I told myself, part and parcel of life on a dairy farm and anyone who is going to be fussy about trampling around in a bit of cow dung isn't going to take too well to life on a farm.

But there wasn't any sitting on top of the load as with sweet smelling hay so it meant a long walk down to the field with perhaps a ride back when the cart had been emptied. Reg and Bob were in the field tipping the muck off the cart and spreading it evenly over the stubble ready for ploughing in later. It was a very peaceful scene, just men, a horse and a cart, small in that wintry immensity, moving slowly over the empty field with only the creak of a wheel or the jingle of harness or the soft word carried on the light breeze under the vast ice-blue dome of the sky above.

No other children were around, there was never any rush to be associated with muck carting! It was getting near to dinner time and I had entered the field with the last load before dinner when there came the sound of aircraft engines from a distance. Nearly all boys at that time were keen aircraft spotters and most of us reckoned to be able to recognise the usual British planes to be seen then. Spitfires and Hurricanes, Wellingtons and Whitleys, we knew them all. There was so much activity in the sky in those days that we had every opportunity to get to know our war-planes and they didn't mind flying low to give us a good look. So hearing the sound of engines I scanned the sky for its source. No warning had gone so it had to be one of ours.

I soon saw the plane, it was flying low, very low, and coming fast towards us from Leighton way. "A Blenheim," I told myself with satisfaction, then clutched hard on the rope with which I was leading the mare as she started to shy away from the thunderous noise. With a roar the Blenheim passed low almost overhead. I saw Reg run to the horse he and Bob were working with, as it made to bolt. I stopped my mare and watched as the plane hurtled towards the Knolls, banking steeply at the last moment to turn well below the summit then heading back towards us losing height and speed with every second. It disappeared from view but a moment later there it was, barely over the top of the tall elms in the neighbouring meadow, its engines cut back, swooping down on our vast empty field of stubble. It touched down perfectly then ran smoothly along the field before coming to rest some way from us.

There it stood, all brown and green and sandy patches, from a distance looking like some incredible giant insect, some titanic locust, wounded and exhausted in an alien environment. Never in my life had I been so close to an aeroplane. I saw Reg and Bob, pitchforks still in hand, striding purposefully towards the aircraft, so I abandoned the now peacefully grazing mare and ran across to join them.

As we came near there was no sign of life on the plane, it stood huge and unnaturally silent so it seemed, ready for some spontaneous activity, possibly sinister. I wondered what we would have done if it had been a German plane. Several minutes we waited, then a door in the side of the fuselage opened and out jumped the pilot, the only person on board so it transpired. Reg stepped towards him smiling and they shook hands. "Hullo then," said Reg. "Can we help you. Are you all right?"

The pilot removed his goggles. "Yes, fine thanks," he said. "Just a spot of engine bother, nothing much but I thought I'd better land. Hope you don't mind me coming down in the middle of your field. Was I relieved to see there were no cables in the way!"

Standing by whilst all this vicarage tea party talk was going on, I was suddenly on active service, part of the mission. The sole survivor in fact of a daring raid on a vital enemy target. Pity all my comrades were killed but that was the way of things in wartime, it had been hell inside with the fuselage all shot up. Honours, fame, promotion all lay ahead. The dream was but a flash, the exciting reality pulled me back. This great bomber right in our field, the actual pilot within touching distance, it was almost too good to be true. The huge propeller blades that might slice my arm off if I reached out and touched them as I felt the urge to do. The plump tyres of the undercarriage, the ridiculous little wheel at the back, the clear dome on top with machine gun barrels poking through, all these details and more I took in as we stood there exchanging chit-chat. Then I heard the pilot say, "I'd rather like to get to a phone. If you could tell me where one is I'd be most grateful."

Reg turned to me. "Well Mick," he said, "you could take this gentleman back to the house couldn't you? Cut across the fields for quickness."

To the pilot he said, "We'll look after this for you."

"Thanks," replied the pilot, "that's very decent of you. They'll probably come and take it away in a day or two."

So the pilot and I set off across the stubble for the farm. His welfare was now in my hands. My mission was to deliver him safe and sound. Could I accomplish this or was he doomed? This pilot's importance to the war was, I doubted not, incalculable, my responsibility therefore weighty. I had already looked him over rapidly for signs of frailty. He didn't look fragile as he strode out purposefully but you could never tell after all he'd been through, so I watched him anxiously as we jumped the brook, wondering if I could carry him if I had to. He managed it okay though, in fact I was the one to get a bootful of muddy water, so I dispensed with the protective attitude and concentrated on keeping up with him as we walked across the meadow past cows idly grazing and on up the road. The pilot was doing all the talking, asking me questions about what we got up to in the village but saying nothing about his activities so I was left to imagine him with his cheery crew coming in low, machine guns chattering, in the way we so often saw them in the cinema, to drop their bombs on the German general's mansion from that Blenheim that stood silhouetted in the field behind us. He was the young and dashing type that easily fitted into my story.

I'm pretty sure we were seen by several children as we walked towards the farm, only young ones though, none of my mates. I was feeling very proud but trying to appear as though it was the most normal thing in the world to be walking along with a bomber pilot in flying kit. That I suppose was my supreme moment of personal glory during the whole war. The one time when I literally rubbed shoulders with that most glamorous and romantic of all war time heroes, the Air Force pilot. It was a pity it was so poorly witnessed and that mostly by cows. I took him to Mrs Costin and he was shown into the front kitchen and the door firmly shut as she came out leaving him alone on the telephone, for this was top secret war business.

Unfortunately I never saw my pilot again, for by the time I got back to the farm after collecting my cart from the field, he was gone. How he went and where he went to I never did discover. Whisked away by police, called for by some official limousine, or perhaps he jumped on the bus to Dunstable. Within an hour a burly policeman stood in the middle of that field to keep inquisitive folk away and we carted no more muck there for a while. Reg told me later that the Blenheim was just being ferried from one airfield to another, no tale of glory and heroic survival in that. But I had the glory of telling the tale to all my friends, leaving out the ferrying bit, and suitably embellished with vague heroics and leaving much to their imaginations for most of what the pilot confided was naturally a sworn secret.

We all went down the road and leaned on the gate where we could get a good view of the plane and just for a few wonderful moments we were at the controls of that roaring, vibrating machine as we raced her over the stubble missing the hedge by inches then soaring up into the blue above the Knolls and away into romantic adventure.

"Was he wounded?" asked Jimmy Knight.

"Well, he . . . " I began trying not to tell a blatant lie but already beginning to see the torn flesh.

"Had he got any medal ribbons?" interrupted Betty.

"I know what the V.C. ribbon is like," said Mac, "it's got a . . . "

"Which base did he come from?" put in Eric.

"They're not allowed to say, you idiot," said Mac. "My dad says so."

"Oh, shut up about your dad," said Aud irritably, "was he good looking this pilot?"

74

"Oh my God," groaned Doug.

I really didn't have to elaborate much, they worked it all out for themselves. They also cursed their luck that they weren't there at muck spreading with me that fateful Saturday morning.

Our Blenheim remained marooned upon the stubble, guarded by the local constabulary, for a week or more before a gang of airmen arrived one day to work on it, and by the time I came home from school it had taken off across the stubble with its spread muck still awaiting the plough, and vanished out of our lives.

Ever afterwards I cast a hopeful eye at any lowish flying plane, wondering if we would get another forced landing to our credit. And oddly enough, quite a long time afterwards, much nearer to the end of the war, we experienced many more landings, voluntary though, not forced. Reg had become very friendly with a pilot, Jim Kempster, who lived in a neighbouring village. This pilot's job consisted exclusively of ferrying planes about all over the country and abroad and many, many times when passing near he would swoop down to rooftop height and circle round and we would all look up and wave and know that Jim was about again. Occasionally he landed in a field for a chat with Reg or a quick visit home before roaring off on his way again.

In those early days of heavy night bombing raids on London the sirens would sometimes go when we were in bed and we would get up groaning and complaining in the darkness and go out to the air raid shelter. Now this was very unusual, for most houses in the village hadn't got a shelter and all their inhabitants could do by way of protection was to crowd into the cupboard under the stairs or under a stout kitchen table. Not that many bothered after the first time or two when most were terrified that the village was about to be obliterated. They soon became blasé, quite sure that the Germans would never find them, so they tended to stay in bed saying that if your number was on a bomb it would get you anyway whether you were under the table or upstairs in bed, and if it wasn't on why bother to get up. But at the farm there was a real purpose-built shelter. This was because Mr Costin's eldest brother was a builder in Harrow, where of course shelters were absolutely necessary, and he'd come down at the outbreak of war with some of his men and insisted on putting a shelter in at the farm. It was just outside in the orchard, a concrete slab affair sunk into the ground with a great earth mound over the top like an ancient tumulus. The thing that nobody knew was, if your number was on a bomb would the shelter cancel it out or was it better fatalistically to stay indoors and take a chance. It was this uncertainty that drove us outdoors on troubled nights.

The shelter was, however, as cramped, cold, damp and uncomfortable as all such places inevitably were, but a shade less disagreeable, larger and capable of inspiring more confidence in survival than our London Anderson shelters. Yet, after we had the experience once or twice of getting up out of a warm bed at two o'clock in the morning, putting on an old coat and shoes and wandering out into the cold and dark, and once in pouring rain across the sheepyard, into the orchard and down into that cold damp hole in the ground, we decided it was too much and preferred to stay indoors in bed and take our chance. It was no joke sitting in an apprehensive, bleary eyed circle in the flickering light of an oil lamp in the small hours, usually shivering in spite of the efforts of a paraffin stove to circulate some warmth. The first time, agreed, it was exciting, even to me. I imagined us as the sole survivors of a massive attack on the village and our senses were all alert, our hearts thumping, for the expected onslaught. The miserable circumstances of the shelter seemed a small price to pay for salvation. But then came the all clear and with it a feeling of anticlimax as though we had been cheated of our due, and we thought, as we trailed disconsolately back indoors, of all our neighbours stirring sleepily in their warm beds, vindicated in their brazen defiance of the instinct of self preservation.

The third time we decamped, more reluctantly, utter peace and calm prevailed again in the starry skies over the village until the all clear went. Again we came forth complaining, beneath those same impassive stars, at the loss of good sleep for no sufficient justification, not even a distant bomb let alone a concentrated attack on the village. "I've had enough of this lark," said Fred, his Special's love of toeing the official line quite exhausted. We vowed then and there as we grumbled our way back across the yard that we'd never again get up in the night for any number of sirens. "I'd rather die in my bed snug and warm," said Mr Costin.

We never did get any value out of that shelter. Abandoned, it just mouldered away, a monument to excessive caution, the home of spiders and yards of fungus, its entrance and surrounding slopes choked with nettles that were very skilled at concealing our cricket ball when we skied it over into the orchard for six and out.

So, very late one night, some weeks after the shelter's final rejection, when the sirens wailed out over the village with everyone in bed, we all stayed there, merely grunting sleepily, rapt smiles on our faces, turning over and appreciating the warmth of bed and our own good sense. Suddenly there came a series of loud explosions, thumping great bangs they were. The house shook, the windows rattled, all creation seemed to shudder and we sat up in the darkness with exclamations of consternation and incredulity. Were we about to pay for our defiance of Jerry and the wisdom of Harrow? How attractive the shelter seemed for a few panic stricken moments! What fools we had been! We listened intently a minute and thought we detected, beyond our own thumping hearts, the faint sound of aircraft engines, then all was complete silence again. Fred, up in his nightshirt at the window, pulled back the blackout curtain but could see nothing.

"I'd better go out and have a look round," he said groping for his Special's uniform which he slipped on hastily. "That lot wasn't far off or I'm a Dutchman."

Bob and I jumped up too and put some clothes on over our pyjamas and went downstairs and were soon joined by Mr and Mrs Costin and Daisy, all speculating freely about the bangs which had really startled and alarmed everyone by their loudness, nothing like it had been heard in the village before. Fred departed on foot up to the village where the explosions had seemed to come from, and we stood around in the yard gazing up at the constellations as if for enlightenment, but becoming no wiser, only colder, we returned indoors and soon to our warm beds again. No question of going into the shelter, the fun and games were over now we felt sure. Everything around was as silent as the grave, no surging anxious crowd in the road outside, no voices in the darkness, no traffic, no flashing lights of course. It seemed as though the village had turned in again if ever it turned out in the first place.

By the time Fred returned the all clear had gone and I was fast asleep again so didn't hear the exciting news till the morning, though Bob had it whispered to him in the darkness of the bedroom. Two bombs had fallen smack in the middle of the main road just below the Memorial Hall. No one had been hurt Fred said, and he didn't think there was any damage to the one or two houses not far away. They hadn't even knocked over the telegraph poles or broken the electric power cables, just made the posts lean a little.

This was our last and heaviest attack of the war and the general concensus of village opinion was that Jerry must have had a fighter after him and jettisoned his bombs which fell on us by mere accident. The school of thought which held that the attack was a deliberate and precisely executed one to cut the village off from Dunstable and thus in some mysteriously subtle way to cripple our war effort, had few adherents even when it was pointed out that several workers at Vauxhall's tank making factory at Luton had been prevented from getting to work the next day. What effect this had on the subsequent North African tank battles, history alas does not record.

On our way to school, which of course did not close for the day though it was only a hundred yards from the devastation, we passed the scene, treading gingerly round the two roped off craters in the road. We paused long enough to search for and find a few bomb splinters which went to augment the collection of war trophies that most of us were keeping. It had been a matter of great regret that I hadn't been able to pull a bit off our stranded Blenheim. It would have given my collection a distinctly enviable advantage over those of my friends.

There were no policemen, fire engines, shovelling workers, sightseers, nothing. Just a rope around the holes until the council road gang, taken off normal sweeping, came along after breakfast to clear up. Daylight also revealed that there was another crater in an adjoining field and we heard that a couple of dead rabbits were found nearby, the only confirmed casualties of direct enemy action in the village itself throughout the war, certainly the only ones eaten. The children who went to school in Dunstable had a day's holiday as no traffic got through. Some of them came up and watched the men shovelling the earth back into the holes and by tea time it was all over and traffic was passing gently over boards placed on the earth. They tarmaced over it quite soon, but for many years afterwards there was a roughness, an unevenness of surface which reminded those who were in the know about that night when the village was shaken to its foundations.

Besides these cataclysmic events we were reminded of the war in many other less direct ways, some of which we came to consider part of the natural order. Perhaps the most obvious was the activity of the local Home Guard. They were generally mustering outside their H.Q. in the old Rechabite Hall as we were going along to Sunday School in the morning. It was a pity really that the times clashed, for the Home Guard could have wanted no keener, more enthusiastic observers and critics to keep them on their toes than the younger generation. Bob was a founder member of the local platoon. At the outbreak of war he was of call up age but exempt by virtue of being a farmer. Several times he volunteered to go in spite of this and on each occasion to his disgust he had been turned down and told to go back to the farm and get on with producing food which was far more important than becoming cannon fodder. Bob was really fed up with this, his best friend Bernard had joined the R.A.F. and of course most of the young men in the village had gone, and there were a few irate outbursts from Bob when his mother had been unable to conceal her relief that he had been turned down. So joining the Home Guard was an important gesture to him and he was a keen and active member through the early dark days of the war. Those days when we saw very few rifles as we walked by the parading lines outside the Rechabite Hall and when a couple of young elms, felled and trimmed of branches, were placed by the roadside as our contribution towards stopping the Panzer divisions.

Another almost daily occurrence that became an accepted part of our life came later on in the war when the Americans were here. We had to get used to the roar of countless giant bombers, Flying Fortresses and Liberators, filling our evening skies like a plague of mechanised locusts as they winged their heavy way to Germany with their lethal loads from bases far out on the flat vale towards Aylesbury and Oxford. Our dawns saw their massed return with often lone and lame stragglers limping along much later with trailing smoke and engine sounds that made us turn our heads and imagine, from the war films that we saw, the devastation and the heroic struggles that must have been going on inside them.

I suppose that no generation is short of the stuff that dreams are made of. Youth will dream. Today's youngsters may dream of becoming intergalactic adventurers, pop stars or sporting supermen but my wartime generation must have had particularly heroic and action packed martial daydreams. The energies of the whole nation were bent, as one man, towards resistance to German conquest and then towards victory. Tales of courage and heroism, even in defeat, pervaded the very air we breathed. There was so little room left for things unconnected with war it is hardly surprising that we boys should reflect those times, especially in our daydreams.

I can vividly recall how, during the long journeys to and from the fields at harvest or haytime, at the head of my immortal unit, I fought savage battles across Europe against the invading Hun, my pursed lips vibrating and my throat rumbling with incessant explosions. I led innumerable forays out of Tobruk against the encircling German armour. Always victorious in my sector against overwhelming opposition which was always finally cut to ribbons, I performed the most amazing deeds of heroism and generalship for which I was regularly decorated with the nation's highest awards for gallantry.

One action completed as I entered the field, if necessary with a quick massacre or brilliant display of tactics, a truce was declared whilst I came back to reality with Reg and Bob, then as I took the return load towards the road I would slip back into fantasy. Occasionally the action was naval, I was in at the River Plate to great effect and often watched with great glee the Graf Spee gurgling beneath the waves. Or again I often served in submarines, upping periscopes and peering over the passing hedge tops at enemy cows wallowing in a sea of grass before releasing my deadly torpedoes. Frequently the action was airborne, as with my heart in my mouth I guided my Swordfish along the carrier's heaving deck, left rein tighter, sharp pull on the right, and we roared up and away, off to plant my tinfish squarely amidships in some German ammunition ship in spite of the curtains of flak they threw at me. It all depended on my hearing of the nine o'clock news on the wireless and a glance at the Daily Express. I must have lived through enough cerebral campaigns to last several life-times, enough to have sated my appetite for action in later years.

I'm sure it was the strong whiff of patriotism in the air that led to my joining the Army Cadet Force on an impulse one day. With Fred in the Specials, Bob in the Home Guard and Reg in the A.R.P. I was, I suppose, duty bound to make my contribution. We hadn't a unit in the village but a platoon had recently been formed at Eaton Bray. It met in a large wooden hut just beyond the duck pond. This was a time when youngsters flocked in droves to the cadet branches of the three services and when old soldiers were in great demand to inspire them and knock them into shape. Patriotism may have inspired me but an essential part of that patriotism was a desire to acquire a uniform to strut about in and to lord it over anyone who would be impressed.

The first two or three times we went – Eric and I went together, Mac for some reason wasn't keen, he liked the R.A.F. which he later joined – I remember we did a bit of drill with wooden rifles, getting fell in, shouldering arms and dressing to the right in that resounding wooden hut. Later, we stood in a long line hearing about how a Lewis gun was put together and taken apart. They had one there with silver coloured dummy bullets, and an old soldier from World War One lowered himself creakingly in his beribboned battledress to a prone position and demonstrated the intricacies of the weapon. It was just a game to us, it never occurred to me that human flesh could be torn to shreds by that sleek looking piece of metal. Then one or two of the cadets, those with uniforms, were invited to have a try to assemble and dismantle it and we all laughed nervously in superior fashion as they made a hopeless mess of it. They also had a hand grenade, a demonstration one that came apart to show how it was constructed and how you made those Cadbury's chocolate squares of metal rip through German bodies.

Apart from trying to digest this information, presented in abrupt, sergeant-majorish tones, I was also greatly concerned with wondering how Eric and I could make good our escape on our bikes afterwards from some of the Eaton Bray lads who resented the foreign intrusion and had intimated that they intended 'seeing' us later.

It was announced one night that when we next met we would be having manoeuvres. It was explained that this was to be like an authentic engagement with the enemy and that thunderflashes would be used. "Heaven help anyone who gets a thunderflash go off in his ear," barked the old sergeant with a glare that wiped the grins off our faces, "he'll be deaf for two days. So keep your wits about you and your eyes skinned. Any questions? Right, Parade-parade dismiss! A quick glance at his watch and he shepherded us speedily out of the hut, leaving himself enough time for a pint or two in the pub opposite.

When the day for manoeuvres arrived I'd had mushrooms with my egg on fried bread for breakfast and one of them must have been a bit off for all day at school my stomach had felt queasy. By evening I was feeling definitely off colour but we went to cadets, Eric and I, and we were issued with our wooden rifles, then the plan of action was outlined. Section A was to attack an imaginary ammunition dump out in the fields somewhere and Section B was to defend it. I can't recall which section we were in, my own internal defences were deteriorating to the point where concentration was very poor. We weren't issued with thunderflashes, I don't know who was. I suppose we just had to fire our wooden rifles and hope that the enemy played fair and fell dead.

In the luminous twilight we slipped out into the Eaton Bray fields, totally unfamiliar to Eric and I who somehow seemed within a short while to be completely on our own, guarding an indeterminate section of the meadow. We hung about as twilight faded into darkness and it grew cold. Gallantly we stuck to our post for ages with nothing happening except that those putrified mushrooms were marching to final victory. I was feeling more and more miserable and less and less concerned with imaginary ammunition dumps.

Then I was violently sick several times. Nobody else was about, no attackers, no defenders, no exploding thunderflashes, not even a stretcher party for the sick, it was all quiet on the Eaton Bray front, they might well have all been annihilated or gone home for all we saw or heard of them. As I was to learn later it was a typical Army caper. I just fled in misery with Eric, shamefully deserting our post and that was the end of my war service. Whether we were posted as missing presumed killed in those mournful fields or dismissed the service with ignominy I never knew, but I daresay our Eaton Bray brothers in arms were overjoyed to see the back of us. Eric and I reasoned with self convincing logic that we had been to cadets four or five times and there was no sign of us being offered a uniform so that cancelled out our obligation. Also at the back of my mind was the thought that one night we might not be so lucky as to slip away before the Eaton Bray boys could 'see' us. Now, if only there had been a platoon in our own village we might have covered ourselves in glory, but you can't really expect boys of different villages to look on each other as anything but enemies even in wartime! It was also quite a time before I would eat mushrooms again.

Our gentlest and most exotic reminder that there was a war on occurred when a group of Italian prisoners of war was sent into the village. They were clearing and deepening the bed of the brook that ran along the edge of the village passing through several of the farm's fields. It was this brook that we were so fond of damming up.

At first when word got round of what was going on we went to see the comic enemy. "Hey, did you know there's some Ities down the brook clearing it out?"

"Ities?"

"Yeah, prisoners."

"No, go on you're kidding."

"Honest, my dad seen 'em s'mornin as 'e went by."

"Let's go an' see 'em shall we?"

"Wha'for, 'oo wants to look at Ities?"

"Waal, it's summit to do. 'Ave a good laugh at 'em too."

The Italian army was treated as joke on the wireless and in the newspapers and we took our cue from them and went down to where they were working, ready for a laugh. Weren't these the army that couldn't even beat the Abyssinians and they only fought with bows and arrows?

Any tendency to make fun of the enemy, however, died before it could find expression. We found a group of twenty or so friendly, darkly handsome young men in strange maroon coloured uniforms with green patches on their backs, working with skill and steady precision, swinging axes, wielding picks and sawing timber to cheerful cries and snatches of song. There was nothing to laugh at there. Aud and Doug, Eric and Mac and I and the rest of our little band stood back uncertainly, still hoping for something to ridicule, and watched the strange scene – the incomprehensible cries, the mechanical digger swinging its great bucket and biting into the stream bed, a couple of British guards leaning on their rifles and smoking – it was all so relaxed, so unusual and unexpected, so fascinating. Apart from the guards' rifles there was no hint of restriction, nothing aggressive in the scene which somewhat resembled a lumberjack camp with small trees and bushes felled and scattered about and prisoners spread out all along the brook, walking around without constraint or strict supervision. If anything it looked as though it was the Italians having the good time and the poor guards who were restricted and bored to death, standing idly about.

After watching for some time we gradually edged nearer. The guards said and did nothing, the Italians smiled at us and hurled loud comments to each other. In another minute, in the way that children alone can accomplish, the barriers were down, we were among them laughing, shouting, gesticulating madly as we tried to communicate with them. It was an incredible mêlée and though we didn't get through to them much on that occasion, or they to us, the one essential point was instantly translatable and internationally recognised – friendliness and good humour – and these made light of all the language difficulties.

From then on the 'Ities' were one of our regular haunts for the next few weeks as they laboriously worked their way downstream out of our territory and into the next village. We boys weren't particularly interested in the Italians as individuals, we soon became keener on the mechanics of what was going on, in watching the progress of the work, the digger and all the tools, in having a try at swinging an axe or lopping branches or piling the bonfires and seeing and tasting what they were cooking for dinner in the big cans heating up over the brushwood fire. The guards weren't forgotten either, they let us hold their rifles, showed us how to load them and laughed as we gazed in awe at real, live ammunition.

The girls on the other hand fraternised with the prisoners as young men, feeling an instinctive attraction to the Latin race, and Aud and Betty and Joan carried on long earnest conversations at a very slow pace with much gesticulation and repetition and fits of giggling. They came to know most of the Italians well, their names and something about them and looked for their favourites each time we came down.

Some of the men showed us attractive rings they made from old scraps of aluminium, patiently filed and polished with nail files and scraps of cloth and leather, anything they could scrounge. These rings amazed us, never had we known such beautiful objects made by hand. We had always assumed such things were made mysteriously in factories by complicated machines. It was quite a shock to see these prisoners handling such desirable objects and telling us how they made them with their own hands in such a makeshift way. Respect for our prisoner friends rose to even greater heights as we recognised their expert workmanship. They were of course, the prisoners' currency and several members of our gang received rings in exchange for bars of chocolate or a few cigarettes. Unfortunately I hadn't any wherewithal to bargain with at the time so never obtained one. We had quite a brisk little business going for a time. The guards didn't mind, they were pleasant, indulgent chaps who just let us all get on with enjoying each other's company.

These gentle, friendly, happy/sad Italians could never again be for us the hated enemy. There was little steel in their make up, more of music than of world mastery, of craftsmanship than conquering ambition. Their primary concern was to be home with their families again, families whose photographs they never tired of showing us with pride and affection.

When the Ities finally worked their way out of the village and out of our lives, only the children had had any contact with them, no adult had come anywhere near so it was only in the children's minds that there grew the puzzling distinction between our likeable bunch of prisoners and the goose stepping hordes of Mussolini that we saw on the cinema screens.

We never came in contact with any German prisoners so it was easy to go on hating the Hun, but I remember Mrs Costin telling me how during the Great War they had a few Germans sent to them to help with the harvest work. She still remembered them clearly and told me what nice fellows they had been, what good workers they were and how friendly they all became, and one or two of them had even corresponded for a while after the war when they were back home.

It was very puzzling to try to reconcile Mrs Costin's story with Germans as we heard about them every day, with Hitler who was the Devil incarnate and with concentration camps for Jews. We could only conclude that they had gone too far downhill now, that the last vestiges of humanity, still latent in the Kaiser's time, were now dead in them. It looked as though the only good German was now a dead German.

Chapter VIII

Remember the Sabbath

Sundays on the farm were always very special days. They had their own undeviating pattern, their peculiar, suspended, inevitable atmosphere. Nobody could mistake those wartime Sundays for any other day of the week.

The day really began when the milking was finished, the cows turned out in the field and the cowsheds cleaned out. No more farm work was done until afternoon milking and nothing again after that. This was an inviolable rule and never once, even at the busiest times with the harvest in the fields waiting in perfect weather to be brought in, do I remember it being broken. Sunday was Sunday, come wartime, food crisis or any other calamity. No good could come from working beyond the strict minimum on the Sabbath. This wasn't just the practice at Manor Farm, it applied to the vast majority of farms in the area. You could look down from the Knolls on a Sunday and see no sign of human activity in the fields for miles around, not a cart moving nor a purposeful horse and certainly no tractor, everything was at rest.

Those early jobs done, an air of quietness akin to mild sanctity descended on the farm, indeed on the whole village. That is not to say that the village church and chapels were crammed full of eager worshippers, though wartime congregations usually exceeded peacetime ones, but rather that having eliminated the noise, i.e, taken good care to send the children off to Sunday School, the men pottered peacefully about grooming the ferret, cleaning the twelve bore, before strolling down to the allotments to criticise their neighbours' gladioli and cauliflowers, stopping to have a yarn over the gate and maybe dropping in at the Duke's Head for a leisurely half pint before coming back home for lunch.

The farm however, had its own peculiar Sunday pattern. For a start the family were strong Methodists, nobody dropped in at the Duke's Head on Sunday or on any other day of the week. So this special Sabbath atmosphere had a strong dash of religious observance about it, serious though never solemn.

With the parish church over a mile away in Church End but the Methodist Chapel only a few minutes walk up the hill, it was originally possibly only a matter of convenience to attend the nearer. But if so, convenience had hardened into tradition and now practically no-one at our end of the village would have considered for a moment going to the parish church. Indeed there was a scarcely concealed animosity between the Anglicans and the Noncomformists, a slowly reducing legacy from the times of open and virulent conflict, conducted now in nods and whispers.

Not many at our end of the village had a good word for the vicar who was in any case seldom seen so far from his church. His appearance, riding slowly on his ancient bicycle, his wisps of grey hair poking out from beneath his black shovel hat, was enough to silence the playing boys and send gossiping housewives scurrying indoors to peer between curtain laces at his progress down the road, watching to see who he would call on.

In the years I was in the village I went to the parish church only once, not to a service but with Miss Jones and the class when she took us to see the perpendicular style windows which she said were its most noteworthy feature. I remember being impressed not by windows but by the atmosphere exuded inside that spacious old building by its ancient stones and furniture. You could sense the centuries preserved there and almost catch the ghostly presence of generations of carpenters, blacksmiths, millers, farmers and peasants, hear them jostling in the venerable pews, so venerable that chunks of them lay about riddled with death watch beetle. On the whole though my mates and I were more interested in reading the gravestones to find the oldest and savouring the flesh-creeping thrill of standing on a grave and trying to picture that person as he once was.

Fred was the Chapel organist and he played for the morning and evening service every Sunday and also helped with afternoon Sunday School, scarcely ever missing a service year in year out. Nobody took holidays during the war, it wasn't the time for such frivolities and anyway most of the beaches were mined and closed off with rolls of barbed wire and tank traps to prevent the Germans landing. So Fred didn't have long for pottering about after breakfast, just time to go down the road to see to his poultry, come back and give the front yard a sweep up then it was time to get changed for Chapel. Mrs Costin's Sunday morning wasn't all that different from other days. If anything it was probably harder even though the same principle was applied to unnecessary work inside as to outside. Cooking a meal of banquet proportions was of course, considered essential.

I remember Mrs Costin telling me that when she was a girl shoes to be worn on Sunday had to be cleaned the previous evening, vegetables prepared on Saturday for Sunday lunch. It was only fairly recently that Sunday papers were admitted to the farm, Mr Costin's father wouldn't have them. "That's silly, I suppose, when you think about it," she said, "after all, the papers are actually printed on the Saturday night." Things were gradually relaxing but in 1940 no Methodist or anybody else in the village mowed his lawn on Sunday, gardened through the afternoon or did anything except what had to be done, or if he did he was not without a guilty feeling about what the elders would have thought.

Being staunch Methodists the farm was on the select rota of houses that received and entertained the minister for the day when he came out from Leighton to preach, about once a month. There was no bus service between the village and Leighton on Sundays or on weekdays, the minister either cycled or depended on lifts, so once arrived in the morning he stayed for the day. These visits had the effect of intensifying the Sabbath aura at the farm, giving it point and added justification, concentrating the mind a little more. We would savour more keenly the slightly pious, more rarified atmosphere of Sunday with the black suited minister at close quarters. No gloom was cast on the hosts by these visitations, indeed they were usually jolly times with much laughter and amusing anecdotes and jokes licensed by holy orders, especially during and after the excellent lunch Mrs Costin had slaved all morning in the kitchen to prepare.

Bob's Sunday mornings were spent with the Home Guard doing we knew not what exactly, as naturally he was parsimonious with his information for weren't we warned on practically every hoarding that 'Walls Have Ears?' So nobody enquired what the Home Guard got up to after they finished their parade. We boys often saw them coming down off the Knolls when we came out of Chapel and suspected them of playing some version of our tracking game. There was no jarring between the khaki uniform in which Bob sat down to lunch and the minister's clerical cloth beside him, church and army got on admirably. Bob put his rifle down by the umbrella stand among the walking sticks, left his forage cap on the sewing machine and came to add his robust military presence to our piously jolly Sunday table.

Sometimes the military presence received reinforcements, as when Daisy's Eric was on leave and both he and Bob were in uniform. It used to occur to me to wonder what Eric thought of those Sunday lunchtime gatherings, with amiable and jovial chattering around the table, the minister convivial as any amidst all the hearty eating. He who only shortly before had seen men blown to bits and bayonneted beside him and who had shot and killed and cursed and been terrified. Did he wonder sometimes and marvel at life's contrasting realities as he sat calmly exchanging civilities with the preacher?

My own attendance at both morning service and afternoon Sunday School was inevitable, given the environment. No pressure was applied, none was needed. Being keen to do the right thing by my foster family I responded automatically to the tradition that pervaded the very air each Sunday. Surprisingly enough for an East End boy I had been sent to church from an early age, Church of England that was, and I was a choirboy. We urchins got paid for choir attendance which must have influenced me favourably in surrendering quite a bit of my spare time to what must have been a fairly irksome ritual. I remember seeing the pile of rubble that was my East End church in later years after my return home and wondering why churches of all places couldn't have been protected by God. "Surely," I told myself, "He could have slanted the bombs to one side a little." It was an oversight that troubled me greatly.

So every Sunday morning before half past ten, all spruced up in our best clothes, we children gathered in groups along the road and wandered stiffly up the hill past the Home Guard elms and a sandbagged dugout nearby commanding the main road to Church End, on past the terrace of three thatched cottages where the Hooles lived with their tiny shop, the two spinster schoolteachers and the Dempsters, then past the Rechabite Hall with the sound of boots on boards within and so on into the Sunday School, a new building tacked on the side of the Chapel. I used to look at the horsechestnut tree that Fred told me Aud and Doug had planted in the plot next to the Sunday School not far from from the wall and wonder if I would ever see it grow to maturity. Three feet or so tall then, its conkers would drum on the schoolroom roof if ever it survived. We were always short of conkers, a pity it couldn't hurry up and grow I thought as I anxiously surveyed it for progress. That set me pondering the age-old question of whether soaking conkers in vinegar made them harder than baking in an oven. We were never tired of arguing such vital subtleties of conkering.

Alongside the road opposite the Sunday School stretched Hoole's spinney, a tangle of hawthorn, sycamore, old pecker-fretted apple, damson and bullace trees. Ivy covered, encrusted with lichen and engulfed by rampant shoulder high weeds and suckers, the whole place was an alluring and almost impenetrable jungle. There was talk of lime pits and shafts in the middle of it somewhere but we never found them on the few occasions, not Sundays, that we invaded it, when we knew that old Mr Hoole had gone up to Dunstable on the bus with his bulky suitcases of combs and ribbons, toys and trinkets to sell from door to door. I always think of old Mr Hoole whenever I see that little sign on peoples' front gates, 'No hawkers or circulars'. There was nothing hawkish about his bulky, slow moving, good natured and nearly circular frame but a hawker he was. Though not a very successful one I'd guess, the only one I ever knew.

Once inside the Sunday School we split into groups by age and sex. We older boys sat at the back with Bob King our teacher, son of old Amos from the thatched cottage beyond the Chapel. Bob worked at the chalkpit and we used to see him cycling home to his council house at Church End, flat capped, his old work clothes covered in chalk dust. On Sundays in formal brown suit not too well fitting and brown boots, he looked uncomfortable but was so friendly, sincere and tolerant towards us boys that we held him in high esteem and never failed to give a cheery wave and friendly shout when he passed us by during the week, dust laden, on his way home. Bob's niece Olive took Aud and Betty and the older girls and his uncle, the aged Arthur King, as superintendent, conducted communal prayers and hymm singing, it was a truly King family affair. Bob was also a member of the Home Guard but was given a special dispensation to miss or to be late for the Sunday parade. He was always a little hard of hearing was Bob, and one Sunday when he was up on the Knolls on some exercise with the Home Guard he failed to hear the whistle summoning

Old Amos King wouldn't see much difference in the outside of his cottage today, though the bungalow next door would send his eyebrows up.

them all down, so still faithfully guarding his knoll had to be searched for and brought down an hour or so later by his wife, with his Sunday dinner rapidly spoiling in the oven.

There were several other prehistoric characters besides Arthur King in the village at that time, so gnarled and ancient, so wrinkled and dried up, so awe inspiring that we children never dared speak to them. A sort of petrified humanity they were, rock-like in their permanence and inscrutability. It always impressed me that Bob's dad Amos had the same name as the Old Testament book. I wasn't sure whether he'd actually written it but in any case there was something magical about that ancient Biblical name, something of great wonder and veneration. Old Tommy Holland opposite Aud and Doug's cottage was another antediluvian figure. He had worked on Manor Farm when Mr Costin was a boy. He was still to be seen pottering about his bit of garden or standing leaning on his stick by his front gate, as immobile and as greeny brown as the moss upon his path.

Arthur the cowman's old dad was another shrunken ancient, with his clay pipe between his teeth and his knobbly stick in his bony hand, a basket for vegetables on his arm, hobbling down to the allotments at a snail's pace. One ancient fellow from Eaton Bray used to preach to us sometimes on Sundays and we would sit as if mesmerised by this aged Humpty Dumpty figure with his large bald head fringed with a few wispy hairs seeming to sit on the pulpit's edge and his eyes magnified grotesquely behind powerful lenses as he piped to us 'dear children' and told us stories we could never follow. We treated him with the greatest respect however, for we knew instinctively he had somehow survived from Old Testament times with all the powers that implied and might be able to do nasty things if provoked. We had all been told the salutary tale of Elisha calling the two she bears down from the mountain to maul the boys who jeered at him and had no intention of risking such terrors even though we felt sure there weren't likely to be many she bears roaming the Knolls nowadays.

Our favourite activity in Sunday School with Bob, I remember, was a game we called Words. Everything had to be a game, we boys weren't interested for long in serious, sober questions. We had to find in our Bibles a word in a given book and chapter chosen by him. We would scrabble eagerly through the pages, fingers stubbing down the verses, half an eye on our neighbours' efforts, until the victorious cry, by way of showing off, came from the first finder. For restless fidgety boys it was probably as good a way as any of occupying us and familiarising us with the books of the Bible. Nothing so frivolous for the girls however. With Olive they had long intimate pow-wows at whose drift we couldn't even hazard a guess and whose cloak of secrecy and deep concentration we could never penetrate with our noisy outbursts of triumph.

After a spell of this we all filed into the Chapel next door and joined with the few adults there in the service proper. We had to try not to fidget when the proceedings became tedious as they often did, and to talk only in whispers. Bob would sit with us to encourage us in these difficult virtues. The art of sitting still requires a long and arduous apprenticeship, with agonies of suffering to endure that adults are only too quick to forget all about. I well recollect as we sat in those hard seats, the demons of discontent prodding me with burning forks in every joint and muscle so that they would, they must, move. To remain still was sheer physical torture. Only slowly and painfully was an accepted degree of passivity acquired and the fever of movement calmed.

We were lucky though in being Methodists for they have an almost infinite variety of preacher, mostly lay, with the occasional visits from the dog collared ministry. There was always something different to divert us. The young and the old, man and woman, sophisticated and simple, the boring, the lucid, the articulate and the near incomprehensible, they all appeared before us over the years in a vast slow-moving kaleidoscope that compensated in some measure for the long minutes that we had to try to sit relatively still in those hard, uncushioned oak pews.

It was the age-old art of storytelling that could freeze us into immobility in those pews and hold us motionless, enthralled, as we hung upon each magic word. He or she who had this art always had our undivided attention.

By far our best storyteller and one whose words left an imprint as of hammer blows upon our minds, was a certain minister who used to cycle out from Leighton, prop the machine against the railings, pocket his bicycle clips and stride in to take the service. He was a tall, shock haired character, lantern jawed with piercing dark eyes beneath bushy black brows, blessed with powerful lungs and given to theatrical gestures, a combination which, with an ability to pick stories of simple dramatic power to tell us, was guaranteed to keep us from pinching each other and from tiresome shufflings in our seats.

You could have heard a pin drop one particular Sunday morning as he got into his stride with a really gripping story with murder, treachery and treasure and a played down dash of lust in which the Old Testament abounds. It seemed as though the ample pulpit would never contain him as he swayed towards us and away, twisting and writhing, arms flailing, hair tossing as the drama poured from him in a cascade of words rising and falling in response to the action. He was approaching the climax of the story, his voice rising to a great crescendo as we sat riveted. Then suddenly in the midst of a powerful utterance, his false teeth flew out, hurtled downwards, bounced on the flat top of the organ immediately below, whizzed by Fred missing him by a whisker and clattered on to the floor. Not an eyelid blinked, not a muscle twitched in all the congregation as the minister, stopping dead, turned and scurried down the pulpit steps, bent, retrieved his erring denture, turned his back to slip them in again then remounted the steps, paused, then grasped the suspended but by now irrelevant story, briefly and flatly ended it, announced the final hymn and sat down to mop his brow.

We fumbled noisily in our books for the hymn, giggling and grimacing to each other below the level of the pew. Once outside and down the road home it was all, "Did you see how they bounced? Nearly knocked Fred's head off. Could have bitten his nose. Lord what a laugh," and we doubled up with helpless laughter. Luckily the minister wasn't staying at the farm that day.

To keep our interest during the service they usually let us take up the collection, which two of us did, clomping noisily out of our seats and smirking in idiot fashion at our friends. It was an open plate, not a bag, so we could see who put a penny in, which was the average child's donation, or who a ha'penny. It also discouraged buttons and foreign coins. Sometimes from the adults, among the threepenny bits, sixpences and shillings, we would marvel at the odd half crown whilst at exceptional times like harvest festival, there was a paper harvest of ten shilling notes and even the odd pound note.

The one time in the year above all other when our active participation in the service was required was the Anniversary. We were all expected to do something. Sometimes it was a case of singing solo or in a small group, or giving a holy or at least a moral recitation. All were difficult, almost impossible. For you could depend upon forgetting your words as your tongue froze and your heart stopped when from the pulpit came the dreaded words, "And now we are to have a recitation from another pair of young gentlemen. Er–Eric and Mick, and their poem is entitled 'The Tiger' by William Blake – let's hear them roar." With sheeplike courage we made our way forward to face the huge flock that turned up for the pleasure of seeing and hearing the children perform, some of them being thankful that they were no longer children. Our tiger made it to the end, just, in a desperately ferocious scramble, leaving the rhyme and metre badly mauled.

As usual it was the very young children that attracted most admiration. Any halting, lisping, incoherent, almost inaudible offering from some pretty little five year old with fetching golden curls, was the object of expansive smiles and the odd dabbed tear from the elders. We older boys, self conscious to an unbearable degree, received only perfunctory and momentary nods and smiles of semi-approval.

There were piles of hymms to sing that day, printed in a special booklet for the occasion, and we had to practice them for weeks beforehand to ensure that we had at least a vague idea of the words and tunes. Once or twice Olive Heley got really ambitious and put on a piece of drama from around the pulpit and the choir seats, a play moreover that Olive and her group of girls evolved for themselves. This was quite revolutionary and was only possible beause there were some good, clever and sensible older girls, all evacuees and including Betty and Aud who could be relied upon to do anything. We boys were pretty useless, fit only for a stumbling reading or a small walk on part in their play which they generously provided for us and which, though endlessly rehearsed, we usually managed to bungle. But of course, the congregation was benevolent and uncritical and smiled indulgently at our stammering and stumbling.

Not long after the Anniversary, and as if in compensation for it, came the Sunday School treat. This might once have been a considerable affair, before the war. I heard tales of outings to Whipsnade Zoo, to Ashridge Park, to the circus in Luton and great picnics and sports on the Downs, but during the war years things withered away dramatically. What with the difficulty of hiring charabancs due to petrol rationing, and food rationing with its effect on such tea essentials as cakes and buns and ham sandwiches, plus the puritanism in the national air which frowned on such frills and inessentials as treats, the poor old Sunday School outing sank almost without trace, postponed until the task on hand was done.

I remember one year we were taken to Hoole's tea garden for our treat, not a hundred yards from the Sunday School. Now the Hooles owned the tiniest shop imaginable, a sort of lean-to box tacked on the end of their cottage. You could get an astonishing range of goods from Hoole's though, a case of a quart from a pint pot if ever there was one. From aniseed balls to Woodbines, from antimacassars to wax polish, with fruit and vegetables in season, all served by the slow moving, slow thinking, slow smiling, ever cheerful Mr Hoole or his sharp querulous wife, who came shuffling or shooting out when the door opened jangling the bell above it.

His tea garden was of the same economical order as his shop, a few benches and tables, painted chocolate brown, around the back with a shrub or two and an overhanging tree to provide the garden. There was no view, it was entirely enclosed, dim and greenish with a tiny patch of sky above.

I daresay before the war he did a fair trade with weekend visitors to the Knolls calling in for a pot of tea and a snack. But rationing and sterner uses of weekends had killed that casual trade stone dead and the tea garden was sadly neglected. But there we had our Sunday School treat. A sandwich, two if you were quick, a cream bun, a goodly slice of floury jam sponge and a beaker of orange squash provided a magnificent feast for us, and of course we had a whale of a time thanks to our own antics and in spite of the disapproving glare of the proprietress as she hovered in the background snatching away plates and beakers once emptied. Afterwards we went over to the lower slopes of the Knolls opposite the Chapel and swung in the great branches of beech trees that brushed the steep chalk slopes, and swarmed all over a fallen tree trunk and had no end of fun.

In spite of all the difficulties of meat rationing, the Sunday Lunch at the farm was still a very substantial affair. Plain farmhouse cooking it may have been with no frills, but good wholesome ingredients were used and plenty of them. The meat coupons were concentrated on the Sunday joint and mid-week was left mainly to rabbits and partridges to help the sausages out. John Thorn the cheery straw hatted butcher from Eaton Bray used to come whistling down the path on Saturday morning, his basket on his arm, always with the same joint of beef, an order that never varied through the years, a joint small by pre-war standards, but John did his best and looked after his valued regulars as well as he was able.

On the table were always several dishes of vegetables and always including one of golden brown roast potatoes. A thick and succulent Yorkshire pudding cooked under the meat always appeared and there was a generous helping for everyone. When the minister stayed there was the same menu as usual but then we always had grace said before we set to.

It was an awesome experience at first for a scruffy little urchin like me to be at close quarters with a minister, within touching distance of the cloth and to observe him whilst seeming not to throughout his meal. It took some getting used to hearing him discuss his row of peas or describing his efforts at repairing some loose guttering.

The first minister I encountered was a man well on in his sixties then, a jolly, large, high complexioned man, round faced, silver haired, comfortable, benign and with a slow and measured way of talking and of eating as though he really enjoyed doing both and wished to prolong them indefinitely. I was surprised at first and a little critical of his obvious humanity. Did I expect ministers to be ascetic, lean and hungry looking, as though they lived on locusts and wild honey? Ours resembled a jolly friar and I felt troubled about it, thinking it was a hindrance and a fault in his job to be worldly. I knew that clergymen were midway between common humanity and the angels, one foot in either camp, it had never occurred to me that they might have the same appetites and preoccupations as ordinary mortals. Ours chewed his food in obvious appreciation, wiped gravy from his chin with a serviette and usually had a second helping whilst protesting that he really shouldn't but, "just this once perhaps."

I gradually came to realise however, that he was both a good man and a good minister, who earned and deserved the esteem and devotion of many a village community like ours. Those ancient villages, comfortable amid their broad and fertile acres, didn't want any emaciated evangelical whizz kids turning everything upside down, spreading discomfort, soul searching and breast beating wherever they went. A steady, settled state of religion was what they liked and needed, comfortable and tolerant, slow moving and fitted to the gentle rhythm and cycle of country life.

The minister's qualities and virtues, as much physical and intellectual as metaphysical, as much human as spiritual, were well suited to his time and place. This was well demonstrated by the fact that he had been prevailed upon to stay in the Leighton circuit for several tours of duty, three years each one, when usually a minister moved on after one tour and was only asked to stay if he was very popular. He was a great favourite at the farm. His visits were looked forward to eagerly by the whole family but particularly by Mr Costin who didn't usually enthuse over much, indeed was canny and non-committal about most things. But the minister he took to as to a long lost brother, his face lit up when they met, he clapped him on the shoulder and shook his hand vigorously and warmth and geniality bubbled from him in profusion.

Nobody at the farm ever went for a walk or strolled about aimlessly or for pleasure, to look around them. Such an idea never entered their heads. They always went out for a definite purpose, to shoot rabbits or let the hens out. They never went strolling on the Knolls to admire the view, most of them hadn't been up there for donkey's years. They were continually moving about through the village for work so the idea of going for a walk for pleasure anywhere in the village would appear nonsensical and the Costins weren't the sort to go prying into other people's business. To a slightly lesser degree that was the attitude of most people in the village, it was only city folk who strolled around when they had no need to. Villagers understood this need of city dwellers to be restlessly on the move in eternal pursuit of pleasure. Life in big cities was so unnatural that it wasn't any wonder they were all screwed up inside. There's none more practical and prosaic than the genuine countryman and of them the farmer is usually the most practical. Whoever heard of a farmer walking around anywhere unless he'd got some particular business in mind?

So Sunday afternoons for the men were spent in the time honoured tradition of masterly inactivity – until milking time at half past three that is. They adjourned replete from the front kitchen to the more spacious and comfortable dining room with the Sunday Express and The People and there passed the entire afternoon, in ritual conversation at first if the minister or other guest were present, but eventually the stage of profound slumber was reached, each sleeper lying back in a big armchair or the chesterfield, legs stretched straight before him, face covered by a sheet of newspaper in summer to keep off the flies. Mrs Costin and Daisy were nearly an hour in the back kitchen doing the washing up and cleaning after the marathon cooking session.

I was left to my own devices for an hour or so until Sunday School time so I generally got a bit bored in best clothes that restricted the range of activities possible. Sometimes Mrs Costin called from the back kitchen, "Have you written home this week, Mick?" The answer was generally no, for like most boys I was reluctant to put pen to paper in spite of those desirable food parcels and the stitched in sixpences that came my way. So I had to sit myself down at the table in the front kitchen and get through the business as quickly as I decently could, my gaze continually wandering to the window and out across the deserted yard, and I was troubled by the sunshine and the swooping swallows and the branches of the big elm in the corner of the orchard.

At other times I kicked around the barns a bit, on the watch for rats – no shooting with the air gun would be encouraged on Sundays – or perfected my patent rat trap invented to catch those brazen rodents who robbed the store of crushed oats I kept for my rabbit, a lovely little Dutch doe given to me by a neighbour. Bob had a rabbit too for a while, a buck, a Flemish giant. He kept it in a hutch near mine. One time he put them in together. "So they can become friends?" I asked. "Well, sort of," he said smiling. I soon twigged when the babies came and added the knowledge to the store of farmyard things I was learning by observation in the absence of any explanation of queer goings on – the antics of the cockerel with his hens and the first witnessing of the bull loosed for a few minutes in the yard with a cow.

Bob used to call my elaborate but completely unsuccessful rat trap a proper Heath Robinson affair. I wasn't sure whether this was a compliment or an insult but as he said it with a smile I concluded it could not have been meant unkindly. I remember the trap as a series of cardboard boxes baited with oats and having cunningly concealed flaps in the floor through which I imagined a rat falling on a preplanned path culminating in a wicked looking rat sized version of the common mouse trap. It must have been an object of great mirth and derision among our rodent population who continued devouring the crushed oats when not laughing out loud. Nothing daunted, I continued for ages refining and improving my ingenious trap, certain that one day I would get it just right, but of course I never did, not so much as a whisker did I catch.

When it was time for me to go to Sunday School Mrs Costin had just finished in the kitchen and would have a wash then get changed into her Sunday dress and perhaps be lucky enough to have half an hour or so to sit down to read the paper, but not to sleep, before it was time to think about tea.

We used to enjoy our afternoons at Sunday School – we who weren't sated with professional entertainment on television were prepared to take our amateur variety where we could find it. Just about all the children were there, with the whole-hearted approval of parents, so anyone missing out would have felt out of it. No one protested about being made to go, you just went, the same as you breathed. And it certainly wasn't that we felt we were being goody goodies, just let anyone try calling us cissies and we would have fixed them, on a weekday. No, it was just the unquestioning acceptance of Sunday that was in the very air we breathed in those days.

Of course we received prizes for good attendance but that hadn't got anything to do with it either, though it was nice when it happened. I still cherish among my books upstairs one of the very first volumes I ever owned and the one that has been longest in my possession, Dumas' 'The Black Tulip', read and re-read many a time years ago, and inside the cover there is a note in Olive Heley's own hand and with Arthur King's signature, saying it was presented to me by the Sunday School for obtaining 104 marks for attendance during 1941, two attendances each Sunday for a year, not one absence, which also says something about the healthiness of country life. From such beginnings started a lifelong love of books – a debt, one of many I owe to that little Sunday School.

Whilst there we had some good songs to sing, good stories to listen to (there's some of the finest bloodthirsty stories I know in the Old Testament, ones that I've never forgotten) a game to play and all with good companions and a tolerant lively and friendly atmosphere – no wonder we didn't object at all to going. We only had the chance once a week and we weren't going to miss it. There was no rival occupation for a Sunday afternoon that could touch it. The few children that didn't come along must have spent deadly dull Sunday afternoons in a time of no trips out in a car and no television.

Afterwards we sometimes wandered home over the Knolls in a group, swung on a beech tree branch, had some target practice with stones, found a skylark's nest beneath a tuft of grass and checked the eggs and collected itching powder from wild rose hips. I arrived at the farm to the sound of the pump going and afternoon milking well under way, and Fred with his best trousers tucked into his wellingtons and wearing his best white milking coat to keep himself clean for evening service.

Sunday tea scaled the highest peaks of refinement and social grace to which the farm aspired. With everyone dressed in their Sunday best, no uniforms or aprons, it was easily the most formal meal of the week and one which at first had me all at sea; I'd encountered nothing quite like it in Poplar. No reaching right across the table for bread and butter, one asked or waited till one was asked, then the plate was politely passed, "excuse mes" flying thick and fast, instead of a slice being unceremoniously dumped on the plate before you. Being shy I sometimes used to sit for ages, nearly dying of starvation before Mrs Costin noticed I had nothing on my plate. We always took Sunday tea two steps up and on another plane in the dining room with its splendid furniture and it was the meal at which we were most likely to have relatives present.

In those days of quite severe food rationing you couldn't just drop in on people and expect a meal. There was no going to the larder for an extra tin of meat to fill out a salad for two or three unexpected visitors. Tins of meat were jealously hoarded up for Christmas when they could be obtained, which wasn't often. But afternoon tea was an easier proposition, tea and sugar were both rationed but were 'stretchable' and most people were either prepared to accept saccharin or had nothing in their tea. Dried fruit for cake making was in desperately short supply but housewives usually managed something, often plain cakes, even if powdered egg had to be used, which it usually did, though not at the farm. So visitors were more easily catered for at tea than for lunch, that is when their petrol ration would run to coming out that far, for it was most often the relatives from Watford and Harrow who came, not the ones in our two neighbouring villages, who because they could be seen anytime, were in fact seldom seen.

Tea wasn't a substantial meal, it wasn't a high tea but a bread and butter occasion, delicacy and finesse figured there more largely than in the other earthier, substantial and more robust weekday affairs. The best silver came out and fine china, serviettes and all the Sunday best. The bread and butter was cut thinner, the triangles were almost transparent, and a plate of delicious little cakes, always the same ones, from Dunstable, appeared with the traditional Madeira with its piece of peel on top. No home made cakes on a Sunday; no rice pudding or cold custard was finished off either. It was a time of animated conversation, especially if guests were present, of impeccable table manners, but nonetheless a time of much merriment and wit.

There was just about time afterwards for the washing up to be done before everyone hurried about getting ready for evening service. No visitors were ever allowed to disrupt custom, either they went to Chapel or, as more frequently happened, they departed after tea. It never happened that attendance at the service was abandoned in order to entertain visitors. This was a service for adults and we children were excused.

In the summer, Sunday evening was a time when a very few of those who were disinclined to attend church or chapel strolled about the lanes and footpaths keeping a professional eye on their neighbours' crops, cattle and general husbandry. It wasn't so much a walk, more a business trip with the mind ever occupied with crop yields, glaring errors and now and again with praise. I often used to go for such a walk with Eric and his dad who very much liked to see what the rest of the farming community was up to. Perhaps it was because, coming into farming late, he never felt really secure and confident in what he was doing and always wanted to compare his own with others' efforts.

We wandered forth when the Chapel folk had gone and the sun was winding down towards the west. The heat haze that had lain all day across the flat vale was dissipating as the evening breezes began to stir. The Knolls rose up five hundred feet to our left hand, cool and green splashed with white, and the high chalk escarpment from Dunstable Downs to Whipsnade ran for miles like a boundary wall before us keeping in the summer heat as in a walled garden. It was a time of lengthening shadows, of rabbits feeding at the cornfield edge, of pheasants clattering their ponderous way into the air, furious at being disturbed, and of clouds of midges ending their daylong dance in the horizontal beams of sunlight.

Along the lanes we'd go, Eric's dad in his grey Sunday suit, flat cap on head, walking stick in hand, in his rolling gait more reminiscent of a sailor than a farmer. He'd run his eye over a field of bearded barley swaying to the breeze like the sea moving in a gentle swell, and being a man of few words his face spoke volumes for him. The stern lines would relax, his eyes leap to life with a merry twinkle and he'd nod a curt "not bad" then plunge into the crop, snap off a handful of ears, examine them intently a moment then on we'd go. Eric and I would gather ourselves some ears, winnow the grain in our hands and chew it meditatively as we strolled along.

On every hand there were fields of rich, fat wheat dotted with scarlet poppies, not too many for that would be a sign of poor cultivation; of graceful rustling oats, ruler straight rows of giant swedes and mangolds and dense green patches of potatoes. Yet this was no land of wall to wall cultivation, barren of tree and bush, a monotonous carpet tile effect of fields, each inch of ground in service. It was a vale of lush, broad hedgerows scattered with shade-casting trees from which as we walked a multitude of birds serenaded us, and corners of fields and headlands full of the colour of flowers and butterflies and vibrant with the chirruping of insects. The land fairly groaned with its burden of fruitfulness which was spread on every hand away into the heart of the great vale. We assessed the crops of several farms in this manner along the brook to Church End during the long summer evenings hardly ever meeting another soul, then wandered back along the road pursued by shadows, ruminating on what we had seen.

On winter Sunday evenings Doug and I often went down to Eric's house and we had his train set out all around the front room. His dad; who looked like a younger version of Pope John Paul II yet who seldom went to Chapel, would be settled in the corner behind his newspaper and clouds of pipe smoke. But he'd soon be tempted out by our railway engineering and operating systems and he'd give advice on the layout and running procedures, stabbing with his pipe stem to indicate just where he meant. All four of us would be happily engrossed until the front door clicked open and Eric's mum was back from Chapel. Aunt Bess, slightly younger than her sister Mrs Costin, Eric's Aunt Em, was blessed with the same sweet and affectionate nature. She was slimmer than her sister, her hair was longer though equally silvery and worn usually in a bun. She'd brought up three boys, two had now flown the nest and were in the army, so that with being a small farmer's wife she had known a life of hard work and insecurity, but nothing extraordinary in that she would have claimed, for she had the same capacity as her sister for cheerfulness. Aunt Bess was unfailingly kind and hospitable to us children. We had huge parties there in the comfortable living room, with plenty of home cooked food, all manner of buns and cakes, a marvel in wartime, and lots of games which must have put her tolerance of noise to a severe test, but she bore it all with endless patience and good humour scarcely considered for a moment by those on whom it was lavished.

It is very curious the capacity of close relatives living near to each other to more or less ignore one another, in the nicest possible way. Mrs Costin and Eric's mum, being sisters separated by no more than a quarter of a mile, scarcely ever entered each other's houses. I can't recall Aunt Bess once coming in for a sit down and a cup of tea at the farm. On the rare occasions when she did come into the house she would say, "No thanks, I've only just popped in for a moment, I can't stay." Nor can I recall Mrs Costin ever paying a social call on her sister. Not that they had fallen out, they were perfectly friendly and there wasn't the least hint of bad feeling. It was the same for the men. Eric's dad never once came into the farm during my years there and neither Mr Costin nor his sons ever visited him. Yet both families were very friendly and hospitable. Obviously being family isn't necessarily the same as being friends, but there was never any formal visiting, out of family duty, particularly from the women who usually enjoy such social contacts more than men. Perhaps they were physically too close and, the novelty element in encountering each other being nil, there seemed no point in visiting each other's houses. If I hadn't been at the farm I don't suppose for a moment that Eric would have had much contact with his only aunt, uncle and cousins in the village.

One Sunday evening in autumn whilst everyone was at Chapel, Doug and I were making the rounds of several poultry houses which had been towed onto the stubble for the Rhode Island cockerels to fatten themselves up for Christmas. We had to shut them in secure against marauding foxes. You only had to forget to shut one lot in once and you could depend on finding a holocaust next day, with poultry indiscriminately slaughtered, many with just their heads bitten off, sheer wanton mayhem and precious few survivors. So we had to be particularly careful over shutting up hen houses in fields. It was most often my job and I've several times, on the point of going to bed, realised I had forgotten to shut some in and had to dash out on my bike and rush down the field in the darkness, cycling over the stubble with my tiny pin point of light showing up the blackness around me. Luckily I was always in time and breathed a sigh of relief as I heard the quiet ripples of cackling from inside as the birds heard me coming in the darkness.

Our last call on that particular evening was to a meadow opposite the Moat where there was also a hen house to be closed up. We left our bikes by the gate and started down the field. There were several horses in the meadow some way from us and as Doug and I walked across we noticed that they seemed agitated, frisking about and dashing around in an unusual fashion. We soon saw the reason. One of the horses had some barbed wire wrapped around its leg and the barbs must have been digging painfully into its flesh, but we couldn't tell from that distance how bad it was nor how long the wire was, though we could see it clearly enough and were discussing the situation as we walked on towards the henhouse.

Suddenly the horses bolted in a group together, galloping down the field to pass between us and the hedge. In a flash and to our horror we saw the huge length of barbed wire strung out across the field in front of us, trailing free and being pulled along at great speed by the bolting horse with the wire around its leg. The wire was snaking straight for us as we turned and ran. I was fortunate, it slashed by me missing me by inches as I leaped above it, but it caught Doug across the calf of one leg and ripped away the flesh down to the bone before it was past.

How we got home I don't know, nor how Doug didn't bleed to death, but providentially no artery was severed and we were near to houses not in one of the remote fields. Chapel was over and there were adults about and we managed to get out of the field and up the road a little to them. Doug was rushed to hospital in Luton and soon recovered, though he bears the scars to this day. It was a strange and macabre coincidence that the field was the same one in which a few years before a relation of the Costins had died in a fire among the corn which grew there then.

Chapter IX
Harvest Gold

It was a sparkling clear morning in early August when I awoke to the sound of the well pump motor starting up outside, and the rhythmical clanking of machinery began that was a sure destroyer of sleep. In that first waking flash I remembered that we were in the school summer holidays so I stretched luxuriously enjoying a slow transition from sleep to the waking world. "We'll cut the winter oats down at Northfield tomorrow if it stays fine," Mr Costin had said the previous day by way of announcing that harvest time was here. I was excited about getting my first taste of it, that romantic time above all other on a farm when every townee thinks enviously of country folk riding about on carts piled high with golden sheaves, sunning themselves and chewing straws without a care in the world.

Having come to the village at the tail end of the 1940 harvest, too late to experience it, I had been forced to wait almost twelve months for this great culminating event of the farming year, waiting with high anticipation spiced with a little trepidation. If we were forking out a few bundles of straw and I worked up a bit of a sweat throwing them into the cart someone would say, "Ah, you wait till harvest my boy, you'll know what it is to sweat then." Or if I were foolishly to admit to having a blister on my hand after using a pitchfork for some small job, the comment would be sure to come, "You wait till harvest my lad, you'll have blisters as big as tea cups on both hands." So I was aware from a string of these remarks uttered throughout the year just how highly they all thought of harvest, how enjoyable it was going to be and that they looked forward to it every bit as keenly as I did.

I lay in bed for a few minutes playing with the light switch that hung from the ceiling on a long flex. It was a pirate ship attacking a Spanish galleon sailing on the sunny Caribbean and we were firing repeated broadsides as I pressed the switch back and forth, with my cut throat crew, cutlasses in mouths ready to leap aboard the heavily laden prize. The sound of dropping chains, like anchors going overboard and the soft clop of hooves on stone told me the milking was over, breakfast would be about ready, so I abandoned ship, dressed in a flash and took the stairs two at a time, sans cutlass, for a wash in the galley.

Sure enough the fried bread was sizzling away in the frying pan and Mrs Costin was keeping an eye on it and the bacon grilling and the kettle coming up to the boil all at the same time. She was getting used to the new gas stove now and confessed that life was a bit easier with the old range standing cold and dead but still glossy black and still securely in position against the wall just in case the new fangled stove went wrong.

With every day that passed my first impression of Mrs Costin had been more than amply borne out and reinforced. Subconsciously, in the casual, taken for granted, offhand way that children have, I realised that here was a woman I could completely trust and who trusted me. And some inarticulate corner of my mind knew that not only trust but a whole host of golden qualities that I could not then begin to name lay in the heart of this most modest, reticent and self deprecating woman.

She was an angel, to everyone not just to me. She was possessed of one of those saintly natures that turned the other cheek, never spoke in anger, was endlessly forgiving and tolerant especially when impatient males, like spoilt children, demanded to know why their dinner wasn't ready the minute they were, or why their bacon wasn't crisp or why there was skin on the custard. To these and many more profound virtues was allied the capacity of a horse for work and the staggering resourcefulness to organise and run, most often single handed, a large house and a demanding family. Having had four sons of her own she knew boys inside out and had exhausted none of the sympathy and understanding she had shown for the little troubles her own boys had got into. She poured oil on troubled waters when Mr Costin grumbled about all us boys jumping about in straw or making a mess in the barn. She could be counted on to smooth our ruffled feathers when told off and to put in a good work for all offenders against outraged authority.

She was saintly in her nature but no mere cipher, no doormat, she was cheerful and lively minded. In her 'spare' time she was president of the Chapel women's meeting, the Happy Sparrows as Fred cheekily called them, which she attended every Wednesday afternoon for years, hardly ever missing a meeting, a welcome little break in her arduous week.

The essence of her character, I saw later, the bedrock on which her marvellous nature was founded was her quiet but unshakable Christian faith. I never heard her say much about her beliefs, she wouldn't have considered herself qualified to discuss religion and she hated talking about herself anyway, but the occasional word merely bore out what everything else about her shouted from the rooftops. She had her quiet convictions and these shone through in her every word and action.

Quiet her convictions may have been but when she had made up her mind to hold a certain opinion or pursue some course of action she could not be browbeaten out of it, no matter how insistent or clever the arguments against her. In other more mundane matters she was as I say a saint, certainly too saintly for her own short term good. At the time I was conscious of very little of this, to me she was someone who was unfailingly kind, not with a polite, formal kindness, a sugar coating, but a loving motherly kindness, genuine all the way through and instantly recognisable and one that forged a bond of feeling between us beyond all words.

"Ready for your first day of harvest work?" she said as I quickly sloshed a little water over my face as Reg and Bob came in.

"He'd better be," said Reg, "we're depending on him aren't we Bob?"

"Not half," said Bob. "I wonder what he'll be doing exactly?"

"Oh, just about everything I expect, running the whole show," said Reg.

"Let's see those lily white hands," said Bob. Then with a sharp intake of breath he added, "It's going to be nasty, we've got to change yours into this in double quick time," and he put his large brown hand with skin like supple leather next to mine.

"You'll be all right," said Reg with a reassuring grin. "Anyway, to start with you can wear gloves if you like."

"No thanks, not for me," I thought. "What do you take me for, a softy?"

The eggs were spitting hot fat furiously and in a moment or two we were sitting down to a hearty breakfast around the big table.

I was eagerly awaiting a discussion on harvesting tactics and maybe some indication of what precisely I would be doing because, since in my own mind my contribution loomed very large, I assumed everyone else must have considered it. But of course it didn't turn out like that. Boys, being the lowest form of farm life, didn't exactly dominate a farmer's thinking and anyway Leighton were playing Dunstable at cricket at the weekend when Bob would be opposing his older brother George, who being a solid and steady solicitor type, played wicket keeper for Dunstable. Bob was Leighton's big hitter and change bowler so there was a difficult division of loyalties for their parents who were nonetheless looking forward to seeing their boys in action against each other.

It always amazed me that George, brought up on the farm, should choose instead to go in for law and be content to work in a sunless solicitor's office in town. I suppose his turning away from farming was one of the hazards of a good education, for all the three younger children, George, Daisy and Bob went to the Cedars private school in Leighton. Fred and Reg, whose school days were fretted away before the Cedars opened, went no further than the village school.

I remember going to Dunstable with Mrs and Mrs Costin to see the cricket match that Saturday. It was after tea when we got there, a lovely, spacious, tree-fringed ground, greenly cool and elegant with a very thin scattering of spectators, mostly wives and children, a typically English scene a million miles from the war. In front of the wooden pavilion was a sprinkling of elderly, blazered gentlemen members sitting around in canvas chairs and each one got up in turn and raised his straw hat to Mrs Costin as she went by. I don't remember anything about the game itself nor which of the brothers gained the upper hand but I do recall that it was all very jolly and hearty with much friendly calling between the players, but the white clad figures seemed so far away and the leisurely action bore so little resemblance to our hectic cricket sessions in the sheepyard that I remained unimpressed.

So with nothing said about my vital role in the coming harvest work we adjourned from the breakfast table. Then some unusual things began to happen according to a well established pattern. Arthur took the scythe to mow a strip around the headland of the field of oats to give access to the binder. Apart from this task and occasionally mowing thistles in the orchard there wasn't much work left on the farm for a scythe, which was a pity for in Arthur's hands that venerable implement was a poem of precise and flowing motion, easier to appreciate than to emulate as I discovered when Arthur gave me some instruction in its use.

"Now, hold it easy," he said, "not too hard, relax a bit and give it a good steady sweep around like this. There, now you have a go."

I snicked tentatively at a few thistles.

"No, keep it well away from you or you'll be the only wooden-legged boy in your class."

I used to like watching him sharpening the blade with the whetstone as with a supple twist of the wrist he'd make the stone glide easily back and forth across the razor sharp edge, bringing both sides of the blade to a shining silver.

Reg and Fred brought the binder out of its quarters in the cart shed behind the big barns and set to, getting it ready for a few weeks' intensive use. It was an ungainly looking machine that rattled its noisy way around the field with its high whirling sails, its flapping canvas and the wicked looking saw-toothed knife hissing in its iron jaws. Awkward it may have looked but what a revolution it must have caused in harvesting when first it scythed its way through the corn pulled by a pair of horses. Instead of the tedious, back breaking labour of cutting the corn with sickle or scythe and binding the sheaves by hand, it was henceforward cleanly and speedily cut, bound and thrown out in neat rows along the stubble, only needing to be stood in shocks to dry.

Bob was sharpening one of the long binder knives. He had clamped it to a four legged metal stand, waist high. Each triangular blade was to be filed to a shining silver, its razor keen edge ready to cut anything in its path, anything. Mental pictures of the grim stories I had heard about children who had fallen in front of the moving binder sent a shudder down my spine as I viewed those cold unyielding blades.

I watched Bob for a while as he gently filed a blade, making it shine silver in the sunlight, tested it gingerly with a finger, filed away a bit more then stood back to survey the result.

"Reckon you could do this job?" he asked.

"Wouldn't mind trying," I replied with cautious enthusiasm.

*This is the house – West View – that Fred inherited from his Aunt Ginny, seen here.
Daisy later lived in it.*

The station at Stanbridgeford by Lower End, Totternhoe, since axed by Beeching.

"Well, you've seen what to do. You've got to do each blade like that. File out all the chipped edges and make 'em really sharp. Oh, and try not to cut too many fingers off in the process. Let's see you have a go."

I took the file and started off as if I was trying to file my way through the bars of Hell. The file slipped off the blade and my hand slid over the cutting edge.

"Hey, not like that!" cried Bob. "Have you cut yourself? You were lucky. Now gently, like this," and he demonstrated again. "Firmly and slowly, stroke it as if it were your rabbit's ears."

I got the idea eventually and Bob went off to wield a spanner on the binder. I coped reasonably well with that job, sustaining only minor cuts, and found it very satisfying as slowly each of the twenty or so blunt and tarnished blades was transformed into a gleaming razor. I felt no end of a fine chap having found my first real job at harvest time. It was a job I did many a time after that for a knife had to be sharpened after each day's cutting; sometimes two a day were needed.

Whilst all this was going on, a brilliant sun that shone from a cloudless sky was drying the dew and justifying Mr Costin's decision that the time and the crop were ripe. By mid-morning the binder had arrived at the field towed down behind the tractor, the rest of us came along in the pony and trap and everything was now ready.

The oats stood dense and tall, their stems and shivering ears of grain a corn-gold jungle, but a jungle that was rich in lesser, lower plants that I could see as I peered into the edge of the mysterious world laid bare by Arthur's scythe. Small red poppies, sinuous bindweed with its pale pink cups open to the sun, scarlet pimpernel hugging the soil and tall white campions crowded in among the oat stems.

"Anything much in there d'you think Arth?" asked Bob as Arthur returned from his scything. Bob's twelve bore lay on his jacket ready for action.

"Some, I shouldn't wonder," replied Arthur. "Four or five rabbits ran back in as I came round by the hedge."

"Rabbit stew for dinner tomorrow Mick, with a bit of luck," grinned Bob.

"Right, away we go!" yelled Reg from his seat high up on the binder. The tractor revved up noisily and the clanking, clattering binder took its first bite of oat stems but hadn't gone twenty yards before Reg banged on the tractor's broad mudguard with his long stick to tell Fred to stop. The binder was spewing the oats out unbound and needed several minutes' adjustment and another false start before the teething trouble was over and it was finally away binding a perfect sheaf.

It was always to me a species of magic that a mere machine could take its string from the giant ball revolving in its position on the binder, lead it through a maze of little eyelets, wind itself around the sheaf, tie its own knot, cut it and do the same all day long. I often peered into the binder at rest and tried to fathom out how it was done, but never could. Knowing how my own fingers had to manipulate to tie a knot, I couldn't for the life of me understand how a machine could dot it, and would no doubt be as baffled by it today as I was then.

The rest of us were shocking for the rest of the day and much of the following day, in fact whenever a field of corn was cut we were shocking. The verb 'to shock' took on a new meaning for me – to stand the sheaves in tents of ten or a dozen – and whatever its origin in this context, I doubt if it was due to anything shocking in the task, which on the contrary was quite agreeable work especially with oats which were light when they were dry. As the day wore on and arms became wearier you'd swear their weight doubled. Later I was to shock the peas and beans and that was much less pleasant, more nearly shocking, due to the thistles that abounded in those crops, hardened sharp thistles dried by the sun and wind to fine needles. It was agony for the fingers that groped for the band, they soon became red and raw with the thistles and the rough stems. On those occasions I was indeed thankful to wear an old pair of leather gloves.

I soon learned not to roll my sleeves up to get my arms brown as I had hoped to do. The oat stems were rough enough to scratch and tear the inside of my forearms and make them red raw where they rubbed against the sheaves, before I yielded to sense and rolled my shirtsleeves down again and buttoned them. I was fated never to get much of a tan though I was out in the sun and wind so much. I wasn't the right colouring for it, being fair. If I did get a dose of hot sunshine, bet your life I'd just go red and peel. It was always surprising to see the difference in the others between the deep leathery tan of their arms and head and the lily white skin just across the border above the rolled up sleeve or below the neckline. Nobody ever stripped off to the waist then, unlike nowadays, partly no doubt because of the roughness of some of the work, but also because it was the custom not to in those unpermissive days.

I worked with Arthur and it was the first time I had been alone with him for any length of time. He usually operated on his own for most jobs save milking when everyone was there. But now all day stretched before us and although he got on at a cracking pace, a pace he could keep up all day, the work left us free to carry on an intermittent conversation as we walked back and forth among the lines of sheaves building up our row of shocks together. Five rows of sheaves we took with the shock being set in the middle one.

After we'd been going some time and made the odd remark about this and that, he began to tell me a little about the one time of great adventure in his life. I knew he'd been in the army in the Great War so was able to catch on when he started up. He didn't elaborate, he never went into interesting detail about anything, the bare minimum of speech was Arthur's style. I don't know what he was like in the Cross Keys after a pint or two, perhaps his tongue was looser then, but I got the impression that Arthur didn't think much of talking, he preferred humming, a low, tuneless, endless humming. So he just laid out the bare bone of his subject as we met to place our sheaves together, dispersing then to seek more.

"Poppies," he said, indicating some on the ground, "I seen the fields of Flanders red with 'em."

Then at our next encounter. "Some mess it was out there, you've never seen anything like it." Even I realised this was probably a considerable under-statement.

He was sucking on his empty pipe as he worked and he spat the words out around the edge of it, his quick eyes flickering with liveliness as he did so, the suggestion of a smile around his stubbly chin.

"Not like this time. Trenches! Lord, I've dug some trenches. He spat on his hands and surveyed them keenly as if looking for evidence of his trench digging.

"Bayonets we had and we used 'em." He did a quick jab to show me and smiled wickedly.

Several minutes later on. "Lord, those Frenchies, they was rum they was. Bonjewer monsewer," and a wry smile lit up his face and he stopped work, stood quite still a moment then took off his cap, a rare gesture, and scratched his flattened hair, a far away look in his eyes. He shook his head speculatively then picked up another sheaf.

In a short while. "Bin over the top a few times. Bin blown up by shells a time or two as well. I was lucky though, didn't have my number of any of 'em. Never had so much as a scratch all the way through."

A few shocks later. "Bigger poppies than these. Red as blood. Millions of 'em. Was I glad to get back home."

"Had some good pals in the Beds and Herts though. We had some laughs together," and his eyes sparkled again as past pleasure sprang briefly to life.

"Done enough wandering, reckon I'll stay put now."

"Not a bad old place down here when you think about it. No place like home. And it's true, it's true all right."

He went on at intervals throughout the morning and I made a suitable audience I suppose, not saying much, not knowing enough to make an intelligent comment or ask a question. He told me how he'd been taken out of the trenches to work with horses in the front line because he'd worked on a farm. They'd got so short of food one winter they'd had to shoot some of the horses and eat them. That put paid to his job and he was sent back into the trenches.

I tried to imagine him fighting heroically as I'd recently seen men fight in the American film 'Sergeant Yorke', all mud and blood and death around but Arthur bearing a charmed life. If he ever won a medal he told no one and I don't suppose he won anything, he wasn't the sort, though he probably earned one. "I just kept my head down and hoped for the best," he said.

He hadn't got anything to say about the evils and the futility of war, he never stocked such notions, just took it all as his row to hoe and got on with it.

He worked away as he chatted, stout booted, leather gaitered against the wire-like stubble, and I tried to see him walking arm in arm with a French girl or drinking a glass of wine at a pavement café, but I couldn't imagine him young

106

and carefree, he had always been old, a confirmed old bachelor, brown and wrinkled and slightly bow legged.

Sharp on twelve by Arthur's pocket watch the tractor and binder pulled away at the corner of the vast rectangle of oats still standing, came to a halt and soon stood silent on the stubble. We all crowded into the pony trap and went cantering off up the road for our dinner, with appetites like ravening wolves. How well Mrs Costin knew her gang! There was a huge meat pie with plenty of thick pastry to compensate for the ungenerous ration of steak and kidney, and tureens of potatoes, runner beans and carrots. It was sheer bliss to sit in the coolness of the front kitchen methodically disposing of a huge plateful of food and sitting back with a self satisfied feeling of fullness afterwards. I was content too, thinking that for once I had earned my dinner. It tasted all the better for it. This was going to be something good this harvest work, and there were weeks of it to come. I liked the feeling of being one of the team.

By the time the jam tart and rice pudding had been seen off and we had sat about for a few minutes feeling good, it was time to go once more, there was never much time wasted in idleness. The news headlines, as ever, were listened to, then we tumbled outside, took the nosebag off the pony and all climbed aboard for the return to the field.

The afternoon was hot. I sweated in my shirt with the sleeves all buttoned up and my thick flannel trousers and leather boots, but Arthur in flannel shirt and waistcoat seemed perfectly at ease. There were by now thousands upon thousands of sheaves waiting to be picked up and just four of us to do it all; the field was really vast. This was where romantic notions of idyllic harvest work could easily crumble and collapse in the heat and sweat. The idea that harvesting is fun and frolic amid the golden corn ignores the reality of the many hours of slogging hard work to be done. When the first flush of pleasure and enthusiasm has passed with the freshness of the early morning, there are still untold acres to be dealt with, unnumbered hours of hot uncomfortable toil still to be endured. He may be a romantic but there has to be steel somewhere in a farmer's make up or he would never survive and it is not surprising that for many the steel soon ousts romanticism.

You had to learn something of the peasant's sense of timelessness, of dogged perseverence, and stifle the town bred impatience and desire for change and variety. As any boy would I found it hard to accept, like an actual physical struggle inside me, that I was going to have to keep on steadily standing sheaves up all day long, no variation, no change of occupation, no going on to something else for a break. Not until I had won that struggle and accepted the long, slow, unchanging hours of work was I able to relax and enjoy myself.

Working with adults made it easier for me to keep going. Another boy or more there and we would have declined into uselessness I've no doubt. Mr Costin had already passed on to me his received wisdom concerning the value of boys on the farm, handed down from his father and heaven knows how many preceding generations. "One boy's a boy, two boys are half a boy and three boys are no boy at all." He enjoyed saying this for apart from concisely summing up his own opinion, it rolled off the tongue in a very satisfying, rhythmical way. He'd often repeat it with a grim smile when a few of us boys were up to something we shouldn't have been.

Arthur left us to see to the milking preparations half way through the afternoon and wasn't I just relieved a little later to be asked to fetch the cows up from the meadow. I jumped the brook and paused for a long drink and splashed water over my burning face, then walked through the cool soft grass, swishing it with my boots, rejoicing in my liberation. Milking brought work in the field to a halt and whilst this was proceeding I went on my usual daily round up of eggs, following the routine I had worked out over the months. Luckily most hens were creatures of habit and tended to lay in the same places, so once you knew the ancestral nesting spots the job was easy. I swung around like a veteran through the sunshine and shadow of sheepyard, rickyard and barns, scooping up eggs where the mote-filled sunbeams hung hot and still in the profound silence of the summer afternoon. Then came tea to refresh us before returning to the fields.

We worked on into the evening with the shadows thrown gigantic on the stubble, the lessening of heat making work more pleasant but tiredness mounting fast, and still the tractor and binder whirred their way around a now quickly diminishing golden rectangle. Eventually, with the light fading fast they stopped and left the rest till day and we others stopped lifting sheaves and left the crop to the serried ranks of shocks to guard till our return.

It was too late to go out looking for Eric or Doug. I wondered what they had been up to all day, I wished I'd been able to join them, I bet they'd been doing something really interesting. But I wasn't too bothered, I was rather pleased and proud of my day.

"Survived your first day of harvest work then Mick," said Mrs Costin as I sat with a mug of cocoa at supper time, aware of most of the muscles in my body declaring their weary presence.

I grinned a reply.

"Ah, we'll make a farmer of him yet, won't we Mick?" declared Mr Costin.

"I wonder what you will do when you grow up?" asked Fred, elbows resting on the table, arms arched over his steaming bowl of bread and milk.

"He won't be a farmer if he's got any sense," laughed Bob. "Too much like hard work isn't it Mick?"

"Oh, I don't know," said Mrs Costin. "How did he get on today?"

"Very well," said Mr Costin firmly. "Arthur says he had a job keeping up with him."

I looked up for the slight twist of a smile that would settle the category of that remark and I saw it.

There was teasing in it and a bit of flattery, and I enjoyed it, wanting the flattery to be true. What would I do when I was grown? I hadn't the least idea what I wanted. Getting a job, the very idea of going out to work didn't really

George Costin, right, and friends.

Ralph Archer, Fred's farmer friend from Church End and also his partner in the Specials, Uncle Alf, with my cousin Doug in front and Fred Costin (left to right). It must have been Sunday, they are in their best clothes. Note the line of elms in the field.

mean anything to me yet. I liked to dream I could be a farmer if I chose. I knew deep down I couldn't of course, I wasn't that much of a simpleton. I realised the unspoken subject, money, came into it a lot, but I was glad they all seemed pleased with my effort so far.

What luxurious fatigue I felt in arms and legs that night as all those miles of stubble tramping and sheaf carrying caught up on untried muscles! The sheer bliss of cool cotton sheets on burning, tired skin, relieved of the weight of blankets. The delirium that enveloped the senses sinking slowly into oblivion! And what a deep untroubled sleep I slept, to wake refreshed for another day among the golden sheaves.

An hour's cutting finished that field of oats but it took us most of the day to stand up all the sheaves. Fred and Reg after helping us awhile had wheeled away to cut another smaller field of oats several fields away so we carried on in our peaceful task monotonously, endlessly in that now silent field, the very routine becoming soothing and satisfying. When we had eventually finished, though weary, I looked around on the rows of golden tents with some pride that I had helped to produce that order out of chaos.

They had brought their guns down with them but there wasn't a thing in the field, not one rabbit, nor a single hare in spite of all the expectancy as the oats declined to a thinner and thinner strip. "They all slipped away during the night," said Reg. "It was a pity we couldn't have finished it off instead of leaving it." He nodded over to the acres of wheat immediately alongside, "That's where they'll be," he said.

We came to cut that wheatfield a few days later after finishing off all the oats. All day long it took, another arduous but vastly satisfying and increasingly enjoyable day. By now I was hardened to the work and although I was tired by evening, it wasn't the tiredness of exhaustion when you were utterly drained, but the tiredness that could soon be remedied by a night's rest or more quickly by Eric and Mac coming whistling down the yard on their bikes for a quick game of cricket before bad light could stop play, then a wander through the orchard down to the brook perfecting our owl hoots to confound the genuine owls beginning their nightly stint.

As we got to grips with the wheat sheaves I soon appreciated the difference between them and the sheaves of oats. The latter's ears had been delicate, well spaced out, they were lighter, non abrasive as they softly stroked hands and arms. The heavier, dense and spiky ears of wheat were, by comparison, harsh, with stems thick and hard, punishing to hands and arms.

The weather remained fine and warm. Large fluffy cotton wool clouds dotted the vivid blue and drifted lazily in the light breeze. We carried on after tea as usual to finish off the cutting and Bob and Reg brought their guns down again. The wheat was down to a long narrow rectangle now, perhaps ten yards wide, but Arthur and Bob and Mr Costin and I were still putting up shocks around the edge of the piece, hours behind the binder. The sun sank lower and plunged into the tall elms in the neighbouring meadow. The golden rectangle of wheat narrowed, narrowed with each broad swathe the binder took. Suddenly Reg stood up on the binder, shouted something above the tractor's roar and pointed into the thin line of standing corn. Bob had been waiting for this, he grabbed his gun and set off running towards the centre of the field. Pat the dog, dozing most of the day and following us as we slowly progressed around the field, sprang up at the sight of Bob's gun and dashed off with him. The tractor reached the end of the strip, turned and came back again. Arthur and I stopped to watch.

The tractor halted and Reg had his gun to his shoulder. Suddenly the field seemed alive with rabbits bursting out of the corn and racing frantically across the open stubble, racing desperately for their lives. Shots rang out, a shattering confusion of noise in the quiet field. No time to reload, the fugitives were gone, bounding away into the dense cover of the adjoining field of potatoes. Pat was going mad rushing frenziedly about. Two rabbits that were sledge-hammered down were searched for and brought back by Pat and they were laid out on the stubble, their grey fur stained with red. We would have our rabbit stew next day. Most of the fields we cut provided a similarly dramatic conclusion as they had been doing for endless years.

The horses were going to play a vital part soon in bringing in the harvest, so on the Saturday before carting was expected to begin I had the job of taking Depper and Dolly over to the blacksmith's at Eaton Bray for a couple of new shoes each. I'd been once before with Bob so I knew where to go. "Don't forget to ask him for rubber soles," said Reg with a grin. He gave me a leg up and I sat proudly astride Depper's ample back with Dolly tied behind and we set off. It was a lovely sunny morning and we went at a steady walk down past the bus stop, with me surveying the world from my high position and feeling grand. I gave some of my friends a wave before we turned off and saw their looks of envy as we passed majestically by. I felt a bit as if I were in a circus procession, so up for show did I seem to be.

Reg knew what he was doing when he entrusted me with Depper. She was a lovely natured chestnut mare, solid and dependable as a rock, not the least flustered at passing buses or lorries. I held the reins but I was entirely in her hands. Her daughter Dolly was more lively and skittish but sobered by her mother's presence. After a marvellous twenty minutes or so ride during which the tiny gnawing anxiety I had tried to ignore was finally soothed away and transformed into a cocky self assurance, so that I felt like some mediaeval knight looking down on the Eaton Bray peasantry, we arrived at the blacksmith's grimy and dim inferno. "Whoa," I called and slipped off Depper's back. She knew perfectly well where she was and stood by the open door to the forge as quiet as a lamb. The blacksmith came out. "Costin's," I said. He nodded, then having no time or inclination to waste his words on a boy, led Depper straight in.

I had nothing to do but hang about and look around me at this strange, dark, iron world, full of mysterious tools and implements. Then as the blacksmith busied himself with our horses I watched fascinated as he fearlessly worked among the horse's legs, his voice full of calm authority quieting her fears. Soon the bellows were blowing the coals white hot and he was beating a shoe into shape on the anvil amid showers of shooting stars every time he struck. The smell of those hissing clouds of fumes that spurted up as he placed the hot shoe on the hoof is one of life's never to be forgotten experiences, unlike anything else ever smelt, acrid and pungent but strangely attractive, its smell still lingers in my nostrils. The hot shoe was dipped into the water trough in an explosion of steam and when the fitting was perfect nails were hammered through the hoof fast and accurate, the horse never stirring, ends nipped off and filed and there was the first shoe on with no trouble. Another horse had arrived outside. This was his busy time, this leather aproned smith, sweating and black faced as he took up Depper's other hind leg to pare off the worn and ragged hoof to prepare it for the shoe. I rode home as proudly as if I'd done the work myself instead of being a mere passenger.

About a week after the cutting had started and with plenty more still to be cut, carting began. The binder took a well earned rest and we began to fetch the harvest in. The rickyard was prepared, a straw base laid out for the first rick and Charlie, Depper, Captain and Dolly were harnessed and hitched up to their carts. I jumped into an empty cart. This was it. This was the real beginning of my harvest, the part I had been impatiently waiting for. This was where a boy came into his own. All that shocking was but the prelude, this was the real thing when I was going to operate on my own, captain of my own cart, master of my fate – almost.

I flicked the reins with a "Gee up Charlie", carefully negotiated the gateway without hitting a post, which wasn't always the case, and we were off on the exciting job of bringing home the harvest. It was marvellous to feel the horse responding to a tug on the reins, to guide the great creature exactly where you wanted it. Nerve racking at first, with experience I soon became blasé and could usually judge to an inch the crucial distance of wheel from gatepost, though with ruts and stones to throw you at an angle it was always a hazardous business.

It was the finest time of my life so far, to be in sole command of a horse and cart at harvest time, a far cry from the previous summer's playing in the streets of Poplar. If anyone had reminded me that I didn't want to come to the farm at the beginning, I would have been hard put to it to have agreed, such doubts and misgivings now seemed incredible, unbelievable.

Now, no longer shunned by my friends as at dung cart, I ran at times a sort of children's shuttle service down to the field as they swarmed aboard for the long ride down where they were always made welcome by Reg and Bob. No wonder I felt more of a village boy than the genuine ones aboard the cart. They wandered or sat about, the girls like bright butterflies resting on the yellow sheaves weaving chains of flowers. The boys looked for mice and pursued them with sticks and loud cries or stood by the horse stroking its nose and asking if they could have a go at pitching a sheaf on the cart. Eventually they got bored and wandered back again behind the load in a long line by the roadside verge clutching small bunches of flowers or plucking ears of corn out and rubbing them between their hands then chewing the grains. After a few days, when the novelty of visiting the field had worn off, I found myself mostly alone on the long trek down and the long walk back with the load.

Passing and repassing along these lanes where there was little traffic, there was always plenty to occupy one's mind. Sitting up high on the cart I could look out over the hedges and ditches on either side into the fields and away down to the railway line with its strings of trucks loaded with lime from the quarry forming a train that shuffled slowly out at half past two each day. Then there were the tiny, one carriage passenger trains, huffing and puffing pompously and all stopping at the little station by the level crossing at Stanbridgeford. And over all, visible at all times, felt even at one's back, stood the Knolls looking down at me green and white and smiling on that long succession of harvest days, always attracting the eye to search its slopes for familiar landmarks and to puzzle over tiny figures moving where I so often roamed.

Mostly when I was alone my head was filled with war fantasies or the burning realities of the moment – would the load get safely to the rickyard without half of it slipping off into the road and blocking it completely, it happened more than once, or would I be able to control Captain, our strongest horse, as he made a mad dash through the rickyard gate?

In the field my job at first was merely to lead the horse between the shocks while Reg and Bob took turns at pitching and being in the cart loading. Then one day as we were going peacefully along, Reg stopped, leaned on his pitchfork a moment, "Dang it all Mick," he said, "jump up into the cart my lad and let's see if you can't learn to be a loader. No sense in wasting manpower is there?"

I'd been having an easy time for a few days, wearing out shoe leather but conserving elbow grease.

I jumped up on the empty wagon very doubtfully. "Now, there's nothing to it," said Reg confidently. "You just lay the sheaves out like this," and he pitched a couple on the back. "No, don't touch 'em, they're all right."

Bob pitched two more beside them and in a minute they had completed the outside edge at the back, all the sheaves lying neatly next to each other, fan like.

"Now put a few in the middle to bind them in," said Reg and he tossed a couple at my feet. I pulled them about to cover the ends of the outside ones.

"And that's the way you go on for the whole cart," Reg declared, "keep your middle full and you'll be okay. Most boys are good at that," he said smiling.

We finished that first load off slowly and with many stops for advice and explanations as the load grew higher. When we'd got up past the side of the cart it was like building a big raft of sheaves, drawing in gradually the higher we went. At the end when I seemed to be standing on the top of a skyscraper, they threw a rope over the top to help keep the load secure on its journey up the road. I slid down clutching the rope and surveyed my first load of harvest. "Well, how does that feel," beamed Reg. "That's a right proper job of work well done."

Those carts contained very big loads because two timber framed extensions were fitted to increase the load carrying capacity, one fitted forward over the horse's back and the other projected rearwards so that the load resembled a stately golden galleon of sheaves, heavily laden and sailing majestically. Sometimes indeed, if the ground was a bit soft and the distance to the road long, the horse would have difficulty in getting out of the field and might have to have a rest. A strong hand at the bridle, shouts and a tap with a stick occasionally had to be resorted to by way of encouragement.

Like most jobs on the farm there was a knack to be learned in loading. Done well, a cart full of sheaves would be easy to unload in the rickyard, it unwound itself almost, systematically. Put in anyhow, Fred would have been puzzled how to get them off in orderly fashion. After a while and a few mishaps – "Bless the boy, what are you up to now?" from Reg. "They're heavy enough without having to pitch them up twice" from Bob as I let some slip down – I managed to acquire the knack of loading and used a small pitchfork to put the sheaves in place quickly and did most of the loading from then on with the two men pitching together and the horse walking on unguided between the rows.

I took great pride in being king of my own load though I was well aware that Reg and Bob made my task much simpler by most often pitching the sheaves, especially the outer and lower ones, exactly where they were to lie. I can't resist a small pang of regret that such a minor skill and satisfaction as loading a harvest cart neatly and competently has been lost for ever. I'm not sure that stowing bales on a trailer provides similar pleasures; I hope it does.

Now and again when spirits were high or when I'd been a bit more cheeky than usual, they'd fling up the sheaves like an avalanche in reverse, completely burying me, then I'd stagger to my feet and fling them down again and we'd all have a good laugh and so the work would carry on with the drudgery and fatigue banished. We became a great team, Reg, Bob and I, as we worked together day after day. The work was tiring, more tiring than shocking, but not exhausting, and after the pitchfork blisters on my hands had healed up I soon became hardened to it.

Sometimes I reverted to driving, sometimes Johnny Janes from Church End, who was about my age, came in to drive too, depending on how far we were working from the rickyard. In succeeding years as I grew stronger I often took my turn pitching and that was real hard work. At first I only managed one sheaf at a time and found even that difficult enough to hoist to the top of a load. But we all want to grow up as fast as we can and I wouldn't rest content until I was pitching two at a time like the men. I did it eventually before my time was up, it was a matter of technique as well as muscle and then I felt the pride of being an equal, or nearly an equal, member of an excellent team.

The sunshine seemed now a warm benediction, seldom uncomfortably hot. We worked in shirtsleeves but I never did acquire my earnestly desired tan, though for many years I was green with envy of those who tanned easily, thinking it was a decided advantage in getting a girl. Eventually I learned to accept my paleness and redness though it wasn't a fashion that ever became popular, Reg wore a large straw hat, Bob went bareheaded or sometimes wore a beret. Always cheerful, always with something interesting and amusing to say, tremendously strong and capable, yet treating me as one of them, they made those days, which stretched into weeks, resuming each succeeding year, pass in a golden haze of hard work made light with good companionship. Was this the romantic ideal of harvest on the farm that townsfolk so obstinately retain? .If so it was hard won and depended as much on the personalities involved as on the occupation.

About mid-morning Mrs Costin would send down to the field a basket with a light snack and some bottles of nectar disguised as cold sweet tea which we consumed between loads, sitting on a flattened shock. "What a way to spend Bank Holiday Monday!" said Reg as we were having a rare and welcome rest while they moved the elevator in the rickyard. A single plane high up, moved with a harsh metallic drone across the unbroken blue dome above. Whipsnade and the long rampart of Downs stood out clear against the horizon, the magnificent chalk lion camouflaged now, a light breeze fanned my cheeks and at my feet some tiny red flowers quivered among the bristling stubble and trailed over the parched, cracked soil. If only this could go on for ever! Bob and Reg a pitchfork length away, spreadeagled and drinking tea to murmurs of appreciation. "Not too bad a way of spending Bank Holiday Monday," I thought.

Back in Fosse's rickyard there was a different atmosphere, one of sober efficiency without the golden spark that made working in the field so enjoyable. Everywhere chickens were scratching amongst the straw, cattle leaning over gates wishing they could get in, pigs in the neighbouring yard squealing and grunting: and in the centre of the rickyard two huge Dutch Barns where our games in the straw had gone on all winter and which would soon be crammed full and inaccessible to all save mice and rats.

At first Fred, up on the load that had just come in from the field, merely had to toss the sheaves down to his father who farmed them out to Arthur as he systematically built up one bay of the Dutch Barn. But as the sides grew higher and climbed over the load so the elevator was brought on. Fred unhitched the pony from the trap and hitched her instead to a stout wooden bar which she pulled around in a circle. The bar was attached to a large and heavy covered metal ring on the ground which turned a steel rod connected to the elevator. As the pony trod her tedious circle the long elevator chains clanked round. They had slats across fixed to the chains with a couple of iron prongs sticking up to keep the mounting sheaves from falling back. This great cumbersome but effective machine that could be raised as the rick grew, would grind on all day, the pony becoming so accustomed to her job that she turned in her treadmill path for hours on end with only the occasional shout to keep her going.

There were often children about, small undemanding ones usually, especially at Fosse's, which was larger and more open than the home rickyard. Attracted by the activity when the rest of the village slumbered in the warm sunshine, the children would sit around on the fence or lounge on a pile of straw and come up and stroke the horse waiting patiently as its load was lightened, or stare at the pony circling, endlessly circling amid its cloud of flies. The load finished, Fred would grab some little boy by the waist, hoist him onto the empty cart and lead it away to an empty corner, the little boy wide eyed with the thrill of having a ride all to himself.

One of the snags about having two rickyards a quarter of a mile or so apart was that the elevator had to be moved between them. It was wound up or down by hand with a big handle that took two to turn when raising. Once folded down upon itself the tractor took the long, awkward, iron wheeled load slowly along the road and with many manoeuvres through the gate posts, into the other yard where it would be set up again for action.

One of the winter jobs every two years or so was to paint that elevator, a daunting task for it seemed to have acres of woodwork. I was helping Reg and Bob do it one year down at Fosse's and was finding the utmost difficulty in working steadily in one place as was needed instead of doing a bit here and a bit there, dodging about all over the place to relieve the monotony. My idea on being let loose on something big like that was to be a happy wanderer. "Do you know what a grasshopper's like Mick?" asked Bob once after I'd been dabbing about in half a dozen places in an hour. Reg tossed his head in amusement.

"A grasshopper?" I queried, "of course I know what it's like. Why?"

"Oh, nothing," said Bob, "I just wondered that's all."

They continued painting steadily and I shrugged my shoulders and went off to find an interesting bit to paint. "Funny," I thought, "he must have meant something by that."

It was hard, hot and dusty work at harvest time under the Dutch Barns as I soon enough found out, for I was drafted in from time to time to help out. We would be getting on fine down in the field, loading away alongside the brook where the plants grew tall and green and the water swished and gurgled in cool delight and the creeping flowers among the stubble created a veritable heaven, when Reg looked up; "Hullo, here comes father," he said as the pony and trap came rattling across the stubble. "I wonder what he wants, it can't be dinner time already."

"Fred's moving the elevator," Mr Costin said as he reined up, "but I'm afraid I've come to take Mick away. I've got to go into Leighton for a couple of hours so he'll have to help out in the rickyard."

"Lucky chap," said Reg smiling.

I climbed into the trap feeling anything but lucky but not minding really. I knew I would be back in the field soon.

The heat close up under the galvanised roof of those Dutch Barns was fiercely tropical, the sweat ran down my face and neck channelling its way through the dust. The sheaves kept dropping relentlessly from the lip of the elevator and each one had to be pitchforked several yards back to Arthur who placed them with his hands tirelessly, hour after hour, humming lightly to himself, exchanging the odd word but mostly working silently. It was hard work, too hard for Mr Costin, who nevertheless insisted on doing it and several times knocked himself up and had to retire indoors to the sal volatile bottle, send for the doctor and be told off by him for overdoing things. "Stubborn old fool," said Fred, "he'll kill himself, then perhaps he'll be satisfied."

When things were really hotting up and harvest work was reaching a crescendo, with every hour of daylight, save the Sabbath, being used to bring the harvest home, Harry Blake would take his week's holiday from the quarry and come to help out on the farm. A big, rough, rock of a man, he looked every inch a prize fighter. His language tended to be colourful too, even when held in check by the presence of his strict Methodist boss. He was one who never quite seemed to make it to Chapel on Sundays. He'd slouch across the yard looking rather punch drunk, his jacket on and buttoned even in the hottest weather, though I occasionally saw him strip off to his thick jumper underneath, climb the ladder to the rick, spit on his hands, grasp his fork and shout down to Fred, "Let her roll," muttering something else inaudibly. Then Arthur would get a good supply of sheaves throughout the day even though he was several yards back under the roof of the Dutch Barn. Slow and slurred of speech was Harry, but for sheer slogging, brute strength it would be hard to find his equal. He always had a soft spot for the farm and seemed to enjoy his 'holiday', it made a change I suppose from prising great blocks of stone from the quarryface with a crowbar.

Harry liked a bit of repartee with us boys and never minded what we said to him. "Worked up a bit of a b . . . thirst today Mick lad," he'd say as he came down from the rick sweating profusely, his tousled gingery hair full of dust and chaff. And off he'd go in the gathering dusk along the road to the Duke's Head to slake his enormous thirst. "See you tomorrow," he'd call, "perhaps get some real work done then."

Arthur used to go home for a wash and tidy up first before following in Harry's footsteps, though if he wasn't too tired Arthur preferred to walk up to the Cross Keys in the middle of the village.

In the evenings after a hard day's work Fred, if he wasn't on duty, would unwind at the drawing room piano, entering his own private world of music, and as darkness began to close down the house would faintly echo to Chopin or Beethoven. This was Fred's other self, the musician that he probably could and should have been rather than the farmer that fate had decreed he should be. Fred, though the eldest son, was the least enthusiastic farmer of the three. He did what he had to do and did it well, but even I at the time dimly realised that his heart wasn't in farming.

Nobody in the family could quite understand and share his love of music and it was the war and his friendship with my Uncle Alf that provided the breakthrough from the tiny music scene of playing the Chapel organ to important friendships in the professional music world in London which gradually developed, especially when the war was over, and which played an increasingly important role in his life. Though he never abandoned farming, it was his piano and his musical friends that he lived for.

Fred's friendship with my uncle became very close; they often went out over the fields together with Fred's four ten shot gun after a rabbit or a pigeon.

Once, Uncle Alf saw as he thought a wild duck down at the bottom of the orchard by the brook and was thrilled to knock it over with a quick shot before it could take off. Only later Fred told him he'd shot one of Horace Henley's Khaki Campbell's that must have wandered away from his duck pond. Which only went to improve the eating!

For all that it was a musical friendship, it was robust and hilarious too, practical jokes and rough houses being the order of the day. Once at the cottage they all set on Fred when he came in, pinned him to the floor and amid shrieks of laughter rubbed his tummy with marmite.

Tired or not there were still the Special Police patrols to do, but Fred and Ralph usually timed matters so that they arrived at one or the other's house punctually at supper time. Ralph would talk farming with Mr Costin and return some of Bob's old Magnets with the escapades of Billy Bunter that he liked to read. He was a very friendly chap Ralph and he always had time for a chat with me and a joke against himself about the Magnets. He was a boyhood friend of Fred's and though not musical had a lot in common with him.

After work Bob would almost certainly go out on his newly acquired motor bike to Dunstable to meet his girl friend Queenie, daughter of a barber in the town, and where I usually went for my haircut, there being no barber in the village and only an austere one-chair place in Eaton Bray. Queenie's dad had two chairs, and comics to read whilst you were waiting.

Those long sunny days of August at harvest cart when it seldom seemed to rain were for me, contrary to the usual way with children, the times of least play in all the year. So August was a quiet month for adventures and expeditions, people in Lower End could sleep easy in their beds free from our noisy games and practical jokes. Work went on till nearly dusk on most days and after work we were usually too tired for anything more than hanging about talking, circling in the road on our bikes. Eric was in much the same boat as I was, for although he had only a small acreage, he and his dad had to do it all themselves.

Later in the evening there would often be just Mr and Mrs Costin and me in the front kitchen. We listened to the nine o'clock news and heard how the war was going, although to us in our peaceful village it must have seemed like the events on another planet that were being described and not our own neck that was in danger of being wrung. It seemed a patriotic duty to listen to it all, the announcer's grave tones implied as much, so we gave serious attention as the seemingly endless list of calamities was described and commented upon, with many tut-tutt-ings and head shakings from Mrs Costin, with the occasional gleam of minor victory to sustain our hopes. Then off went the set, out came Mr Costin's farming magazine, he fitted on his pair of gold pince-nez and he was gone into the national agricultural scene. Mrs Costin, if she had no darning, settled down to her chief daily relaxation, the Express crossword, which she sometimes let me help her with, otherwise I'd read any book to hand. Soon after starting school in Dunstable I went into the little public library there and discovered Jeffery Farnol and for some months devoured every book of his I could lay my hands on so fascinated was I by his romantic tales of a bygone rural

England, a fascination with a rural past to match the love of a rural present that day by day drew me, all unknowingly, under its subtle spell.

The room was quiet for long periods as darkness massed outside the windows and the air was warm and heavy with the fragrances of summer. Then with an exclamation Mrs Costin jumped up and closed the heavy curtains. "One son a Special, another an Air Raid Warden and here we are breaking blackout regulations!"

So the August days slowly passed, the rickyards filled and the harvest gradually came home, with interruptions for a day's rain and thunderstorms which sometimes flattened acres of corn making the job of the binder very difficult and the loss of some of the crop inevitable. But on the whole my memories are ones of enormously successful harvests, of yards overflowing with ricks, every available inch of space having to be used to store it all, as farmers, keen to provide rationed Britain with every possible ounce of food, ploughed up steep and stony land that hadn't been cultivated since the Great War and made even the thin chalk soils blossom as the rose.

When for some reason there was a short lull in our operations, a field not quite ready for cutting or the shocks needing a day longer to dry out, we sometimes went over to Eaton Bray to help out Mr Costin's brother John, a hearty old widower, sharp as a razor. Hook nosed, brown booted and brown gaitered, bowler hatted, check jacketed and bow legged, he'd burst into the yard waving his stick and in a town crier's voice launch into a story at a distance of twenty yards. With the young men away in the forces he found it difficult to get help at busy times and the family rallied round and did him proud. The other farming brother Will, at Stanbridge, had sons of his own and didn't need our help.

When I went up on the Knolls in early August the whole vale, as far as the eye could distinguish detail, seemed crammed with fields of shocks, regiments of grain marching with Guard-like precision to the distant horizon. Gradually as the weeks passed, I saw the landscape empty until by early September the fields were almost bare, the harvest was mostly in and already the first ploughs were in the fields turning a furrow for the next year's crop, and the farmers were busy working out their yields per acre, assessing their profits and making plans for another season.

On Saturday mornings Mr Costin used to go to the bank in Dunstable and when he came back he'd pay out the week's wages. Fred's, Bob's and Reg's were always put on a high shelf on the big dresser in the front kitchen and they'd come in later and take it down casually, flick it through non committally and pocket it, and of course the details of that were unknown to me, money being one of those things never discussed in the presence of children.

At harvest time I received a generous payment each week and knew for a while the unusual satisfaction of the crackle of crisp paper money in my hand. But at the end of harvest, at the last paying out before I went back to school, together with the money Mr Costin brought out of his pocket a chunky silver pocket watch. "Here you are Mick," he said, "you've not been a bad boy as boys go, so it's about time you had a pocket watch like all farmers have."

He handed the watch over to me who'd never dreamed of owning such a thing. Only people of substance and standing had one of those, objects of solid worth as they were. Was I to have one too? It was something way beyond all my expectations. I could scarcely say anything, only a mumbled word of thanks. He was a hard man in many respects, Mr Costin, hard but scrupulously fair and harder on himself than on others. He'd been brought up in a hard school. But now and again the horny shell opened to reveal a man of a generosity and warmth unsuspected by many.

With the watch was a heavy silver chain with a bar to fit into the buttonhole of jacket or waistcoat. All suits were three piece then and all us boys wore waistcoats and old ones were worn by men and boys for working. Mrs Costin stood by as I handled my watch wonderingly and slipped it into my waistcoat pocket to see the effect. That watch served me well for many a year and in my eyes its value never lessened, and far from the farm its sight and touch could transport me back in an instant to fond memories of its donor and the days of its best use. It wasn't until many years later that I put it by and bought one of those new fangled wrist watches that gradually ousted pocket watches in popularity.

Chapter X

Country Pastimes

There was nothing Mr Costin liked better than a game of dominoes in the evening and when it was raining outside or too dark to play Eric and I often gave him a few games. We played Fives and Threes and Running Out, and tense and exciting sessions they became as the matchsticks in the scoring board crept nearer to the end. Pretty tame stuff it was no doubt, compared to the nightly feast of violence and horror that children are favoured with today on television, but then our expectations were much lower and we came away well satisfied.

I learned to pick out the double blank when the dominoes were shuffled around, pips down, for us to take our hand. When counting out at the end of a game this often proved to be to my advantage for the one with the fewest pips was the winner and Mr Costin could never understand how I managed to have it in my hand so often.

"Well I never," he'd say, "you've got it again. How the devil . . . ?" and he'd pick it up and scrutinise the back of it closely. "I can't see anything different about it," he'd say. Next hand I'd pick it out again.

There was a full sized dartboard in the front kitchen, hanging in front of the bookcase and we'd often use it when we were forced to stay in. The books not covered by the board bore testimony to our inadequacies in this game, also to our perseverence, but fortunately they were mostly old textbooks with the Cedars label inside the cover and school stories long since closed for good. Like most practical and very busy people they weren't great readers of books at the farm. Life was too active and full, its satisfactions leaving little room, desire or need of literary pleasures. No mobile library came round in those days and the nearest library was in Dunstable, but the three miles might as well have been three hundred for all the difference it would have made.

We played cards quite often. Everyone had Happy Families and we also played Beat Your Neighbour and Knockout Whist and half a dozen others that

121

I have forgotten, at the farm or at Aud and Doug's or in Eric's house, wherever we felt like going. Often the adults joined in and then we had an uproarious session. On a slightly higher level were the village whist drives which continued with scarcely diminished ferocity all through the war and which Fred loved to attend. He was a great favourite at these functions in all the villages round, as I saw for myself on the few occasions when he took me with him. He was the epitome of the gay bachelor and was the centre of attraction for the many spinsters and wives who had left their husbands at home. But Fred would have fun and tease and joke all evening then leave alone and come straight home to mum, leaving no doubt many a yearning heart behind.

So we had our round of games and distractions for the long dark winter evenings when, because of the blackout which was very strictly enforced, there were no street lamps for us to congregate around. At that time there were no organisations in the village for children to belong to, no Guides or Scouts or Youth Club, we were strictly on our own but found no fault with that. We read of course when we were alone. I don't know whether we read on average more than children of today. I suspect we did, with a peak in midwinter because apart from those darkest of days we spent most of our waking hours outdoors. Wet weather was no great deterrent for there were always barns we could play in, and of all the barns available to us Manor Farm had the biggest and the best with more variety of lofts and ladders, dark corners, piles of straw, bins, sacks and things to hide behind or under than anywhere else. We disappeared into the barns and for hours at a time played, hid, fought, climbed, tunnelled, always on the move without once appearing in the yard. This was very useful, for Mr Costin wasn't all that keen on having hordes of children rampaging in and out of his barns, but providing we slipped in quietly when nobody was about, kept inside and didn't raise the roof with our noise, we could play undisturbed for as long as we liked.

After threshing, part of the loft over the cowshed was used to store loose chaff. It was in a great block about six feet thick, extended across the width of the barn and stretched back five of six yards. It was dim and cobwebby up there, a glimmer of light came in through a dust shrouded piece of opaque glass in the roof and you had to duck under the two feet wide roof ties when walking about. I loved it in that huge loft which ran the whole length of the barn, a considerable distance.

One day when I was on my own there looking for something interesting to do, I decided to tunnel into this seam of chaff. It had lain long enough to be quite compressed and made an ideal medium for tunnelling, rather loose perhaps and there were many tricklings from the roof, mostly down my neck where it itched like the devil as I squirmed my way forward on my belly like a giant mole. But my tunnel with the floorboards as base, progressed rapidly and I had visions of creating a veritable warren for future games. We could chase each other through the tunnels I thought. Naturally I was in a dreadful state when I had to abandon work for dinner, chaff is not the best material to have embedded in hair and clothes, but I wasn't worried as I walked over to the house leaving a golden trail behind me.

After several more sessions of burrowing on my own, sustained by the novelty of the idea and with the unveiling to admiring friends in mind, I was going great guns when I had a major chaff fall as I was about my body length in the tunnel. The whole thing collapsed around me and I was totally immersed, my eyes, mouth, nose, completely enveloped. I pulled myself out gasping and spluttering and spent some time trying to get the stuff off me and even then Mrs Costin asked me what I had been doing to get in such a mess and it was rare for her to say anything. "Digging in what? In chaff. Bless the boy, whatever did you hope to find in chaff?" After that I gave up the idea of underground games in the loft, abandoned chaff as a tunelling medium and never really took to the prospect of a mining career.

Another unique feature of our village was the chalkpit. This was once a small local quarry, biting or nibbling into the chalk escarpment of the Chilterns of which our Knolls was part. But with the rise of cement and concrete as building materials the need for chalk escalated dramatically and a big national cement company moved in on our chalk and the pit had grown wider and deeper, its sides of dizzy height as great bites were taken into the hillside, so that by those early war years there was a monumental hole half a mile or so across and profound enough to hide a church, spire and all. All day long on terraces that ringed the sides the excavators and mechanical diggers tore away huge mouthfulls of chalk, attempting to satisfy an insatiable wartime appetite. By the side of that huge enterprise the tiny original quarry firm went on quietly digging out its stone with crowbars and sending it away by the occasional lorry load as it had done for generations. The quarry was by far the biggest single employer in the district for several miles around as every night the chalky, dust laden cycles fanning out homewards in all directions testified.

At weekends the quarry was ours whenever we wanted it. It was so vast a place that nobody bothered about a few children wandering around or could have prevented it had they wished. A network of narrow railway tracks patterned the quarry floor and climbed some of the terraces. Lines of little trucks to take away the chalk were hauled around by tiny, motor driven locomotives. These connected with the main railway sidings where a long line of wagons was loaded each day and sent off to the Midlands. We roamed all over this blinding white desert finding fascinating things to do everywhere. It was a glorious place for echoes and we terrified the spirits of the place as we outyodelled the Swiss and bounced our screams and roars off towering snow white cliffs.

Truck riding was our favourite occupation. When we found one in a good position at the top of a long incline we piled aboard, released the brake and went hurtling down headlong, bumping and clanking on the rough, uneven track which at every moment threatened to fling us all off, yelling at the top of our voices to keep terror at bay. Sometimes we found a whole line of trucks, then we had fun for an hour at a time. Luckily for us the locomotives were locked away in boyproof engine sheds. I think we would have fancied ourselves as breakneck drivers hurtling round the rails and satisfying that ambition which is said to lurk in all small boys.

We devoted part of our time in the quarry to gold prospecting. Just as did the old timers in California in '49, we stumbled on nuggets as big as our fist just lying on the surface near where the diggers had been ripping the chalk walls. Just as eagerly as them we pounced rapaciously on our finds, our eyes ablaze with gold fever. One of the outstanding differences with California was that instead of being incited to robbery and murder we would break our nuggets into several pieces, hitting one against the other, the split portions shining silvery-gold in their close lined structure, then share them generously around.

It may only have been fool's gold but we treasured it and searched avidly for it, but like happiness we usually found it when we weren't looking for it. We could never understand how such stuff could get there in the midst of all those millions of tons of chalk which we vaguely knew had been formed under the sea. Had someone been dropping pieces in? Such conundrums and considerations only added to the mystical value of our finds which we hoarded jealously at home along with our shrapnel and bomb splinters, our incendiary bomb fins and our spent bullet cases.

We searched in a desultory way for fossils too. It would have been nice to have unearthed a dinosaur or two. I could picture myself coming into the farmyard carrying a mighty claw or monstrous head and watching Fred's face as I casually laid it down. But though we always cast a hopeful eye on the walls of the chalk canyons for even a fish's fin or a few shells, we sadly concluded that they couldn't have liked our chalky sea for we never found any. It did tend to get a bit tedious poring over chunks of chalk, there were so many. It was rather like the enthusiasm I once felt for searching in coal for fossils. I used to be out in the coal house for hours at a time with a hammer smashing up the large pieces the coalman delivered and eagerly surveying each piece held in blackened hands, hoping, always hoping for a bone or a wing or even a leaf. It was an activity not entirely disapproved of provided I didn't grind the coal to dust, because it saved someone the job of having to break it up. But the exercise never brought me any profit and sadly I eventually gave it up though continuing to run my eye over the pile as I passed by and even now I still feel the pull to start turning over the coal in my own bunker to see if I can't find just one clear cut, undeniable fossil.

One Saturday afternoon we were wandering across the hills near the edge of the quarry, on the far side away from the village, and were debating whether to go down into the pit, when we came across a group of soldiers around a large anti-tank gun. "Hey, look at that!" cried Mac who happened to see them first. We stopped and stared, amazed at the sight. A gun on our hills!

Suddenly with a great roar the gun fired. "Crikey," cried Doug, "what are they up to?" There'd been no firing before or we would have heard.

The gun was pointing down into the quarry. There was a flurry of activity among the soldiers and it fired again with a deafening crack that rebounded over the chalk hills. We stood rooted to the spot in fascination. Surely the Germans hadn't landed and occupied the quarry! We hadn't seen or heard them, there had been no little parachutes swinging in the sky. Again and again the gun fired. We saw the spent shell cases come bouncing onto the ground. No answering fire came. The Jerries were lying doggo perhaps, but we were flat on our bellies by then in the rough grass just in case and watched another three or four shots go crashing into the quarry. As the smoke cleared the soldiers relaxed, stood back from the gun and started talking among themselves.

"They're practising," said Eric.

"Yeah, just practising," we all said jumping up.

Thus reassured we sidled nearer and came up to the edge of the quarry.

"Wow, what do you make of that?" breathed Mac as a hundred feet below us one of our trucks trundled along over the quarry floor drawn by a wire. It was supporting a large, square, black painted target, unblemished.

The soldiers snapped back into action again and fired off several shells as the target rolled slowly along. Great puffs of chalk spurted up from the ground, miles away from the simulated tank. If there were Jerries there they'd be laughing. We knew we could do better than that.

"Pity we can't have a shot" grumbled Doug.

"Ask 'em" said Mac brightly.

"You ask 'em," retorted Doug.

We edged closer wondering if we dared ask for a go on their gun. Firing was still going on but our ears were getting used to the explosions and we kept our eyes on the target which was still untouched as it trundled tantalisingly along.

The sergeant looked around menacingly as we came within a few yards of the gun. "Clear orf!" he spat out as another spent case came hopping out of the breech.

"Can we 'ave one of the empty cases please?" asked Mac bravely, trying for the lesser prize first.

"I said clear orf," hissed the sergeant drawing himself to his full height. "Now git! We don't want no kids round 'ere."

We took the hint and wandered disconsolately away, bemoaning the fact that it was ignorant regulars and not our own Home Guard who were doing the firing. "Our lot would have given us a go I bet," declared Eric.

"Yeah, rotten lot," snarled Doug.

"Rotten shots too!" I hurled back in a quiet shout.

"Couldn't knock the skin off a rice puddin'," yelled Doug as another round of firing began, as inaccurate as the others.

That was the one and only time we knew the quarry to be used for firing but ever afterwards we had a good look round when we were down on the quarry floor, to make sure before we started riding the trucks that we didn't land up dodging anti-tank shells. You could never tell whether they might have improved their aim.

A mile or so farther along the chalk escarpment was the old abandoned quarry workings at Sewell. We sometimes walked along there, skirting our own living quarry on the way, and clambered over the silent, dead ruins and roamed around the deserted quarry floor where nature was gradually moving back in with plants and small bushes somehow getting a foothold in the solid chalk. Mosses, grass and flowers were spreading and beginning to tone down the stark and sterile white of naked chalk to softer shades, forerunners of the coming coat of turf. You no longer had to shade your eyes in bright sunlight as you did in our quarry.

It was mostly in Spring that we walked Sewellwards for it was an unparalleled place for obtaining pussy willow and we used to come back with great bundles of branches of those soft woolly buttons that everybody seemed to love to stick in vases. We stopped usually at a clear cold spring that gushed copiously from under the chalk by the broad grassy lane, and drank long draughts of that champagne of waters from our cupped and brimming hands.

That landscape of my wartime childhood was not very well endowed with woodland. Cultivation had long since destroyed the primaeval forests that once covered those fertile lowlands. Now throughout the broad vale there were only occasional groves, copses and spinneys, such as Hoole's spinney opposite their shop. On the Knolls we had our beech groves, Nature's cathedrals, with their majestic columns rising smooth and grey to a green vaulted roof, their clear untrammelled naves devoid of undergrowth, in perpetual semi-gloom in summer with an atmosphere almost as solemn and ecclesiastical as some austere twelfth century cathedral. But once again, these magnificent beeches were all man planted, a wonderful legacy to us by men of vision of bygone generations.

But again we were luckier than most villages for we had the Litany. This Litany was our nearest to true woodland, a dense, damp, haphazard mixture of hawthorn, oak and ash. Not only that but for added good fortune there was Black Grove Wood bordering the Litany on the Tilsworth side. This was a mixture of tall mature trees growing amongst coppiced hazel and our expeditions used to carry us through both stretches of woodland.

It was my first experience of wild forest, its bluebell glades, its standing pools beneath the trees, its fallen logs, its face lashing jungle of undergrowth, its deep mysterious places, its sinister inexplicable sounds. It was a lonely, deserted, totally isolated place the Litany, near no road that we knew of, no farm, no house nearby. I don't recall that in all our many expeditions there we ever met a single soul. Something of this isolation, this strangeness, this lack of human contact, was in the atmosphere of the place. It was as though, we said, something terrible had once happened in these woods and the memory of it still haunted the place. But what it was, if indeed it was anything beyond our volatile imaginations, we never did discover, but I don't think anything would have induced us to stay there after dark. All of which, of course, only added to the daytime lure, the fascination of those wild woods.

So the Litany frequently drew a gang of us out of the village, along the road past the Duke's Head and past the quarry entrance with its railway sidings where Charlie Brooks often gave us a wave from the cab of his shunting engine, down along the lane between hedges whitened with chalk dust, over the railway line where we lay on the track, ears to the rail, to see if we could feel the vibrations of the Flier that we could see thundering towards us straight as a die down the long incline from Dunstable. Over a stream we went to the great low lying tract of waste country where our Litany flourished amid its streams and pools.

We rambled over the wood climbing anything climbable, swinging, leaping, searching for the perfect stick, poking for nests, investigating holes in trees, balancing along a huge moss grown log and, according to the season, gathering armfulls of bluebells or searching for hazel nuts. We always argued about whether there were any deer in the wood, we never saw any but admitted that our progress through the trees was rather like that of a herd of elephants. The odd deer was seen in the fields from time to time, escapees so it was reckoned from some big estates several miles away. To be on the safe side though we cut and sharpened some spears just in case we came upon a wild boar. "They can rip your guts open with their tusks," Eric assured us smilingly. The thought of our entrails spilling out on the ground so far from home was enough to make us cautious for a few minutes until we forgot all about it.

Tracking was our big adventure as on the Knolls, and in the green silence of the deepest thickets we would stand or crouch still as statues as our pursuers crashed around, their ears alert for the slightest telltale snapping of a twig. Was it in those tense moments with every sense doubly receptive, my mind a sentient sponge, that the spirit of woodlands got itself well and truly planted in me, as awareness of stem, branch and leaf, dappled shadows and all the multiplicity of woodland sound and scent were caught and stored unthinkingly?

An hour or so of this, during which we traversed the entire area of forest, for it wasn't very large, and we would return content, stopping perhaps at the stream to see if we could capture sticklebacks or tadpoles for the jars we brought for the purpose. Upon our arrival home in Spring nearly every windowsill in Lower End had its bunch of bluebells and our hunger for woodlands had been appeased for a few more weeks.

Ferreting was one of our minor distractions. In those days of a meagre meat ration, rabbits played an important part in village economy and the rabbit was plentiful, pestilentially plentiful in those pre-myxamatosis times. Along with the twelve bore and the snare the ferret played an important part in the rabbit stew strategy and was widely kept and frequently and skilfully used. We tried our hand at setting snares too but like most country crafts it was more difficult than it appeared. It needed an intimate knowledge of the ways of rabbits and a slowly acquired experience of where and how to set the snare before you could hope to catch anything.

We went around carefully trying to identify the run of a rabbit through the long grass, looking for where it was flattened at the sides as in a tunnel. When we thought we had found a run we set the snare, placing the hoop of wire, so we imagined, to let the rabbit's head go through but not the rest of its body. But our bungling attempts never had a hope of success though for a long time we went blithely on expecting bunny to commit suicide. There was many a man in the village however, who knew all about the ways of rabbits and how to set snares and they saw to it that their families didn't go short of meat.

Bob had a ferret which lived in a hutch near to my Dutch rabbit, too near for the latter's comfort I daresay. One Saturday morning Bob decided to go ferreting and Eric and I went to assist him. We took a dozen or so nets and a spade in case the ferret had to be dug out, there'd been trouble with the line getting caught around tree roots before.

We fixed on a warren on the far side of the orchard near the hedge.

"The first job is to net as many holes as we can find," said Bob. We took some nets and started to cover the obvious holes, pushing the little pegs well into the soil.

"Trouble is," said Bob standing up and looking round at our efforts, "we're right by the hedge and I'll bet there's holes in there where we can't see 'em."

There was a thick bramble patch spilling out from the hedge and plenty of nettles where a couple of strands of barbed wire ran to keep the cattle from breaking out. We poked around but couldn't find any more holes. Bob reached into the sack carefully and brought out the ferret, a dirty white, pink eyed, sinuous and ferocious killer, rippling over the ground as if made of rubber. He attached a line to the little collar around its neck. "Right, here we go," he said. "Now be ready, try and grab any rabbits that come up into the net. Stand back behind the holes so they don't see you."

The ferret was slipped under one of the nets and we waited, thick sticks in hand as Bob paid out the knotted line. Nothing happened for a few minutes. We stood with bated breath awaiting the rush of rabbits then the ferret popped his pink nose enquiringly out of the hole, blinking in the sunlight, and had to be re-directed down. "That's a fine start, doesn't seem very eager does he?" said Bob. "He ought to be though, seeing as he hasn't been fed for a couple of days."

All was quiet again for another couple of minutes, then suddenly there was a flurry of grey fur and two rabbits exploded into the nets, two more bolted along the hedge from a hole we had missed. Bob rushed in and grabbed one of the rabbits, disentangled it from the netting, held it up by its back legs and broke its neck with a jerk, quickly and cleanly; it twitched a little as it died. Eric was hitting the other one with his stick as it lay bundled up in the net. Bob grabbed that one too and despatched it speedily as he had the first one, then laid them out side by side on the grass.

"That's it for this morning," said Bob, "we'll get no more here, they've all gone. Time's getting on anyway." He had a cricket match to prepare for in the afternoon. So we packed up considering it a moderately successful hunt, one for our pot and one for Bob's girlfriend's family.

It took some time to pull the ferret back up the hole it went down, but it came in the end, blinking and sniffing, suspecting it had missed all the action and eager to get its teeth into rabbit flesh.

I've often watched Mrs Costin skin and clean out a rabbit, for we had rabbit to eat quite often, it was a great favourite with all the family. She would slit it open with a sharp knife, disembowel it expertly and with a few deft tugs in the right places strip the fur right off cleanly, chop the head off and there was lean, pink fleshed rabbit all ready for the pot after a good wash under the tap. I used to find the smell disgusting and knew I could never do that job, yet she did it with no hint of displeasure but with a no nonsense, clinical detachment as if she were cleaning out a dirty saucepan. "I've done this job ever since I got married," she told me when I expressed my dislike and wondered if she shared it, "I never even think about it."

Besides rabbits our diet was often supplemented by hares and partridges and less frequently by pheasants and pigeons. Not surprisingly for a place so far from the sea and from fish shops, fresh fish was a rarity in our diet, though sometimes when Mr and Mrs Costin went up to Dunstable to do some shopping after tea on Saturday, they brought back some newspaper wrapped fish and chips which we would have for supper. In those days before the great explosion which sent chips into almost every household and into every meal in the land, they were reserved exclusively for fish and were never home made.

A time or two I went with Bob fishing in the Grand Union Canal near Ivinghoe. We cycled the six miles or so on a Saturday with our rods strapped to our cross bars and in our rucksack a tin of gentles dug up in the rickyard just before starting out. That corner of the rickyard yielded a rich harvest of worms and maggots for it was where diseased chickens, calves and piglets were buried. We had a pleasant time fishing, the tranquil scene being disturbed now and again by the passage of a string of brightly decorated canal boats which set our floats a-dancing and our minds wondering about the romantic gipsy-like figures who waved to us as they chugged by. We failed to contribute any fish for the table, not that that was our chief objective. Our best efforts were a few small gudgeon about four inches long. Bob settled to waiting patiently in the sunshine but I remember boredom and restlessness setting in after about half an hour in spite of the pleasant surroundings. I longed to be up and doing, always thinking that a few yards further on would be the best place to set my float bobbing on the murky water. Perhaps that is why I have never since cast a hook in anger. Although as an excuse for a peaceful nap on a warm summer's day I can see that angling might now have its attractions.

Chickens which abounded on the farm were hardly ever eaten. Farm poultry was of two main sorts. On the one hand there were egg laying birds, too valuable to kill off for dinner, their eggs indeed being almost golden at that time; those that died, being mainly diseased were never eaten. And on the other hand there were cockerels being fattened up for the Christmas trade, once again too valuable to eat. Bred to be at their best in December, there were no New Year survivors. At a time when the term battery hen would have been incomprehensible, or perhaps taken to mean some kind of mechanical chicken, when fridges were almost non-existent and deep freezers not yet invented, fowls and cockerels for the table were still very much an expensive, Christmas only treat for the majority of people. There was usually such a plentiful supply of wild creatures to be had for the cost of a cartridge that we were never driven to kill chickens for the table.

It was on my fourteenth birthday that we were cutting spring oats down at Far Corner alongside the brook. The rest of us were shocking as usual. Reg had brought his gun hoping for a rabbit when the piece was finished. Halfway through the morning when Fred stopped for a few minutes to refuel the tractor, Reg came over to me with his gun. "Like to come over here a minute Mick?" he said, and I followed him wondering what was up as he walked towards the brook at a spot where several willows grew tall along the bank. "How would you like a shot with the twelve bore?" Reg said.

I could hardly believe my luck, I'd never shot with anything bigger than an air gun before. "Call it a birthday present," he said smiling.

"Now look," went on Reg, breaking the gun and slipping a couple of cartridges in, "up in that willow, can you see, near the top there's a pigeon's nest. Got it?" I saw it after a moment, among the shading leaves.

"Can you just see the head of the pigeon poking out the top?" he asked. I could see a small shape which I took to be the pigeon. "Well, here you are," he said giving me the gun, "see if you can bring it down." A quick glance around as I took the weapon showed me that everyone was standing watching at a discreet distance. "Just one barrel," whispered Reg, "then the other if necessary."

I raised the gun, sighting along the glinting barrel, feeling the weight of it and pushing it well into my shoulder. After a seeming eternity of trying to stop it waving about I pulled the trigger. There was a terrific crash, a kick in my shoulder and a great cry from Reg. "Well done, you hit it boy!" and I saw the heavy body of the pigeon tumble to the ground and the nest disintegrate and rain down around it. I gave the gun back somewhat deafened and stunned and secretly amazed that I should have hit the target. But chiefly I was thrilled that Reg's confidence in me had been justified in front of everyone else in the field and grateful to him for my most unusual birthday present ever. I went back to shocking at least two inches taller than I was five minutes before.

I remember clearly the first time I ever wrung a chicken's neck. I should have thought that I was much too squeamish for such a task but one day Fred caught hold of a hen that had been standing about not feeding, not active and chirpy but huddled up, hardly moving even when you walked right by it. "I'd better put you out of your misery old girl," he said as I stood by watching him. "Here Mick, would you like to do it?"

My instinctive reaction was to turn away, but unwilling to be thought a soft townie, unable to face realities, I took the hen. As I held its legs it just hung there inertly. Fred told me what to do. I gave its neck a sharp, hard jerk and the bird went limp in my hands. Fred threw it on the steaming dunghill and I stood puzzled a moment at the ease with which my hands had changed life into death. But I had no part in the large scale killing of the cockerels at Christmas time. There were scores of them and the men used to sit on upturned buckets and boxes in the barn plucking them. The feathers were saved and used I daresay to stuff mattresses and cushions. It was the end of a road that had begun the previous Spring with dozens of tiny, golden, one day old balls of fluff cowering together in the incubator's warmth, cheeping plaintively and pecking eagerly at the special Chick Mash that was put down for them.

Laying hens were particularly valuable of course at a time when eggs to rationed city folk were like gold dust and practically all cooking was done with dried egg powder. Mrs Costin always put several scores of eggs into waterglass to preserve them for winter use so that when the hens went off laying we never went short. Following tradition all the profits from the sale of eggs went to Mrs Costin and was no doubt a welcome boost to her housekeeping.

There were usually a few eggs in a paper bag slipped to visiting relations or special friends from town, just a nod and a wink and a grateful gleam in the eye from the recipient, for it didn't do to talk about such things. Butter was a rarer gift and was even more rarely discussed. We made enough for the house, in fact making it was one of my regular jobs on Saturday morning. Mrs Costin skimmed the cream off the milk in the dairy each day and by Saturday there were several pints of cream which were tipped into the glass churn. It was always cool in that stone flagged dairy, down a few steps from the general level, no milk ever went off even in the hottest weather.

I knew what lay in wait for me on Saturday mornings even if I was mending my bike or cleaning the rabbit's hutch out, and eventually I'd wander into the back kitchen and there it would be on the table waiting.

All ready for it then Mick?" she'd say, being as cheerful about it as she could, for she knew what a hard slog it often was before the butter came. Before I took the job on she'd always done it and was very grateful that I'd relieved her of that particular chore.

"Let's hope it comes quickly this week eh?" she said.

"Yes, I hope so," I said without much optimism.

So I grasped the handle, held the top securely with the other hand – it was just like a big hand whisk but with wooden beaters at the bottom – and started turning. It went so easily, the cream swishing around and spurting up the sides of the churn. I started off as if my arm were iron, tireless, piston-like as I turned at a steady, deliberate rate, completely in control.

Mrs Costin was busy in the kitchen cutting up steak and kidney and peeling vegetables, and now and again she'd come over and peer into the churn as if willing the butter to come. After a few minutes of god-like rhythmical turning, a weariness began its insidious invasion of my arm muscles. I'd try to ignore it, "Not yet," I'd say to myself, "it's too early, not yet please." The steady, machine-like power began to falter, the ache spread, stabbing at my shoulder and ravaging my biceps. I stopped, or rather was brought to a halt and looked searchingly into the churn but it was only early stages yet. I knew what agony 'ay ahead.

I turned the churn around to use my left hand and the procedure was repeated, less effectively for my left arm weakened faster than the right and didn't turn so smoothly. When somebody else came into the room I did my best to appear to be turning as nonchalantly as if I'd just started, but eventually I was brought to a stop again.

"Let's have a look," said Mrs Costin, knowing full well the situation. "Mm, no sign yet. I know, I'll put a spot of colouring in, it's looking rather pale."

Whilst all this went on I had a welcome break. Then the right hand took over again and we started off hopefully once more. "If only," I said to myself behind gritted teeth, "if only I could do it all in one go without having to stop. Then I'd be really strong, strong as a man." If only! I was furious with myself as the ache in my muscles struck more quickly next time, and my turning became less smooth, more desperate as I drove myself on to prove I wasn't a weakling.

I stared long and hard into the churn as I changed hands yet again. "I don't think it will be long now," said Mrs Costin encouragingly. Some weeks the butter came quickly, and what a delight that was, more often it came slowly, reluctantly, protestingly, but come it always did in the end, depending on the temperature I think, the warmer the cream the quicker it became butter.

I'd go on, changing arms at shorter intervals, despairing of ever finishing the job, until at last, miraculously, when I seemed about to collapse in an exhausted heap, there was a sudden change in the note of the paddles inside. "Ah!" exlaimed Mrs Costin at once, "you're nearly there." Indeed the cream was separating itself off into tiny particles of soft butter, the whey sloshing about like water. A few more turns, easy all of a sudden, and the tiny particles merged into large lumps, the paddles jammed and the job was finished, the butter had come.

"Well done. Good boy," said Mrs Costin. "You can have a good rest now. Oh, and here's sixpence for doing it so well."

"Rest? Me?" I said to myself, pocketing the money, "I'm all right, I don't need a rest."

Mrs Costin took the butter out and with a pair of wooden butter pats shaped it into a block and patterned it nicely and then it was stored carefully away in the fridgeless dairy for use during the week to help out the pathetic ration from the grocer.

Much more to my liking was partridge shooting. After harvest was the best time, when the coveys were fully grown and were working the stubble for the corn left lying around. It needed real skill, the hunter's ability to move silently, to use any cover to hand in order to get within shooting distance of a covey of partridges. One heavy step, sneeze or click of trigger and with a flurry of whip-like explosions they would rocket into the sky and be gone.

Many a time I've gone with Bob across the evening stubble fields in pursuit of partridges, many a time we've returned empty handed, having put up a covey or two, sometimes the same one twice for they often landed again not far away after taking fright. But sometimes Bob's knapsack was stuffed full of birds when we returned as twilight was fading, for when with luck or skill we managed to get quite close to a covey, using the line of a brook or squirming flat on our bellies over the open stubble in poor light, then put them up deliberately, both barrels could bring down as many as ten or a dozen at once so close together do they fly.

Killing was an integral part of life in the village and on the farm. It had its rightful, controlled place and no one questioned it. There was no sickly sentimental attitude towards either domestic or wild animals. Rabbits were shot or trapped to eat. A farmer shot a fox if he caught it stealing his chickens, though more often than not the fox got away with it. We never had any controversy over fox hunting in the village and the only complaints I ever heard were ones of damage done to hedges and crops, for which compensation was paid.

The genuine countryman is neither a romantic nor is he cruel. He is a realist, he has a farm to run or a family to feed and he knows his business. It is the city dweller with little knowledge or experience of country life and armed only with his arrogant sensibilities, who would often smother everything in his tenderer-than-thou sentimentality, an attitude which is, perhaps inevitably, sweeping this modern world.

In those days when the word conservation still slumbered in the dictionary, most of us boys had our birds' egg collection. I inherited Bob's collection in a handsome case and I added to it modestly, though someone gave me an emu's egg which I had to keep in a shoe box. We'd be well satisfied with one of each kind, never took more than one from a nest, and learned to be efficient at blowing them. Pigeon's eggs we were encouraged to be ruthless with. As eaters of vast amounts of corn, pigeons were depicted as enemies hand in glove with the Germans and farmers were urged to shoot as many as possible.

Those were a few of our principal occupations when we weren't at school or helping with the work, and we usually seemed to have plenty of spare time. They were country and farm activities which I took to naturally and pleasurably and which without me giving it a thought were bringing about a permanent change in my outlook whereby city life would from then on be a poor second best.

Chapter XI

Love is in the Air

For us children life in the village soon became one we had to leave behind each school day and resume each evening. Secondary education called us away inexorably and we would leave our essential being and put on, like changing into Sunday clothes, another existence, no less real perhaps but ill fitting and uncomfortable, to be taken off with relief as we dismounted from the school bus home and slipped happily back into the well worn, loved attire of our real life. Not only did we have to leave the village but we left each other and went our separate, individual ways. When we stepped off the bus going to school we were reduced, weakened and each became a mere figure in a large anonymous crowd, and it was only when we were reunited that our strength and individuality returned.

We all went off in the same bus together, some to Luton, the rest, myself included, to Dunstable. On the bus we had to contend with a group of half a dozen or so Dunstable Grammar School boys from Eaton Bray and Edlesborough. As they were fee paying, these butchers', farmers' and millers' sons considered themselves a cut above us and we professed scorn and derision for them, jumped up peasants. On the infrequent occasions when we had the top deck to ourselves the bus became a travelling battleground, not with fists but paper pellets shot from an elastic band stretched between thumb and forefinger. The Grammar Gang, getting on the bus first, had choice of position and usually took the front two rows of seats. We were at the back and the air between hummed with our missiles, small but if one hit you in the face you would know all about it. Ducking behind seats, peering from satchels held as shields, we would suddenly let fly and this in turn provoked a volley in reprisal. The ammunition was inexhaustible as it was used over and over again. Our school caps with peaks pulled well down were a good protection but it was still a wonder that no one had his eye knocked out.

When the conductor, hearing triumphant whoops or yells of agony from upstairs came with heavy tread to investigate, we would all be sitting demurely in our places, whistling and looking out of the window, missiles and firing apparatus clutched in our palms. Devoid of evidence, he growled a deeply suspicious, "Look 'ere you lot, be'ave yerselves or I'll chuck you off," and retreated downstairs, whereupon battle would immediately recommence.

It was a friendly, cheerful and inevitable war which broke out nowhere else save on the bus. There was no bitterness or animosity on either side, nobody ever won and each side was willing to admire a good performance from the other. Eventually, after we had fought more or less to a standstill and began to grow out of childish things, we gradually lapsed into a cessation of hostilities and became, well, never quite good friends, but friendly and with well founded mutual respect.

My school was struggling to survive, sharing one building with the local occupants. Originally a boys' school it took girls for the first time the year I joined. Running a school in those wartime evacuee conditions must have been a nightmare of organisation but we were scarcely aware of such things, our concerns were only with ourselves.

Eric and Mac and I were in the same building but they were pupils of the local school and I seldom saw them, everything was separate including playgrounds and meals. I remember seeing Eric one day come out of a classroom with a long line of his classmates and walk in silent file along the corridor. We gave each other a sheepish grin, it didn't seem like the Eric I knew, the village Eric, thumping a cricket ball or chasing rats. It was a strange feeling meeting like that in a different existence.

Rita was the only one from the village with me; we joined at the same time from the Memorial Hall and were in the same class. Rita was billeted opposite the Chapel in old Amos King's thatched cottage. After starting school in Dunstable, when we were thrown together much more, it was as if I saw Rita for the first time. She was short and dark haired with a cheeky Cockney grin, lively and with a quick mind and a way of laughing at once infectious and disturbing. In no time at all I was enslaved. One day I was quite normal, girl hating, girl avoiding, girl ridiculing, the next the secret switch was thrown and Rita was desirable, miraculous and awe inspiring. Never since has raven hair curled so bewitchingly over a clear rose-like complexion, never have deep brown eyes twinkled so alluringly or such ruby lips curved so finely over perfect teeth. When in her company I thought of nothing but the desire to hold her hand, and oh, those lips – I hardly dared look at them.

None of my friends seemed to have this strange affliction, they continued to treat girls as nuisances in a perfectly normal, straightforward way as I did myself of course, except in the case of Rita. I didn't try to analyse the malady, just accepted it as inevitable, like spots. This after all was what grown ups were like all the time wasn't it? I told myself, so it couldn't be anything dangerous to health. And I was more or less all right when I wasn't with Rita. She haunted my thoughts but didn't get in the way of tree climbing or lasso making or anything important like that. It was only when I was with her, especially alone with her, that I felt that disturbing churning over sensation, that loss of thought and action, that semi-mesmerised feeling that was new and peculiar, as if I had been taken over by some alien being within me.

Then from being chronic the malaise took a turn for the worse and became critical. I began to plot how I might be with her more often. Of course I was terrified of being rejected and perhaps ridiculed, so I professed public indifference and even contempt for the idea of liking a girl and I'd have been deeply ashamed to admit to my friends that I had this fever for Rita.

In school at least I saw her all day, but although we were in mixed classes, boys had to sit with boys and girls with girls, each on their own side of the room. I could at least sit and look at her surreptitiously and try to be clever and give right answers just to prove to her that I was no fool. Rita was very good at her lessons, her quick bright intelligence was strongly in evidence and I strove in plodding fashion to match her performance, giving more attention than would come naturally to the strange stuff that was served up for us to learn, treating French and theorems as a way of forcing her to recognise my brilliance. At the end of the first year after all our exams she was declared top of the class and by the greatest of flukes I was pronounced second. It was to me as if it were a sign written in the stars that we were meant for each other.

After Sunday School one day Aud, for reasons I could not fathom, only marvel at, asked Rita if she would walk down the road with the group of us on our way home. She came, the first time ever, and I was delirious, though I did my best to disguise it with some oafish clowning with the other boys.

When we came to the farm I walked on past with the others instead of going in, muttering something about having to check on the hens behind old Tommy Holland's cottage. We reached Aud and Doug's cottage and split up, Eric and Betty and Joan went on down to their houses, Jimmy Knight went in, so did Aud and Doug.

I stood irresolute and glanced for justification into the orchard where the hens were scratching peacefully needing no assistance from me. Rita said lightly, "Oh well, I'll go home now I suppose."

She turned in her new bright orange coat and set off back. There was an agonising second's indecision then I shambled round, kicked a stone and walked back nearly at her side. She chatted away with supreme lack of concern, bright and chirpy as a sparrow but as we walked I hardly heard a word she said for the confused maelstrom of passions I was experiencing, my ears were buzzing, my heart thumping and my hands went all clammy. I'd given myself away, declared my weakness for all to see. This was the very first time I had ever walked alone with a girl, intentionally.

We came to the farm again and I walked quickly by. Rita didn't say anything, or at least she didn't stop whatever she was saying, but she must have known the die was cast. We went on up the hill, aware of being intentionally together now. I would willingly have stopped there with her in suspended animation for the rest of my life. It was enough, I would live off her words and glances for the remainder of my days. We came again to the Chapel where I said an off hand

"Cheerio". Rita went running in and I returned to the farm bouncing off clouds. "My very own girlfriend," I exulted. "She likes me, I'm sure she likes me." I could have died then and there for the sheer bliss of it.

From then on we were betrothed. But unfortunately Fred had seen us go by together as he was cooling the milk and for weeks he teased me unmercifully. "Hey Mick, Rita says she's coming to your birthday tea. I invited her for you."

For a moment I didn't know whether to believe him or not, but his face broke into a grin as I looked at him searchingly. We had a nice little all male tea party in the back kitchen, Eric and Doug and Mac but not Rita. I'd have died of shame if she had come.

"Had a nice day at school then?" Fred would say as I came down the yard. "How's Rita today? Told off were you for talking to her in class?"

Like a fool I blushed crimson at the mere public mention of her name and could only mumble incoherently and think of nothing sharp by way of reply, which rejoiced Fred and the other onlookers greatly. Only Mrs Costin took pity on me and gently chided Fred for so embarrassing me. No teasing however, was able to dampen my ardour and I still lived in torments of anxiety lest I should miss her when we got off the bus to walk to school or when we were coming home. In class I was unhappy till she acknowledged me, which she often did, but if anyone else was looking I ignored her.

The whole gang of us went tracking on the Knolls one fine evening; Rita was with us and our two teams for once were girls against boys. I was puzzled and worried that she giggled and flashed a saucy glance at me whenever our eyes met, whispering to the other girls and falling about with laughter at some secret joke. But in the chase I made it my business to pursue Rita and when I eventually caught her and grabbed her laughing and struggling as we fell together in the grass, there was something more than just innocent childish play in the thrill that electrified me as my arms encircled her and as I pressed against her as we struggled.

We played until the last gleams of light were fading from the western sky then came down off the hill to the road in a boisterous, well satisfied group, with Rita as teasing and provocative as ever, and me as full as ever of secret, dumb desire to be near her and excited at a bold plan I had earlier conceived and was soon to put into action, if I dared.

We split up outside Aud and Doug's cottage as before, and as before Rita's way led with mine past the farm, the only ones who went that way. We walked along together, she chattering on as usual, me silent and thoughtful, determined now that the decisive moment was coming, but scared.

We came to the farm and I went on with Rita up the hill. It was so dark that I couldn't see her face and I was glad mine was hidden. She made no mention of me walking on with her, and with her still talking almost compulsively, it seemed, we passed along the darkened road till we came outside the locked Chapel gate. I stopped in the silent darkness, so did she. I could see only the dark shadowy outline of her now. Surely I could find the courage to kiss her in the dark! I stood a long minute sweating, locked in inactivity, there was no word spoken. Then bursting as it were an invisible bond I seized her hand, lurched forward into the darkness and kissed her briefly on her upturned lips, lips that to my shocked surprise returned my kiss with interest. Then she went, slipping like a shadow across the lane and into the house. I stood there a few minutes spellbound then floated down the hill on wings of ecstasy, life's highest aim accomplished, the peak of amorous experience scaled.

Each day of the following week was lived with only one thought in mind, the evening assignation with Rita. Whatever else we were doing I'd find her before it grew too dark and walk with her. Holding hands in the gloom we'd wander slowly, with me in a state of acute excitement and awareness of the exquisitely beautiful and vivacious creature beside me who actually wanted to be with me. Our kisses in the dark were long and lingering now like those we were used to seeing in the cinema and sent me rolling home head over heels in ecstasy down the hill, joy and exultation bursting out of me in crazy shouts and gasps and whisperings to the darkness.

She went away afterwards, suddenly without warning. I looked for her on the bus one morning and she wasn't there, and I gazed dully at her empty place in class all day thinking she must be unwell. Nor did I see her about the cottage on our return. I remember the despair I felt, whilst feigning disinterest, on being told that her mother had come suddenly to take her back to London. I felt for the first time the callous hand of fate dealing out injustice and was plunged headlong into that uniquely agonising despair that attends blighted youthful romance. Fred's teasing stopped, whether by chance or design I didn't know, and after a day or two's utter misery other things began to dominate my thoughts again. Perhaps the greatest casualty of this tragic affair was my scholastic future. For now that Rita had gone my classroom performance immediately nose dived and found its true level around the middle of the class and never again rose to dizzy heights.

I didn't see Rita again for several years but somehow I kept her London address intact in a corner of my memory and one evening on a short leave from the army, having impulsively scribbled her a note, I went to call on her in her parents' little terraced house in Kentish Town. We had a good night out in the West End, a meal, and acres of reminiscences as we walked the streets afterwards, but somehow it was not the same, our paths had diverged too much and the magic had flown in the intervening years. I took her home, we said goodnight, I kissed her once more and parted never to see her again.

School after Rita went was henceforward just school, not the magical place it had once been. It was, as I have said, labouring under immense difficulties with regard to space, for now I recall there was a party from a third secondary school using those same buildings for some while. Three headmasters sitting at three desks in one office! How three schools managed to jam into premises built for one I'll never know, for I think it is pretty general experience that scarcely any school has an excess of space and our school alone couldn't have numbered less than two hundred, which of course is a tiny number to provide secondary education for, but the resources, judged by today's standards, were as limited as the number of pupils.

As serious as were the physical problems of how to accommodate all the evacuees, they were dwarfed in importance by the problems of obtaining staff and of maintaining an adequate curriculum. So many teachers were called up that schools were sadly depleted, specialists were taken away with no hope of replacement.

The result was of course that standards could not be maintained. Our report form showed Spanish as one of the languages studied; the Spanish master, who was also in charge of French, was called up shortly before I arrived, so we didn't have a single lesson, which is only one of the reasons why I have never sampled the delights of the Costa Brava. Our woodwork master left after I had been there a few months and after that we only had the occasional lesson when some retired teacher could come in to take us, a circumstance that I have ever since used to excuse to myself my utter incompetence with anything involving wood.

I remember having poetry lessons sitting on benches in the woodwork room. The elderly headmaster, on the point of retiring, took us through and through Macaulay's 'Horatius'. We each had to read in turn all through the interminable poem and I can still hear William Warboys trying to say, "Then out spake Spurius Lartius", without letting his voice rise at the end of Lartius. "No, not like that," said the head with massive patience, and he'd read it for him again, "just keep your voice level to the end of the line." But poor old William just couldn't, up he would pipe on the last syllable. The head's grey locks seemed almost to whiten perceptibly. No wonder I've remembered much of that poem word for word ever since. The head employed the same technique with 'How They Brought The Good News From Ghent to Aix', and 'The Pied Piper of Hamelin'. We dwelt on them so intensively that the story came through so vividly it has never been forgotten.

Just one science master was left to cover all the varied aspects of his subject and to try and waken some sparks of scientific interest among us. It was a hopeless task, though he was a good teacher and struggled manfully to cope. Our geography master left after my first year and wasn't replaced, which I regretted because geography with its implication of travel and flavour of foreign parts, surviving all the dusty text book treatment, was the one school subject that I loved.

So the specialist teaching which we increasingly needed became increasingly lacking. It was part of the price of war and at the time we were not concerned; few were concerned, they couldn't be with a fight for survival going on. We even considered ourselves lucky that we were having an easier time than we should. French was bad enough, there was one French master left – unfit for military service – but to have had to learn Spanish too would have been dreadful, we said, and all that science homework. No, we congratulated ourselves on our good fortune, practically no homework of any kind, plenty of time for an afternoon's gardening on the school allotment at the edge of town, plenty of time for football and for the perfection of our handwriting, a circumstance from which mine has never recovered. Plenty of time too, for some mysterious and seemingly purposeless activity called bookkeeping that a steely eyed elderly dragon forced down our unwilling throats each week.

The school meals service, I remember, was just painfully emerging, even as forty years later it is now painfully declining. We had to walk in a long crocodile down into the centre of town each dinner time, rain or shine, to a vast wooden warehouse type of building where with children from other schools we queued for ages for our meal. Later on things improved and we were able to have our meal at school in the large hall that had just been built.

In our lunch break we were free to do as we liked and a small group of us often walked down town to a little herbalist's shop and drank a glass of sarsaparilla and sat around on the stools and felt sophisticated young men about town. Then we wandered over the road to inspect the cattle market beside the busy Watling Street. Outside the Town Hall we stopped to see how much had been collected so far in the 'Wings for Victory' campaign. A wooden Spitfire on a long painted board climbed higher with each thousand pounds or so collected. We sometimes mooched around the grounds of the old Priory Church looking for conkers, and on our way back to school we passed a little bakery where we watched wholemeal loaves being taken out of the brick ovens and sometimes we bought a loaf between us and tore it to pieces all hot and steaming as we broke it, and devoured it as we walked along, and never has bread tasted so good.

I never had good friends at school like those I had in the village. One or two that I got to know and like in the first year left and returned to London. Yet those who were left were London boys like me and of my own age, we ought to have had a lot in common. I understood them perfectly and we were good enough acquaintances. But already, after one year in the village, I felt a growing unwillingness to acknowledge my city origins. I was turning into a country boy and had a burning desire to think of my life as being only in the village and had no wish to talk to these townee schoolfellows about life on the farm or take them into my confidence about our escapades, they wouldn't have made sense to strangers so I kept quiet. They were only too willing to discuss their life in Dunstable for they all lived in the town, I was the only one from the country. Without exception they longed to get back to London and in varying degrees disliked their life in the little market town. Their separation from their families was in no way compensated for by the attraction of life as evacuees and I have no reason to suppose that I would have been any different from them but for the happy chance of living in a village and on a farm.

None of the teachers ever asked me about living on the farm, I've no idea whether any of them knew where I lived. There was as I remember, no contact at all between home and school, save for the annual report. We appeared at nine o'clock from some unknown limbo and returned there at four. The two worlds of home and school were utterly divorced from each other and we who moved between these two existences took it all unquestioningly as right and natural.

140

There was no special school bus in those days to take us the three miles or so into town and bring us home. We used the ordinary service which took us to the Town Hall, five minutes walk away from school. Coming home it happened now and again that we missed the bus or it was full and pulled away without us, though it would have to be really full for that, there was none of the present day nonsense about only a few standing, they crammed them in as tight as in the Japanese metro. But if in spite of that the bus pulled away with the rear platform almost on the ground and we were left behind, it was an hour before the next bus so we often walked unless the weather was too bad.

So, satchel on back, we would start out on the long tramp up the slope to the Rifle Volunteer at the foot of Dunstable Downs by the California Swimming Pool which on hot summer days we sometimes visited. It was there at the foot of the Downs amid the rising thermals that in later years as the war drew to its close, gliding began again after its enforced suspension. The road divided here and our way swung round towards the top of Lancot Hill where the view was superb and the thirties' rash of houses stopped save for one estate a little way ahead which marked Dunstable's furthest extent. We were high up, the air felt clearer, cleaner, the wind blew freely and one's vision leaped ahead a dozen miles across the broad vale and into the dark blue distance. To the left above us the faded green of the bare grass slopes of the Downs stretched in a long, unbroken, treeless arm to Whipsnade, after which the chalk hills curved back out of sight. Onwards again the eye took in the long spur of Ivinghoe Beacon crouching like a giant Sphinx above the plain, and on beyond that again to the western horizon, ridges of distant unknown hills, vaguely wooded. It was a different angle on the view I loved from the Knolls. As you walked along you could pick and choose indefinitely the different things to focus on and think about. The eye, and the mind behind the eye, was liberated and could roam unhindered within that expansive view.

Our pace quickened a little now we were over the crest and the way led downhill. The ploughed fields to our right showed white chalk through the brown soil and ended in wooded coombes where more chalk hills edged the eastern vale and ended in our Knolls, sharply outlined ahead with its thick coat of beeches warmly wrapped around its shoulders.

Bit by bit along the road and all down Lancot Hill where fields of wheat grew beside the road, one savoured the approach to the village, seeing it in all its splendid setting. Descending as it were from the clouds, one's view was slowly circumscribed as the outskirts of the village were reached until finally in Church End by the Recreation Ground one was on the flat valley bottom. If a look back up the long slope of Lancot Hill showed a toy sized bus coming we'd wait and catch it there, but if not we'd carry on the final mile to home past both the schools, with the road skirting the wooded Knolls which dips steeply down to meet it there, then on past the Cross Keys and the Chapel. Most of the way through the village the road runs on a ledge a little way above the valley floor so there is always an interesting view out over the fields and orchards.

Once past the Cross Keys one had the real feeling of being home, of knowing intimately every step of the way now. It was all our territory. Each cottage, stretch of hedgerow, every path, each tree and bush had our special stamp of ownership upon it that we casually recognised as we passed along. It was then that the special magic of Lower End was felt and that more strongly when we walked alone and went undistracted with eyes and every sense receptive to the many powers that combine thereabouts to weave a spell so powerful it in no sense diminishes by absence however lengthy it may be. It is a magic invoked by the bold slope of the Knolls towering above the road, its beeches majestic with their exquisite colouring whatever the season, from tenderest early summer green to golden autumnal glory and shining winter grey. They descend to the roadside and are forever trying to cross and would eagerly take the fateful step one feels, were it not for the cottages and orchards which guard and ornament those lower slopes. Every step now deepens and extends the magic of the place, both by its natural beauty and by its intimate associations to produce the feeling of being home.

If it were the winter season darkness would be closing in by then as we made the final descent to Lower End, to our hidden village sheltering below the hill. Somehow there'd never be the same desire to do the journey in reverse, to walk the long uphill road to school. On the rare occasions that the bus failed to turn up or we could not get on, we let it go at that and had the day at home. Everyone seemed to think that was fair.

View across Church End towards Ivinghoe Beacon, looking as good now, and as productive, as it was in wartime.

The Cross Keys as it was in wartime, where Arthur took his customary pint.

Chapter XII

Awash with Fruit

Soon after the end of August, depending on the season, and when most of the harvest was in, Mr Costin cast a more than cursory glance over the orchard below the farm when the horses were let out to graze at the end of the day. He walked out over the concrete mud and looked hard up into the plum trees. Fred, wandering down into his orchard by the bus stop after letting his hens out in the morning, pulled down a bough and sampled the fruit. Bob and Reg surveyed the plums and greengages in the orchard by Tommy Holland's house as we took the cart down the road to start the day's harvesting. It was the time for plum picking and everyone could see, especially where Fred's trees overhung the road, that the fruit peeping between the rough green leaves had changed from tiny green bullets to large deep purple ovals with a sky dust bloom upon them. Scores of folks in all the villages round about had just that day taken a plum from a branch, squeezed it a little in the fingers to loosen the stone, split it open and sampled the dull yellow flesh. If ripe it was firm, not juicy, and had a pleasant, semi-sweet flavour, not sickly cloying like a dessert plum, but a little sharp with character about it.

Of course nobody thought of asking us boys about the plums. Yet we were the ones who knew, the undeniable experts. We had our fingers on the pulse of plums in every nearby orchard. For several weeks past we had been sampling them, at first screwing up our faces in disgust at the sourness, but gradually as the hot sun bore down on the trees day by day, we'd bite and swallow with diminishing grimace until at last that well satisfied gleam in the eye at tasting told whoever would see that the crop was ripe.

There was never any need for the Costins to be on guard against small boys stealing plums. The children were so few and there was so much fruit all over the village. In practically every garden and the many orchards the whole village was awash with fruit at that season. And of course as is the way when there is such plenty, hardly anyone used to bother to eat it seriously and nobody minded when they did. Apple and plum trees leaned so frequently over roadside verges that you didn't have to enter private property, just reach up an arm as you walked by.

The matter of plums would be thoroughly thought about for some days and then discussed over a meal as were all important issues at the farm.

"What do you reckon about the plums down your place?" said Mr Costin to Fred.

"About ready in a week I should think," said Fred pushing forward his dish for another helping of rice pudding.

"The 'gages down at Tommy's are ready now," said Bob, "I tried several last night."

"I reckon the plums up here will be a few days yet," said Mr Costin. He paused for a moment or two's thought. "We should finish off that bit of barley down at Double Gates by tomorrow night, Friday," he said speculatively. "That leaves the peas and beans. They won't be ready for about another ten days from what I saw of them this morning. So I'll ring the agent and tell him we'll start picking 'gages on Monday. Going to be a fair number this year don't you think?"

"A fair old crop," said Bob.

Fred nodded. The discussion ended, the wireless was switched on for the news, just in time.

"Hm," said Mrs Costin getting up to clear away. "That means I'd better look out my jam and bottling things, I'm going to be extra busy next week by the look of it." Each year she bottled about a hundred pounds of fruit, mostly plums and greengages, and she made countless jars of jam. For months past she had been saving a little of each week's sugar ration and hoarding it jealously away. It was surprising too, how grocers could find the odd bag of sugar over and above the ration for old and valued customers. Beyond that, saccharin had to be resorted to when all else failed. The deep cupboards in the corner of the front kitchen next to the fireplace held all the jam and bottled fruit and it was a sight to draw gasps of admiration and envy from visitors, especially in winter time as a bottle of plums was taken out to make a pie and the vast treasure of fruit, row upon row of jars, was revealed.

Mr Costin switched off the wireless and picked up the 'phone. He pushed down the lever to call the operator. No reply. He pushed it down again several times. "Blast 'em," he said loudly, "they've all gone to sleep."

Several more times he tried to get the operator. "Hullo, hullo," he bawled into the mouthpiece. No success. We sat around the table entranced. Fred's eyes swivelled upwards with a slight toss of his head.

"Hullo, hullo," went on Mr Costin flicking the lever furiously, "answer blow you! Ah, at last. Are you there? I say, do you know I've been trying to ring you for these last ten minutes? What! Don't you argue with me! Are you saying I'm a liar? No, well you be careful what you say. And I've got better things to do than hang on here while you have a good chin wag with your mates. Now, you get me this number straightaway please."

Mrs Costin, tut-tutting and shaking her head in disapproval went on collecting the plates, Bob stared into the distance and Fred went outside. Funny how aggression flows easily along telephone wires!

In a day or two the skips arrived. Strongly woven round baskets, they stood in tall piles about the barns and yard. The barley having been duly finished on the Friday night, on Saturday morning the tall splay footed ladders and some shorter ones were wakened from their long rest in the implement shed behind the barns and thoroughly inspected, any weak or damaged rungs replaced and everything got ready for the Monday start.

We were a cheerful band that set to work that first Monday of picking 'gages. Everyone was looking forward to it, even those like Mr Costin who had harvested plums during a long lifetime couldn't conceal their pleasure at the prospect of climbing up into trees once more and picking fruit. His sons were positively vibrating with good humour, even Arthur, dour Arthur, licked his lips and popped an imaginary plum into his mouth by way of greeting, with a knowing wink.

For plum picking is one of those tasks wholly delightful in prospect and with no apparent unpleasant side effects or disadvantages. The thought of unlimited ripe fruit which may be eaten at will and involving little effort in the culling, merely the leisurely stretching out of one's hand to ease the ripe fruit from its stem, is surely an attractive one. Add to it the prospect of sunshine and a leafy paradise and the idea of plum picking seems to have been conceived in heaven.

After we'd had breakfast and cleaned out the cowsheds we all went down the road to the orchard behind Tommy Holland's cottage. Everything was ready, ladders, skips and picking baskets with hooks attached to hang on the ladder to give you two free hands. It might just have crossed my mind that almost exactly a year before I had arrived in the village, stepped off the bus and seen my first plum tree. Now here I was twelve months of farming life later about to put my ladder in a tree and start picking as an equal, almost, with all those others, unknown a year ago, who were pushing their ladders into trees around me. I might have thought along those lines but I doubt it, I was too full of the pleasure of the moment. It was like going to a party, we were all calling light heartedly to one another before the games began, and the clear sunny air had the headiness of champagne about it. Someone came to show me how to put the ladder into a tree, slide it in sideways and make it rest securely on a thick bough, and soon we had all abandoned the solid earth, gone aloft, and the first green-gages were dropping into baskets and everyone but me was settling down to work steadily in an atmosphere of satisfaction and good humour. What sheer bliss, the flavour of a ripe greengage eaten on the instant from the tree. That divine flavour, juicy and sweet, and the aroma of the freshly picked fruit haunt me still and bear no comparison to the same fruit bought from the greengrocer's shelf.

Height was my big thrill at first. I climbed straight to the top of the ladder and gazed around at the new angle on life. I couldn't in truth see so very much. I was in the trough of a green wave whose crests reared around me and rolled away in a billowing leafy sea, wave upon wave to some distant bounds. But looking down at the firm ground below me I seemed to be enormously high, the ladder swayed beneath my feet and I imagined crashing down to lie broken in the grass. There was the spice of adventure in it, a dash of riskiness which with the licence to eat fruit at will, combined to produce in me a feeling almost of carnival.

It took a few days before I became hardened to the work, adept at moving a ladder, patient and with expectations a little lower than the Elysian Fields. But once acclimatised the task is indeed agreeable, though as with many jobs about the farm, harder than it may at first appear. With one person to a tree I found it difficult to pick patiently every greengage there was, turning aside the clumps of leaves to find the greengage that's out of sight. After a few minutes in one place gathering the obvious accumulations of fruit, I looked around, saw thick clusters a little way away and wanted to go down and move the ladder round to get at them. But that of course would not do, so I had to learn to stay hardly stirring from one spot for many minutes at a time until everything within arm's reach had gone.

Only in this way could I pass Mr Costin's searching scrutiny when he came round to the tree I'd just left to see how the new plum picking recruit was shaping up. "Few there you've missed Mick," he'd say and back I'd have to go to gather in the few stray fruits. So we'd be spread out across the orchard in trees of our own choosing and a watcher might stand ten minutes and hardly see a movement, so plentiful was the fruit and so patient the pickers. But even when there was not much movement there was usually a fair amount of noise from disembodied voices floating over the orchard like calling birds concealed in the greenery.

They were large trees planted many years before, with stout branches, so that for a change or when the ladder rounds were pressing painfully, I'd step off and stand upon a bough and pick from there and enjoy the freer movement of climbing among the boughs. Those plums were a particularly fine and free harvest to reap, for I never knew the trees to be sprayed or pruned or given the least attention, saving taking away a fallen branch, yet year after year they provided bumper crops from the three main orchards on the farm.

After the greengages it was the turn of the much more numerous blue plums in the farm's four main orchards.

The whole area for miles around was renowned for its plums, they had been grown for generations, the soil and the climate being just right. I was appalled to hear that most of the plums went not to greengrocers' shops but to factories, they had some industrial use as a dye apparently. It was too awful to think about, all that delicious fruit going to waste like that. It was a beautiful sight to look out from the Knolls in Springtime to see the soft white mist of plum blossom like unseasonable snow drifting for miles across the vale. Ours I was told, the whole crop, would be sent to Covent Garden and at once snapped up, the dealers could not get enough. Years afterwards when I visited Covent

Garden market and was overawed by the mountains of fruit on the move each day, I could put our seemingly vast sea of plums into its proper perspective as indeed a very tiny drop in a vast ocean. But at the time I had never seen so much fruit. All over the orchard as the day progressed skips would be filled to the top with the dark purple fruit then taken up to the barn to be weighed so that by evening the barn floor would be entirely covered with plums and the air delicately perfumed, until the lorry came to collect them and leave another batch of empty skips.

At first I found myself eating a plum every few minutes when I came across a tempting one, but as with any fruit one can soon have a surfeit. And so I found. After a while I could scarcely face another plum however ripe it may have appeared. Also I soon found that in quantity they had a disastrous effect on the bowels. "Black coated workers, just like prunes," grinned Fred as he warned me, too late, against them.

There was no shortage of spectators and assistants for fruit picking. Like vultures the smaller children would huddle in the long grass beneath the trees and poke about for fallen fruit. Fred would often tease them and joke with them then toss down a handful of greengages for them to scramble for as with pennies and oranges at a mayor choosing. For pure pleasure Eric used to come and help us pick when his own work was slack but Mr Costin daren't let any others climb the ladders in case they fell for he'd be liable.

Sometimes we'd be picking away quietly with Mr Costin away at the bank or gone up to the farm with a load of skips then suddenly there came a great crash by my ear as a plum smashed through the leaves. I looked around but all was perfectly normal, plums going steadily down into buckets as usual. I resumed picking, on the alert. Another great hiss as a plum whizzed through the leaves above my head. This time out of a watchful corner of my eye I'd seen it was Reg. "Hey," I shouted, "here's a plum if you want one," and steadying myself with one hand I threw one back hard.

"What's up Mick?" called Eric in the tree next to mine.

"They're at it again," I replied.

"Is that Mick throwing plums again?" came Bob's voice. "Right, you're asking for trouble this time," and plums started to zip and crash around us and we returned the fire with interest. The bombardment went on for several minutes whilst laughs and shouts and curses echoed around the orchard before we settled down to work again, with only Arthur's ceaseless quiet humming to himself to break the silence among the trees. Fred played the elder brother role, disdaining any involvement in such childlike antics.

In the farmhouse the activity in the orchard was reflected in the kitchen. Mrs Costin gave her orders each day for such and such a quantity of fruit and we had plum pie for dessert, tart with plums, stewed plums with custard. No one was fussy, we'd eat cooked plums for days and come again for more each time and I'd line the stones around my plate and count out a different future each time.

Then there was the jam. A great copper pan was used expressly for the job

All over Lower End splay footed ladders came out at plum picking time.

Cultivating with a pair of horses in Lower End. Tall elms like those in the background were everywhere.

and we'd come home to a sweet fruity smell around the house and rows of shining jars cooling on the back kitchen table. Another day it would be the turn of bottling, and batches of brass capped jars would be simmering away in a large pan then stood upon the table to cool, their rubber sealed contents destined for our winter pies.

All this activity with cooked fruit was too good to be missed by the local wasps. The buzz went out the length and breadth of the county so it seemed and they zoomed in on us in hundreds, stings at the ready, droning drunkenly around the kitchen, forcing the closure of all doors and windows and much swatting of the ones who nonetheless got through. The whole place was alive with wasps, you walked through clouds of black and yellow stripes to get indoors, it was a wonder we weren't continually stung. I was goaded into taking counter measures to this invasion. I rigged up wasp traps, jam jars with water in them and a little jam and a paper top with a small hole, secured by an elastic band. I'm not sure whether these traps attracted still more wasps to the house or took their victims from the ones there already, but my jars, left outside on windowsills, were soon filled to overflowing with trapped and drowning wasps and had to be frequently renewed.

Hornets were the creatures we children were terrified of. There was a mythology of horror stories of attacks by hornets, so every time I saw a wasp-like creature on the larger size than normal I gave it a wide berth just for safety's sake. No sense in being the subject of some future hornet horror story in which someone always knows of someone who knew a boy who was stung by one of these ferocious monsters and died an agonising death.

The apple trees, though not so numerous as the plums were stripped in their turn whilst we were in the orchard. They filled a skip quicker but were otherwise more difficult to pick as each one had to be placed carefully in the basket lest it be bruised and then coaxed gently from basket into skip. Having eaten one ripe apple one's appetite was satisfied for quite a long time and what with dropped and damaged fruit there was enough lying about for all the hungry monsters who still stood around. After a while they wandered away sated, having thrown the cores at each other, to seek a more exciting occupation such as an examination of Bob's flock of Aylesbury ducks who frequented the pond behind Tommy Holland's cottage.

The apples for storing were kept in the apple loft over part of the shed around the sheep yard. The pick of the crop, they were spread out on deep straw safe from the severest frosts and provided a continual supply of fresh fruit throughout the winter. I used to open the door, savour the delicately scented, cidery air and reach out for an apple whenever I felt like it. The apple loft also made a good hiding place in our games. Being in an out of the way corner it combined difficulty of detection with an ideal occupation whilst hiding.

Those fruit picking days of early September, long, sunny and clear, were some of the finest days of my life and in terms of pleasure the most fruitful too! I wished for them never to end but that all our days could be spent in such a delightful and deeply satisfying occupation. The work grown easy, the pace leisurely amid the cool leafy trees, with ripe fruit on every hand in careless abundance and with good company and cheerful conversation to pass the long hours and days suspended between earth and heaven as golden summer slowly merged into mellow autumn. We worked all day easily and without strain, enveloped in pleasure and plenty and ended the day without exhaustion, ready to enjoy the leisure hours.

This was also the time for blackberries of course and we took our quota, but it was mostly an incidental occupation. We seldom set out with baskets to bring blackberries home, that was too much like work, the berries small, the containers large, and we became impatient with it. We left that to the adults with their walking sticks to hook the best ones down that always seemed to grow out of reach of our fingers. No, we would be tree climbing or on our way to the quarry or the Litany and we'd stop by a promising patch of brambles to stuff ourselves for a few minutes, our minds on other things.

At the farm one of the Sunday pies throughout most of the year was blackberry and apple, using bottled blackberries which had their place among the rows and rows of kilner jars. But those blackberries, strangely enough in the midst of all that black treasure of the hedgerows, came mostly from the allotments, cultivated ones passed in by old Mr Waters in great basketsful in thanks for the milk he picked up each morning as he tottered down the hill with his walking stick to do his bit of digging for victory.

Crab apple trees grew in the hedgerows and kept already busy mums even busier making crab apple jelly if they had enough sugar. Some even gathered rose hips and made a jelly, ideal so it was said for babies. But only a few went that far, though at a time when most staple foods were rationed every one was very food conscious and wasting food was almost a criminal act. Posters everywhere exhorted us to 'Waste Not Want Not', 'Dig for Victory' and many others. I remember our art lessons at school were given over to the production of such posters for a long time and we became expert at drawing garden forks and parsnips. Mothers can never have had such ideal conditions for getting their reluctant offspring to finish up their spinach.

All sorts of things were used as substitutes for unobtainable ingredients. The virtues of grated carrot were extolled I remember, as a replacement for currants and sultanas in cakes and things were so desperate that housewives actually used this and many, many other weird yet officially recommended recipes. Strange sorts of tinned fish swam into view. Snoek was one of them and provided many a laugh in the music halls. Whale meat was also in good supply and had its supporters. It followed from the general food shortage that it was a patriotic duty to use everything that grew wild and free to ease the burden on food supplies. This was so close to country ways anyway that it was merely a slight intensifying of what was regular practice. I never remember hearing the words "self sufficiency" but the villagers were past masters at it by nature.

Many a time in autumn I've gone out before breakfast over the meadows soaked in dew, searching for mushrooms when everything seemed to have been created anew overnight. The grass, brambles, trees, so still and shiningly clear cut in the early light as the first softly diffused sunbeams gently brushed away the slumbering mist. The world had that newly minted look about it and everywhere was festooned with dewy spider webs stringing their silvery beads in grass and hedgerow. The sheer ecstasy of being alive there, alone in the midst of such miracles was further sharpened by the sighting of those small white buttons in the grass, often pushed over by a browsing cow or horse, and gathering them up I'd wander back and be in time for us all to have them, cooked in a moment, with our breakfast eggs.

This season of plenty and the farming year culminated in the Harvest Festival. Practically everyone in the village had a hand in what went on, providing the fruit and flowers that had been safely gathered in and once again the children featured prominently in the day's proceedings. No one had then started to confuse matters by bringing in a scuttle of coal or a can of oil or making arrangements of fishing nets and green bottle floats. It was still the simple and straightforward rural celebration of the products of farm and garden. The tiny chapel was decorated to saturation point. Rows of shining apples glowed warmly along the window sills, sheaves of corn stood upright on either side of the organ with, between them, an enormous and magnificent harvest loaf with its decorative twists and frills, trails of ivy and clematis round polished posts. Every little ledge and unused step was crammed with vast marrows, turnips and cabbages. Lines of runner beans dotted off with tomatoes sent their message in vegetable Morse Code. Pots of dahlias and asters atop the organ and great bunches of chrysanthemums and golden rod around the pulpit almost concealed the specially invited preacher for the day, who peered out at us as from the jungle's edge. It was the overflowing outdoors swallowing up the indoors, moving in and swamping it, making of the Chapel a covered Garden of Eden.

It was as good a village produce show as could be seen for miles around and with some heart warming singing of favourite old hymns and a sermon that was down to earth and understood by all, it was a natural crowd puller. Even those who never normally came to chapel came to Harvest Festival. Even Eric's dad came!

We had our part to play in the morning and afternoon services, filing in and bringing our gifts and with some readings, singing and recitations, though nothing on the scale of Anniversary fortunately. Then just this once we came again in the evening and went upstairs with the other young bloods and the courting couples. Even with a few dour elders up there to keep things restrained there was an almost carnival atmosphere as we nudged and winked and whispered and pointed things and people out to each other and gazed at the fruitful scene below. It was like going up in the circle at the cinema in Dunstable but better for being a live show.

The Chapel was full to overflowing in the evening, chairs having to be brought in from the schoolroom and placed in spare corners and down the aisle to take the extra people. Some deep, subconscious reservoir of feeling for the land and its marvels and mysteries had been touched and the Chapel roof almost leaped off with the charge of emotion and enthusiasm that burst forth at the singing of the hymns. The choir stalls were brimming with eager singers and local soloists were brought in specially to sing some appropriate pieces and often Uncle Alf was one of them, his fine baritone voice was very popular with Chapel folk.

Thankfulness for all the plenty on display and for everything produced in field and garden was intensified in those desperate wartime days by the knowledge of the stranglehold that the U boats had and were always trying to tighten on our imports of food. It was heartening to see so much provided by our own efforts, there was a direct connection between growing more and better potatoes and winning the war and it was the awareness of this aspect of Harvest Festival that lent it even more fervour than usual. The bounteous harvest was proof, if any were needed, that the Almighty was indeed on our side.

The next evening in the schoolroom the great auction sale of all the produce was held. We children were there early with our pennies and our threepenny bits, giving the stuff a good look over to see what we would like to buy. The schoolroom soon began to fill up with a cheerful, raincoated and stoutbooted stream of adults and soon all the chairs were taken, the walls lined and the doorways bulging, and the volume of excited chattering grew deafening. Then Bob King called everyone to order, extended a brief welcome, said a short prayer and handed over to the auctioneer.

Everyone could see that all the fruit, the flowers, the vegetables that had filled the Chapel the day before were as the mere tip of the iceberg as far as all the produce donated was concerned. There were mountains of things that there had been no room for in the Chapel, including a few really rare and precious items like a packet of dried fruit, a tin of peaches, a packet of tea and the two crowning pieces of the evening, three oranges and a banana.

He didn't waste time, our auctioneer, but plunged in fast saying they'd be there till midnight unless he hurried. A few of us boys were soon recruited as delivery boys and were kept busy running here and there with bunches of chrysanthemums and plates of apples for their purchasers.

"Now ladies and gentlemen, we have here the high spot of the evening," boomed the auctioneer whilst pockets and purses were still fairly full. He lovingly took the banana and, holding it up as if it were the finest porcelain, fairly purred at the assembly. "Take a good look ladies and gentlemen, you're not likely to see another banana for many a long day." We nudged each other excitedly, the taste memory of those oranges and that banana was driving us frantic. Murders have been committed for desires less strong than those we were feeling then. We hadn't seen a banana for twelve months or more, let alone eaten one. Boiled parsnip with banana flavouring was a recommended replacement for the real thing in banana custard.

"Now, what am I bid ladies and gentlemen for this one gloriously, deliciously ripe banana? Look at it, go on, it's just ready for eating." He held it up lovingly, sniffed it rapturously and slowly waved it in front of the audience who gazed back in rapt bemusement as if hypnotised.

"Anyone start me off at ten shillings?" There was silence in the room for a few moments save for several sharp intakes of breath at his audacity. Ten bob for one banana, the man must be insane!

"Thank you Charlie, ten shillings I'm bid."

A hundred pairs of eyes swivelled to Charlie and marvelled at the extravagance of the man.

"Fifteen shillings anyone? Thank you Emmy. Can you almost taste it my love? Mm, wish I could."

"Oh, one pound over there. Thank you Frank, your missis'll love you for ever. Now, twenty five bob I'm bid in the far corner. One pound ten anyone?"

We could hardly believe our ears, everyone was going mad.

"Right Mr Horton," went on the auctioneer, "thirty bob it is. That's more like it. Come on ladies and gentlemen, this beautiful banana's worth more than that, just think where it's been . . ."

The sale proceeded for a while in an atmosphere as near to rivalling Sotheby's as we could hope to come. The banana was finally knocked down to a retired farmer for thirty seven and six. "Obviously in his dotage" was the general opinion as a wave of excited comment swept the room. The oranges caused only marginally less hysteria and were eventually sold for a week's wages.

The rest of the sale was a noisy, good humoured affair at which most of us boys had to settle for a bunch of beetroot or a few rosy apples instead of the bunch of grapes or basket of yellow pears we had our eyes on. Some of the farmers had given hundredweights of potatoes and sacks of swedes and these were speedily sold along with just about everything else. At the very end everyone staggered out into the night clutching their purchases, well pleased with their 'bargains' which generally cost a sight more than they would have done outside.

After Harvest Festival autumn dipped slowly but surely towards winter, and one morning in that dead season at the end of November I awoke to find the world enveloped in a dense grey blanket. The usual sounds from across the yard were muted, disembodied, and peering out I saw the softly blurred glow of the hurricane lamp in the cowshed and the dim, ghostly outline of the barns as all around swirled the concealing mist. This was the thickest fog I had seen in the village, reminiscent to me of those still thicker sulphurous fogs, those peasoupers I had known in London.

It was Saturday and there was nothing important to do, nothing anyway that couldn't wait an hour for as I was dressing an exciting idea had come to me. How thick, I wondered, was this mist? If I should climb the Knolls to the very top, would I come out above it? I had no way of knowing, but it was such a thrilling possibility that I decided to find out.

After breakfast the mist was thick as ever in spite of my fears that it would evaporate as the earlier, less substantial ones had done. As I went out into the yard all was leaden grey with no sign of thinning overhead. Even the sheepyard was so curtained that cricket would have been an hilarious farce. Out over the orchard gate the world ended twenty yards away where trees changed to phantom shapes before being swallowed up entirely. The tall elms at a little distance had lost half their height and below on the grass the cattle stood disconsolately about, anxiously swishing their tales waiting for the gloom to lift.

I walked up to the road and watched a few vehicles creep past, their hooded headlights full on but making little impression on the swirling grey wall which opened only to swallow them again immediately. This was the moment. I'd said nothing about my intentions, the plan was too precious to divulge. I crossed the road and started climbing up the steep path. Turning after a few moments the house and barns were but the faintest of forms and in another upward pace or two were gone completely.

I reached the top of that first slope and stood upon the level ground again, a spot from which I usually surveyed the fields and farms out over Eaton Bray and several miles around. Today nothing but gently floating wraiths of mist and all around me grass and bushes glistening with tiny silver droplets and strung with jewelled webs amid an eerie silence which made me feel more utterly alone than anything I had known before. The mist was as thick as ever as I started across the mass of little hills. Luckily I knew every step of the way, but I imagined a stranger wandering there and saw him baffled, lost, stumbling around in circles until eventual exhaustion overtook him, and I peered about wondering if I should stumble upon his bleached skeleton.

I was enjoying myself so much I could have wished that time itself would stop so that for ever more I could feel the intense delight of wandering in that insubstantial fairyland. But I was drawn onwards and upwards, and confident of my way and sublimely happy in my private miniature moving world, I walked on following the little paths that opened up ahead then closed behind me like the doors to an exotic magical world. I knew how vast a view there was to see yet saw nothing, no matter how intense my gaze, always the slowly stirring veils past which I could not see.

I reached the foot of the great rampart with still never a sound, no cheep of bird, no skylarks soared this morning, no fellow explorer looming phantom-like out of the mist, not even a rabbit to be seen. I was alone in this whole vast eerie wilderness.

Or was I alone? What was that blurred form moving slowly at the limit of my vision? I stopped a moment, chilled by fear. The ghosts of the old defenders of the castle? Would they be on the prowl across the hills? Did the mist call them out and send them restlessly drifting in this formless element? I stepped towards the shape and the mist thinned to reveal a small hawthorn bush. I savoured the flesh tingling eeriness of standing still a moment longer then, "Now for it," I thought, "Will the mist hold out to the top and beyond?"

I began to climb the steep slope eagerly and as I did the mist slowly thinned, the heavy grey above became a little lighter. My view extended some yards but still presented me with a grey nothingness. Then as I neared the top I looked up and saw the greyness swirling and dissolving into blue, yet at ground level the writhing grey phantoms still barred the view and hemmed me in though loosely now.

It was the same as I topped the rampart and stood upon the flat. My anticipation shrivelled to disappointment — I could see nothing save a patch of blue immediately above me, it was as if I was at the bottom of a whirlpool with only a tiny window to the sky.

But how about the top knoll? Hurriedly I made for it, my last slim hope, and climbed its steep but short side. As I did so and came on top, the very top, miraculously the last veils of mist melted away and I emerged clear and free to be met by a sight so amazing that I still recall it as vividly as if I saw it yesterday.

As far as eye could see, maybe twenty miles, maybe two hundred, the whole world, everything was submerged beneath a great sea of mist rolling steadily away in gentle billows to the horizon. A sea which shone bright silvery white in the brilliant golden sunshine under a cloudless blue sky. The air was so shining pure, so clear and clean, it seemed to my impressionable mind that I was standing at the very gate of heaven itself and that this was no earthly light that met my eyes and welcomed me. I had won through, struggled up through the deadening grey of the lower world and now stood triumphant in glory above it.

My feet were solidly on the ground however, and the mist washed over them and around my knees. I climbed up on the top of the Home Guard dug out and stood at last completely free of mist on my own tiny point of undrowned land. I could make out now, as I looked around intently for other survivors of this second flood, the very top of Ivinghoe Beacon, all that remained of solid earth. It was a splendid sight and my very own, my secret and unique vision that not one of all the thousands down there in the gloom could have any conception of. I gazed my fill before plunging back down into the greyness, taking with me that scene which I have never again experienced nor ever could experience again in quite the same way. The murky world below remained enshrouded till nearly dinner time.

Chapter XIII
Off Colour

I woke up early in the morning not feeling at all my normal self, hot and with an unpleasant soreness in my throat and a headache. The morning was as dull and miserable as I felt, but for once I was interested only in the inner not the outer weather. Bob and Fred were up and the grey light of morning filled the room as I tossed and turned restlessly. Eventually I gave up all hope of sleep, lay on my back feeling wretched and wondered if my last day on earth had come. Was I to be cut off before my prime, before I could make my impact on the world? What bitter injustice, what cold and cruel fate!

"Hullo then," said Mrs Costin as I shuffled into the back kitchen. I managed a rather wan, sorry for myself smile.

"Are you feeling all right?" she asked glancing up from the frying pan.

I shook my head, muttering lugubriously.

"I can see you don't," she said anxiously.

"The smell of eggs frying in smoking fat was turning my stomach over, a sure sign that something was wrong. I wandered over to the sink followed by Mrs Costin's worried gaze. "What's the trouble?" she asked.

I reeled off the main symptoms, then paused to consider if there were any minor ones worth mentioning. "And I feel funny," I concluded.

She removed the frying pan from the heat. "Let's have a look at you," she said turning me to face her. "Mm" she said, "you look hot. Let's have a look at your tongue." After a close inspection of that furred and furrowed organ she pronounced, "It's back to bed for you I'm afraid my boy."

It was a great relief to hear that. I was sure then I wasn't malingering, up till that point I had a gnawing suspicion I was.

"Hullo, what's this?" said Fred as he came in and sized up the situation. "You've never been struck down surely? Or have you got algebra at school today?

157

I grinned a bit sheepishly.

"You go back to bed now," said Mrs Costin, "or do you feel like some breakfast first?"

I shook my head and moved towards the door. "Well I never," exclaimed Fred in mock astonishment, "no breakfast eh! You must be in a bad way."

Upstairs again I peeled off my clothes and got back into bed. So I really was poorly, that was official now. No school today anyway, that's for sure. I lay back luxuriously, concerned, and wondered what I'd got. The thought of the Church End girl who had died suddenly a short while before of meningitis sent a cold chill down my spine. She'd been fine one moment apparently, like me yesterday, then suddenly . . . I didn't mind a reasonably serious illness, one to keep me in warmth and comfort for a while and give me a break from school, but nothing worse than that, please, please.

After breakfast the telltale sounds of work around the yard ran their course and faded. The pump's loud clanking was stilled, the clatter of milking pails, the rolling of full churns up the slope to the road, the shovelling of cow muck and the brushing out of cowsheds and all the accompanying voices were stilled at last. Fred and Bob popped up to see me and to congratulate me on fiddling the time off school and to hope it wasn't the plague I'd caught. Fred said he'd sent for the vet. Then there was silence as the men had gone off to various jobs. Mr Costin to market in Leighton, Fred to ploughing, Reg and Bob to fence mending and Arthur to thatching the ricks.

It was strange how every little sound carried, seemed exaggerated. Things I'd never thought of listening to I heard with crystal clarity in that mid morning stillness. A gate squeaking slightly on oil starved hinges, each individual hen clucking in the yard, the bull stirring in his pen under the deserted cowshed, rattling at his chain at some late flies perhaps as he faced the waste of another day of close confinement, the calf, which had been calling plaintively all night long for its mother, moving in its pen next to the pig sty, the guttural grunting of the sow as she luxuriated in her deep litter.

Then the doctor came over from Leighton. A tall dignified old man in a blue-grey suit. I'd seen him before when he came to look at Mr Costin after he'd knocked himself up at harvest work. Visiting royalty could have been received no more deferentially than the doctor was. It was as though a god had suddenly appeared in our midst, and this god's smart town suit in the house in mid-week was sufficiently unusual in itself to make everyone feel uncomfortably on edge. Voices were subdued, loud footsteps quietened. Tones were reverential. It was "Yes doctor, no doctor, straightaway doctor," and a china bowl from the best bedroom brought with soap and hot water and a clean towel for the doctor to wash his hands after touching the patient.

There was no doctor in the village or in any of the villages round; he came from the town so was not summoned lightly, for no one wished to cry wolf in case the day of the wolf might actually come. There was no chemist in any of the villages either so the doctor brought his own medicines. The little dark bottle or box of pills he dispensed was received with awe as if it held the key to eternal life. Mr Costin might say in an offhand carefree moment, "Oh, old G.... he's no good, he doesn't know anything about it," and refer to him as a quack, but as soon as he was ill and terrified of dying, he was as meek as a lamb when old G. came to see him, submissive and equally as deferential as Mrs Costin, clay in the doctor's hands.

The doctor had bent over me in the big bed upstairs with Mrs Costin hovering, the room quickly tidied before he came in, looked at my tongue, felt my pulse, then said to Mrs Costin, "I'm pretty sure it's measles. A mild attack fortunately, only the suspicion of a rash. Two or three days in bed I think, then he can probably get up." He turned to me, "How will that suit you, young man? A little time off school eh? A little holiday in bed."

That suited me fine but even more important, "Are you sure it's measles doctor, it couldn't be meningitis could it?"

"Meningitis," he echoed with a laugh turning to Mrs Costin. "I don't know where they get their ideas from. No son, it's not meningitis, I can promise you that."

I breathed a great sigh of relief and began to feel better immediately.

He took out a large bottle of medicine from his bag and doled out a big spoonful of it which I swallowed with revulsion. "That's the stuff," he said with a smile, "all the best medicines taste horrible. I'll call again in a few days," he said as he went out.

"Ugh, some start to a holiday," I muttered trying to swallow away the last of that foul taste in my mouth.

I was left with the pleasurable feeling of being the centre of concern yet anxious that a mere evacuee should put everyone to so much bother. I must have started feeling better quite quickly for I soon began visualising a vivid deathbed scene when everyone who knew me, all my friends in Lower End, were grouped around sad and weeping, leaning anxiously over the bedspread bemoaning my imminent departure and listening for my final words of wisdom, though I couldn't bring myself actually to look at the corpse.

With the doctor gone I lay propped up on double pillows feeling so much better I began to wonder how I was going to pass the time. I lay back luxuriously, tucked my knees up and formed in the earth's primeval, bedclothes crust a towering mountain range, eroded in an instant to a level plain. Successive Everests arose and fell at the whim of knee joints and there at last, with Mallory and Irving failing, I panted up the final slope to plant the flag on earth's highest pinnacle.

The solid earth dissolved before my eyes as giant waves raged over seas of eiderdown and my piteous crew fearing the edge of the world begged me to save them, which I promptly did and steered our ship calmly into harbour to discover America and in a second with upstretched leg raised a novel skyscraper. Then with knees collapsed I gazed upon an endless icy plain and from my turned up toes of tents I walked with Oates out into the storm then returned to watch as Scott sat writing his final letter home.

My head rested back on the pillow and my eyes ranged over the wallpaper counting the repeating patterns in a variety of directions. Up on the ceiling I traced the tiny cracks along miles of navigable waterways in my birch bark canoe, leaped giant rapids till at last I came to Niagara itself where to my horror I plunged helplessly over, falling, falling — to awake with Mrs Costin standing over me with a glass of orange squash in one hand and that horrible bottle of medicine in the other.

Luxury of luxuries, I'd pecked at a little lunch brought up on a tray. I heard everyone come in downstairs to eat, and strained without success to interpret the jumble of sounds that wafted up. Then they had all gone back to work. And was I really still ill, I wondered? I didn't feel so bad now, no searing pains, no agonies, I ought really to feel worse than I did, I thought a little guiltily, I wasn't giving good value for the concern shown and the doctor's special visit. But no, I remembered thankfully what the doctor had said. I was protected from guilt, for he had pronounced judgement that I wasn't swinging the lead; I could legitimately enjoy my little illness.

The trouble was, how to enjoy it? Mrs Costin had brought me up some books and comics so I read in a desultory fashion some of the exploits of the legendary Wilson and the stupid sounding goings on of Billy Bunter. What else was there to read? I sorted over the books. Cronin's 'The Stars Look Down', I'd seen that among the dart-holed books downstairs before, but hadn't felt like getting beyond its maroon cover. I suspected there weren't any pictures anyway. 'Carisbroke Castle'? that looked interesting. I flicked the pages over and saw some line drawings of knights in armour. I read half a page. It was a romantic tale of medieval chivalry and heroic deeds. I closed it up. I'll read it later I thought. 'Ungava Bay', now that might be good I thought as I turned the pages, looking at the drawings and reading a line here and there. Obviously an adventure story up among the Eskimos. The trouble was I didn't really feel like reading at all, I was becoming restless.

Every few minutes I looked towards the window listening for sounds of life outside and pining for freedom. The afternoon was long and boring, I dozed part of the time and awoke to hear the cows coming into the yard with Arthur's quietly encouraging voice as he went around fastening their chains. "Good," I thought, "the day will soon be done." I definitely wasn't enjoying my day in bed. I felt I ought to, but had to admit I longed to be on my feet again. Why aren't things ever as they should be? The morning's thrill at the prospect of a few days in bed had crumbled to ashes; I was fed up.

By the morning of the second day and after a good night's sleep and more spoonsful of that revolting medicine, I was feeling so much better that the thought of another day in bed filled me with panic, and I begged to be allowed up in spite of old G's edict of two or three days in bed. Mrs Costin gave me a long searching look. "Hm," she said, "can you eat any breakfast?" The vision of my usual egg on fried bread set my mouth watering and brought a sparkle to my eyes. "Yes please," I said.

"Good," she declared, "when you've eaten your breakfast you can get up.

I'll go down and cook it in a few minutes."

So after duly clearing my plate I was allowed to come downstairs and sit about in an old dressing gown of Bob's. It was a very strange 'fish out of water' feeling to be loafing around through the working hours in the front kitchen where one normally only sat during meal times and in the evenings when one had earned the right to lounge about. Strange how awkward and uncomfortable it seemed in that room just because it was the wrong time to be there. Like a sort of purgatory between being bedridden and real outdoor fitness.

"You can write a letter home to tell your mum you're on the mend," said Mrs Costin, "it'll pass the time away."

In the afternoon I was allowed to get dressed as it was obvious that anyone who could put their dinner away as I despatched mine couldn't need to lounge around in pyjamas and dressing gown. In the evening Eric came up, "I've had measles," he said, "and you can't get it twice can you?" We went round the clock on the dart board then had a few games of dominoes with Mr Costin. It was grand to be back in the land of the living! Next day I was allowed out. They phoned the doctor to say he needn't bother to come again as I'd pulled through!

A few days later Mrs Costin decided that I ought to have a bath as a sort of ritual cleansing after sickness. Having a bath was not very easy at the farm as there was no bathroom. Naturally it wasn't a subject that appealed to me much. I was quite content to go on washing the visible parts if I must and leaving all other parts to look after themselves. The adults managed in various ways peculiar to themselves, bathing wasn't a topic that I recall occupying very much open discussion time, though I do remember that Bob used to go up to his brother George's house in Dunstable to have a bath. However, now and again I was subjected to the ordeal by bath in the back kitchen. A long and narrow zinc bath tub brought in from the coal store was filled with water from the copper, which still had the fire alight from heating Monday's washing water. Actually, having a bath wasn't an entirely new experience for me. Aud and Doug had an old hip bath in the cottage which was in fairly frequent use and I'd sampled that during my stay there. Before that even, in London, I'd been once or twice to the Poplar Public Baths in the Roman Road, so I knew roughly what having a bath was all about.

When the water in the copper was hot Mrs Costin tipped it in bucketsful into the zinc bath, then some more buckets of cold water followed until a few inches of fairly hot water lay in the flat metallic bottom. It was considered unpatriotic to have deep baths, water and energy were not to be wasted on such frivolities, three inches was the officially approved depth.

I undressed, got in and went through the business of washing as quickly as possible, encouraged by several chance wanderers into the kitchen who leaned over the clothes horse draped with towels that Mrs Costin had placed alongside the bath. "Thank goodness for that," said Bob coming in just before Fred, "I didn't like to complain but . . ." and pinched his nostrils.

"Oh my God! exclaimed Fred, "it's 'orrible. Here use this scrubbing brush," and he tossed the brush from under the sink into the bath. "Shall I do it for you?"

"Here, come on, give the boy a bit of privacy," said Mrs Costin coming along the passageway.

"Just being sociable, aren't we Mick?" grinned Bob.

Afterwards all the water had to be emptied by hand and all in all it was such a laborious procedure that it was no wonder that it happened only rarely, for which I was profoundly thankful.

All my friends in the village had baths, if they had them at all, like I did. Bathrooms with panelled baths and flush lavatories were only for towns and not by any means for all their inhabitants either. It was only as the war was coming to an end that a bathroom and toilet were built at the farm, in a corner of our big bedroom. All white tiles, mirrors and gleaming chrome it was, and the chamber pots, the washstands, the ewers and buckets all passed away and were no more. Bob and I had moved out some time before, into the smaller bedroom next door which had been Daisy's, leaving Fred in sole occupation of the end bedroom where we had all three been for several years. By that time I'd got so used to the little shed along the garden path with its two-level seats over the big drop, that I actually missed it.

There was a spartan coldness about those bedrooms that is becoming harder to find in these centrally heated times. Is there any connection, one is inclined to wonder, between the widespread use of central heating and the obvious disintegration of the national character?

This spartan quality applied equally downstairs of course where the only heating even in the severest weather was the fire in the front kitchen. All the other downstairs rooms were like ice boxes, even the back kitchen, now sadly missing the old range's warmth. But we used to sit around the fire and feel very warm and comfortable, enjoying the liveliness of the crackling logs and the glowing coals and accepting the cold when we had to move. There was no form of heating upstairs at all, though Fred occasionally brought up the copper warming pan filled with hot coals and passed it between the sheets to take the icy chill off.

No one had hot water bottles though there was a stone one for visitors, and electric blankets were still some way off in the future. In all weathers the windows stood open and on a winter's night the temperature was distinctly low as we came up from sitting around the fire. We didn't hang about. Undressing was done at speed, pyjamas donned in a rush and a quick dive made into bed, which with cotton sheets was, for the first few minutes, like sliding between slabs of ice. I used to lie as still as the shivers would allow, all tense and rigid, until eventually a blessed pocket of warmth developed around me and I could relax in comfort, although stretching one's legs brought ice to the feet again.

There was very little sickness in my years at the farm. Mrs Costin never had a day in bed all the time I was there, nor did Mr Costin, though he was the vulnerable one and had the doctor several times for working as if he were a young man.

He had to take things easy for a day or two each time, sat about in his big chair and had recourse to the medicinal whisky but never stayed in bed. Fred and Bob too never had a day in bed for sickness. Accident was a far likelier cause of confinement to bed. When Fred was a boy, Mrs Costin told me, the elevator had collapsed on him severely injuring him about the face and knocking out all his teeth. Fortunately the scars healed and with dentures there were no visible signs of an accident that could easily have killed him.

Bob, off to play cricket one day in Leighton, had only just started out on his motor bike with his big cricket bag slung over his back. We'd seen him off and wished him good luck. At the fork in the road by Reg's house he smashed into a lorry coming the other way and was very badly injured. He was rushed off to the Luton and Dunstable hospital where he stayed for some weeks and made a complete recovery. That particular cloud, however, had a solid silver lining, for he fell for, and later married, the lady surgeon who treated his injuries.

Chapter XIV
Machines – old and new

By the end of harvest each year the home rickyard was crammed full of wheat, oat and barley ricks and usually one of peas and beans, about eight or nine in all, and all of which Arthur thatched so they could stand snug and dry throughout the winter. Down at Fosse's yard the two Dutch barns were full of wheat and a hayrick or two stood in the open; sometimes there was also a hayrick in a field due to shortage of space in the yards. These and thousands more like them were the farmers' answer to the nation's need for more and still more home grown food.

Mr Costin used to laugh ruefully and say how odd it was that the nation had to be practically on its knees before the Government gave much thought to farmers. "Now when the country's in a desperate way for food they look to us to get them out of the mess. They couldn't give a damn about us for more years than I care to remember. We could rot along with our crops for all they cared." That hard light in the narrowed eyes and the grim expression on the lined face, I'd seen in many farmers of his generation in and around the village. No wonder they had grown a tough shell, they'd come through tough times.

One day, usually during the winter, the threshing circus would hit the farm. It arrived in the evening having finished work at another farm earlier and was a sight guaranteed to bring out all the small boys. A great giant of a traction engine, all gleaming black and shining brass, steam hissing from its tall funnel, came lumbering majestically along the road on huge rear wheels that scarred the surface like battle tanks. The driver, a grimy, boiler suited figure standing high among clouds of steam, spun the wheel frantically to steer by means of heavy chains as the awesome giant rolled slowly along. Behind it was towed the red painted thresher, that large mysterious box of tricks that fed on sheaves and as by magic converted them to cascades of chaff, mountains of straw and flowing rivers of corn. A final little blue painted trailer completed this highway train that puffed and hissed and finally eased itself between the gateposts and into the yard and lined itself up alongside a rick ready for the morning's start.

Next day, whilst milking was being finished off and breakfast eaten, the driver of the traction engine would be lighting his fire, getting up steam and going thoroughly round all the equipment with his large oil can lubricating everything that moved, ready for the hard day ahead. The giant canvas belt from the engine to the thresher would be put in place along with other smaller belts on the thresher itself and soon the great machine was steaming gently away, flexing its muscles to indicate its waiting potency.

From then on it was a day of steady work, tiring but not frenetic, the yard a place of varied activity that kept the child watchers by the fence satisfied and soothed for hours on end. It was noisy not with the hum and hiss of the engine itself but with the clanking and bumping and banging of the innumerable working parts of the thresher as it devoured the steady stream of sheaves that was poured down its gullet. Two were needed on the rick, of whom I was often one, to keep a steady supply of sheaves to the man on top of the thresher who cut the bands and fed the corn into the monster's ever open mouth. The driver had no hand in all the work around him, the machinery was his sole concern and lovingly and expertly he attended it throughout the day, controlled it, kept it sweet, making it perform the tricks the farmers all depended on.

Who they were, the crew of this machine, and where they came from I never knew, for they didn't deign to notice boys and nobody else ever said. But I did notice their bikes slung on the back of the little blue painted trailer, so they must have had homes to go to each evening and didn't camp out with their machine in whatever rickyard their caravan had rested.

At the far end of the operation huge sacks of chaff filled steadily and were carried away on Bob's or Reg's shoulders to the chaff loft above the cowsheds. The wheat or oats more slowly filled their sacks and these as well when full and extremely weighty were taken away on shoulders across the yard, up the ladder and into the loft and stored in great bins for grinding up for cattle food or left in sacks for collection by merchants later. Finally the steady stream of straw was built up by Arthur into a new rick to balance the one descending at the start. When the straw rick rose above man height the elevator added its clanking to the general noise, and Polly the pony once more began her endless treadmill trek.

For us boys the crowning excitement was the rats. These had for several months been settled comfortably in the ricks eating their fill, having the unlimited run of their huge hotel, completely protected from cat and dog and human. We saw the holes they burrowed in the thatch but could do nothing to get at them. Threshing was the time of reckoning for rats. The shout would go up as they left the sinking rick, now only a few feet high, in a mass exodus as if at some pre-arranged signal. We grabbed a rick peg, Pat the dog dived furiously in and for a few minutes there were wild beatings and hollerings around the straw covered yard, kicking, stamping and much dashing about. Sometimes we killed a rat or two if we were lucky, some mice more likely, but most of them escaped to another rick or out into the orchard with its impenetrable stands of nettles along the fence.

At the end of the day the engine's giant flywheel slowed to a stop, steam hissed gently and the thresher ceased to rattle as quiet descended on the yard. Arthur humming gently combed off the new straw rick, others leaned about on pitchforks awhile and spoke softly, without strain, feeling the pleasure of a job accomplished. Just a few minutes, then ours moved off to other things, the circus upped its pegs, packed away its props and shuffled off along the road to keep its next appointment, followed by its retinue of admiring boys.

Rats were always present on the farm and always in good numbers, quietly taking their percentage of food in spite of all opposition. Occasionally in the yard in the quiet of a Saturday afternoon I came across one drinking at the cattle trough quite openly. My reaction then as now was instinctive hostility and I grabbed a stone and hurled it furiously but never accurately enough and the repulsive creature slipped contemptuously away and waited until I'd gone before continuing his drink. We had a cat, a good tabby someone gave me rather than have it drowned, and it did its best and was quite a good mouser but the size of some of those rats would make a cat think twice before attacking. They dwelt securely beneath the wooden floors and in the countless dark and inaccessible places that abounded in those old barns, and no one seemed to mind unduly — rats were accepted as part of farming's natural order.

Sometimes I took an air gun and hung about the barns and yard confident that I would make significant inroads into their population. But it was uncanny how, after one shot, I'd never see another rat so long as I stayed there with the gun. It was like the rooks who soon learned to recognise the difference between a man with and without a gun walking through the fields and would take off or remain accordingly. In the barns I often had the creepy feeling that I was being watched by countless pairs of wicked beady eyes whose owners were debating whether one quick concerted rush would settle matters their way.

One harvest time towards the end of the war a strange new machine made its appearance in the village for the first time, though seen in films before and vaguely known about as part of America's mid-western farming scene. Down in Tom Turvey's big field of wheat towards the station and right opposite Costin's fields we saw a combine harvester at work. As we were cutting with the binder and setting sheaves in shocks to cart with horses later, we could see the bright red monster with its long low sails whirring and doing with one man and in one smooth operation what we were toiling many days and even weeks to do. So we were working out the final page of one chapter of the farming story as our neighbour opened up another and ushered in a whole new era, one as revolutionary as anything so far seen upon the land. Machines and highly skilled mechanics would finally supplant the skills and strength of human hands that farms for generations had depended on. Arthur and his like, once they faded away, would never more be seen upon the land. He never drove a tractor, knew not a thing about machines, always milked by hand. Milking parlours, rotating and with music, farms where everything is run like clockwork or nowadays computerised and one man does the work of six, were all unknown to him.

Though the great threshing machines went on for a few years yet to call from farm to farm as they had done for the life time of even the oldest in the village, their time was fast running out. Soon those magnificent traction engines, like their cousins the steam rollers, would become mere museum piece attractions at rallies and agricultural shows, and the threshers themselves would gently rot away in forgotten corners of yards the length and breadth of the land.

Chapter XV

Looking Beyond

With the slow passing of the years we entered more fully into our teens and began painfully to discard those activities and ways of thinking and of being that had long been ours. The sloughing of those skins of our former selves and the emergence of the new, bright and glistening creatures that we were becoming was remorseless and inevitable.

Unspoken doubts and anxieties loomed large, mostly they were dreads and desires of the unknown world of sex we were drifting towards. No longer did we wish to scoop up handfuls of clay from the brook and work happily in water for hours at a time. Many a good tree with inviting hand holds and forks went unclimbed as we mooned disconsolately by. Now we scoffed at the idea of hours of tireless tracking on the Knolls, as when with unflagging muscles we had bounded like deer across the hills to fling ourselves at last upon the grass and in its coolness feel a oneness with the crawling insects, the pollen-seeking bees, the flowers that nodded level with our eyes and the butterflies and birds we knew as equals and as friends.

We began to look beyond our close, intimate and homely world for our distractions. Eric began to play cricket for Eaton Bray on Saturdays. He wore whites, bowled well on a level grassy pitch and was away out of our company for hours at a time. To my surprise I was invited to play for the village football team on the Recreation Ground and used to cycle there on Saturday afternoons, apprehensively at first because I was the only one from Lower End and would be among our former enemies from ancient battles on the Knolls. But they were friendly. We used to enjoy the game, laugh and joke together before I cycled home with my horizons expanded, the bounds of the unknown pushed farther back.

My ambition at the time was to be a professional footballer. It must be heaven I thought when play was your work and when you were paid for doing what you would cheerfully do for nothing. Playing for the village was a start.

I was also a regular member of the school team now, if only because numbers were so reduced that almost anything on two legs could get a place. My main source of inspiration for this footballing ambition was our visits to Luton Town. A group of us from Lower End would cycle in the six or so miles, put our bikes in the tiny back yard of an acquaintance near the ground and stroll along to see our favourites.

How we loved our team! And cheered them on always from the same spot behind the goal. Those were the times when Arsenal's immaculate Eddie Hapgood played as guest for Luton; he was in the Air Force stationed nearby. Bob Morton from Eaton Bray, rocklike Horace Gager and dashing forward Duggan, we loved them all and watched them many a time in games where, with big crowds and scarcely a policeman to be seen, there was never a suggestion of violence. Sending offs and cards of various hues were unknown and the language such as would scarcely bring a blush to a bishop's cheeks. Star players then were bought and sold for as much as £10,000 though most often four figures sufficed.

Once I came in on the back of Bob's motor bike and felt the thrill of speed and the wind snatching at my face for mile after mile. The exhilaration of the ride was matched by the quality of the game and maintained for the return journey to make it a memorable afternoon. It wasn't often that Bob went to watch Luton play, he was almost as good a soccer player as he was a cricketer and he played regularly for a good Dunstable club among a sprinkling of part time professionals.

It was about this time that we began to go on long bicycle rides. Mac and I were the cycling partners; Eric was far too sensible for such fanciful activities even if he hadn't been playing cricket. Together Mac and I visited undreamed of towns a world away from the village. Bob was aghast when I casually mentioned that we were going to cycle to Hitchin on Saturday. "Hitchin!" he echoed, "you'll never get there, it's fifteen miles away at least."

Heaven knows why we fixed on Hitchin, because it was there I suppose, but get to Hitchin we did. We fussed over our bikes beforehand like anxious nannies, pouring oil liberally onto everything that moved, cleaning unheard of amounts of dirt and grime away, lingering over saddle heights, carefully inflating tyres just so and generally carrying on as if it were the Tour de France we were embarking on. We visited Hitchin's Woolworths I remember, and found that threepence and sixpence bought exactly the same as in Dunstable, which we found supremely satisfying.

As travellers abroad recognise, it is very comforting in an alien land to come across an authentic piece of home. A London double decker bus in France draws Englishmen to visit it who never give a second glance to one in London. That's what Hitchin's Woolworths meant to us.

Mrs Costin breathed a sigh of relief when we came cycling down the yard in the evening having confounded our critics and exhausted ourselves in the process. It hadn't exactly been enjoyable. Nothing pleasurable had happened but at least we knew now that we could cope with conditions in foreign parts.

We'd had no great problems, we followed the signposts without difficulty, luckily they were no longer covered up or turned round to confuse the Germans. We managed not to get knocked down and felt that what we had done for Hitchin we could equally do for other towns maybe even further away.

A few weeks later when I dropped the name Watford as our target, shoulders were shrugged. "Watford! What's at Watford?"

Once again, nothing. Nothing that we discovered anyway. We found the football ground and had a rest on the sparsely peopled wooden terracing and watched the game. It was the getting there that was important, the conquering of the miles, the punishing effort, the defiance of our elders' wisdom and of course the seeking for something to do with ourselves now that former pleasures palled, some distraction for our troubled minds and uncontrollable bodies. A restlessness which demanded movement as its only consolation.

The cycling continued getting more and more outrageous. Northampton, Oxford, fell to our desperate pedals, all profitless, pointless conquests, and still the fever raged. What did we know or care about the priceless treasures of Oxford? We cycled down a street full of shops, people and traffic and that was another place ticked off on our list of conquests. We sat on our bikes by the kerb outside Woolworths and ate our sandwiches then started back straightaway in case we shouldn't arrive home by dark, for we had no lights.

One pleasant cycling occasion was when a group of us went down to St. Albans: Aud and Betty and Eric and Mac, we visited the ancient Abbey and the Roman remains of Verulamium, actually stopped and took a good deal of time to look at something interesting. It was a straightforward ride down the Watling Street from Dunstable, through Markyate and along the ancient Roman Road, and the traffic was light enough to make cycling pleasant. I remember my front tyre burst with a loud explosion in the centre of St. Albans, the casing was worn threadbare by so much heavy use and I was lucky the repair held till we got home.

I'd never seen anything Roman before and what really surprised me, I remember, among all the many beautiful ornaments, the coins, the glass and pottery and the skilfully made tools and weapons, was the cement. I'd somehow imagined only modern times used it, as witnessed by our huge chalk pit. The sight of neatly pointed Roman walls looking as if made only yesterday, impressed me no end. I wondered if our tribesmen on the Knolls had trouble from the Romans or perhaps caused them trouble. I couldn't see our hilltop bands standing much chance against all the formidable power implied by what we saw at Verulamium.

The final cycling excess was a proposed trip to the Lake District in our school holiday. I knew nothing about the Lake District except that Wordsworth had seen some daffodils there, our poetry lessons in the woodwork room had taught me that, and that it was mountainous, and it was the latter point that clinched the matter for me for I had never seen a hill higher than the Knoll's five hundred feet and felt a burning desire just to see and, even better, to climb a mountain.

I managed to persuade Mac into accompanying me; he had a tent, which was essential. Heaven knows what his mother thought, for she was a timid, anxious soul who worried about everything. We were about fifteen at the time, old enough to look after ourselves to a large extent, and should have been old enough to have more sense. I can only marvel at our blithe disregard of huge distances and enormous obstacles involved in the planning of the trip.

It was a hopeless, crazy scheme from the outset but to her credit Mrs Costin let me go ahead with it, though not without grave misgiving. We didn't plan to cook, we'd live pretty rough on odds and ends, drink water from the brooks and so on. We had a few pounds each for food and a map. For clothes we had just t'ose we stood up in with a spare pair of socks stuffed in our bag and we reckoned we'd be away anything between a week and a fortnight. What staggering self assurance we must have displayed! Oh, it was a long way, we knew that, but it was only a case of doing over and over a few times what we had often done before. We would get there all right, they'd soon see. "We'll send you a card," we promised.

We started out cheerfully in good sunny weather, and full of confidence cycled northwards all day on the Watling Street and finished up near Rugby, where we pitched our tent in a field corner a little way off the road. We were tired and, after eating the sandwiches we'd brought with us, we lay in the tent wrapped in a blanket on the hard unyielding ground. We were quieter now, the exultation of the adventurer strangely muted. Our morale had gradually ebbed away with each mile that took us farther from home.

I think it was then as twilight faded into night that the enormity of the task we had undertaken hit us with all the reality of an explosion. We were completely on our own, no hot meal or comfortable bed to return to as when we'd been to Hitchin. There was no one to turn to, not a friend in all this unknown land, just mile after mile of punishing roads into the unknown. And all this just to see some mountains! We suddenly perceived how thin was the ice we were skating on.

"It's no good," Mac burst out at last, "I'm going back."

There it was, he'd said it. He'd voiced the mounting doubts of both of us.

"We're not giving up already," I said, "we've only just started." The thing had to be argued out, though I knew well that we were both on the same side.

"You can go on," muttered Mac sullenly, "I'm going home."

"You've got the tent," I pointed out, "I can't go on by myself."

"You can borrow it," he countered.

"Couldn't carry it all," I said, "too heavy."

"All I know is I'm not going on," he declared stubbornly, "it's mad. It's too far and it's too risky. What if something happens to our bikes?"

So there it was, he'd thrown in first, for which I was relieved. I'd got my answer to the scoffers when we returned, tail between legs.

"Let's go tonight," Mac said eagerly, "we've got lights."

"No, not tonight," I protested anxiously, picturing me knocking on the farm door at midnight. That would be too shameful. "Look," I said, "we'll go first thing in the morning if you're still feeling like it. One night in the tent won't hurt us."

"All right," he agreed reluctantly.

The crisis passed, we fell asleep quickly as darkness descended on our lonely field corner.

I awoke soon after daybreak stiff and cold and went outside. It had been an uncomfortable night with frequent awakenings on the rock hard ground, it was a relief to stand up again. That was a thing we hadn't counted on, the hardness of the ground. Neither of us had ever camped before. There had been a heavy dew and the grass was silvery and sodden but it was a fine clear morning with only a carolling blackbird to break that living early morning silence. "Are we right to give up?" I wondered. I felt in the rosy flush of dawn that perhaps we could go on, that it would be intolerably feeble to give up so easily. But no, the impulse wasn't strong enough, the instinct of self preservation won over the call of adventure and I knew that I was only more cheerful because we were giving up.

When Mac woke up we didn't say much. I didn't need to ask him if he still wanted to go home, his silence was eloquent. We packed up, turned our bicycles back the way we had come and with a light heart headed for home, gaily abandoning the project that had pre-occupied us for weeks.

Mrs Costin seemed not at all surprised to see me back, I'm sure they all banked on our early return. We didn't get our legs pulled much about the fiasco, I suppose everyone was so relieved it had ended without disaster. The bubble had at last burst, the cycling fever was over. No more marathon journeys, no visiting distant Woolworths; still consumed with restlessness and discontent, we harboured them at home.

It was soon afterwards that Joyce came briefly into my life. She was a dark haired, brown eyed beauty with a dreamlike quality about her pale, alabaster features and she bowled me over from the moment I first saw her. Not since Rita's departure had there been anyone in the village to disturb our male society, with its derision for and its secret dread of girls. But now Joyce on a short holiday visit immediately concentrated all those vague, diffuse stirrings, the restlessness that filled our days and which, unrecognised and unacknowledged, filled us increasingly with unfamiliar miseries.

We met as darkness fell, Joyce and I, partly to avoid the inevitable teasing that would follow detection in daylight, but partly as a cloak to our own hesitancy and shyness. With Aud as an entirely acceptable chaperone we walked and talked smoothly and seriously in the dark, holding hands. Moments that were clear, unruffled pools in the muddier waters of day to day life.

I never got to know much about her, I wasn't interested in finding out. She was quite unlike the boisterous Rita. Joyce was a magical, mystical creature, existing only at dusk like some exotic moth and having for me no other being. An apparition, food for my fevered imagination, she didn't burden me with a mundane, routine life but came gliding on the shadows, to melt, after an enchanted assignation, into the night.

We finished up most often in the garage, Aud by the entrance, concealed from anyone who passed on the road or went into the house, and there for all eternity we stood close, our silhouettes touching. I could feel her warm breath on my cheek. Then I kissed her quickly and briefly and that was it, the consummation. She slipped away into the darkness and as the two of them went off I returned indoors to a quizzical glance in the bright light from Mrs Costin. With the wireless on I'd sit exulting, outwardly calm and with thoughts that paid little heed to news of battles which for once I didn't hear. I was busy thinking of tomorrow.

There were however, very few tomorrows, and none for us to brave the daylight in, before Joyce's brief stay was over. She went away and we never met again.

The war drew on. Daisy's husband Eric, a corporal at Dunkirk with the dispirited B.E.F. was now a captain, smart and confident in his splendid uniform. A nephew of Mrs Costin, raised in a Dunstable council house and joining the army as a private, had lately been promoted to lieutenant colonel, and George, prised from his dusty legal chambers, after briefly enduring the Pioneer Corps was discharged on medical grounds, still a private. The white starred vehicles were familiar on our roads, their smiling, gumchewing occupants besieged by clamouring children whenever they stopped. The war news was no longer a catalogue of disasters. The allies were back in Normandy and another army was pushing up through Italy. Hitler's European empire was crumbling. The tide had turned and there was no doubt now that we were going to win, the only question was, how soon?

The war had in fact lost its immediacy, that concentrating of the mind when the tiger was at our throats. Now for us at home it had lapsed into a subject of absorbing interest. We could afford the luxury of following its details with fascination and with calm appraisal, each of us his own master tactician. Not like those days in 1940 when the whole nation was united in grimly holding on, bearing with wholesale disaster, death and destruction.

Everywhere evacuees were returning home and our little community of children at Lower End was disintegrating fast and soon only the villagers would be left, and all the good and the bad times and the people that made them would, for the returned evacuees, be reduced to memories. Bombing raids were mostly one way now, we were dishing out instead of receiving. The tube stations were no longer crowded dormitories at night, although in fact the final terrors of the buzz bomb were just beginning and the V2 rockets were still to come. Families that had been separated for years could no longer be kept apart by terror from the skies and were rushing to be reunited. So it was convenient that my time at school was running out as the war was running out. After leaving my school desk for the last time there would be no reason for me staying on at the farm, I could return to London and find a job.

I didn't consciously try to picture life off the Mile End Road after years on the farm below the green chalk hills but I knew that I lived with a daily increasing inarticulate dread and a growing frustration that I was helpless to do anything about it. It was hardly surprising that in four years, four short years though they seemed, I should have put down tenacious roots. But if I had to keep a stiff upper lip when I first arrived unwillingly, it was no less so now that my unwilling departure was inevitable and imminent.

A few weeks before I left I was in the back kitchen cleaning a pair of shoes when Reg came in after milking to wash his hands at the sink. No one else was there. He was usually so full of talk that I waited for some remark. He was staring out of the window into the garden and there was an unaccustomed air of solemnity about him somehow; I wondered if something was wrong. Then he spoke, still looking unseeing into the garden. "I can't tell you Mick, how sorry I am you'll be going soon." He shook his hands dry and turned to me. I just looked down, a funny feeling around my eyes. "If it were up to me," he went on quietly, "I'd offer you a partnership, but as it is . . ." his voice trailed off as his words burned themselves into my brain. Fred came in noisily and the moment was over and Reg went. I stood there polishing mechanically at the shoes, excited and proud at what I had heard but knowing that it was hopeless yet wishing so much that it wasn't hopeless.

High summer it was as my time ran out. Harvest work was just beginning and I joined in as usual for my last few days, desperate to pretend that nothing had changed. Everything in the harvest field was as true to its nature as it had always been and always would be, the yellowness of the corn, the spaciousness of the field with the Knolls rising green and white behind, the smoothness of a pitchfork slipping through the hands, the good companionship of Reg and Bob.

On the last day they all said their goodbyes, then went off to the field saying that of course they would see me again soon, I would come to visit for a weekend as soon as I got settled in at home. Mrs Costin walked with me down to the bus stop, the same at which I had arrived four years before. We were very cheerful. The plums were taking on a purple tinge I noticed, they would be ripe in a few weeks. The bus came, we shook hands and she kissed me lightly on the cheek. I climbed aboard, stowed my case, found a seat and waved as we gathered speed and she waved back encouragingly. As we roared past the farm and up the hill I suddenly knew that it was over and yet that it would never be over, that from then on in spite of both time and distance, this place would always be home. But for now London lay ahead and I would have to cope with it.

THE END

Books Published by
THE BOOK CASTLE

JOURNEYS INTO BEDFORDSHIRE: Anthony Mackay
Foreword by The Marquess of Tavistock
A lavish book of over 150 evocative ink drawings.

. . .

LOCAL WALKS: SOUTH BEDFORDSHIRE and NORTH CHILTERNS:
Vaughan Basham
Twenty seven thematic circular walks.

. . .

JOHN BUNYAN: HIS LIFE and TIMES: Vivienne Evans
Foreword by the Bishop of Bedford
Bedfordshire's most famous son set in his seventeenth century context.

. . .

DUNSTABLE IN DETAIL: Nigel Benson
A hundred of the town's buildings and features, past and present, plus town-trail map.

. . .

ROYAL HOUGHTON: Pat Lovering
Illustrated history of Houghton Regis from earliest times to the present day.

. . .

OLD HOUGHTON, INCLUDING UPPER HOUGHTON, NOW PART OF DUNSTABLE: Pat Lovering
Over 170 photographs of Houghton Regis during the last 100 years.

. . .

A LASTING IMPRESSION: Michael Dundrow
An East End boy's wartime experiences as an evacuee on a Chilterns farm at Totternhoe.

. . .

ECHOES: TALES AND LEGENDS OF BEDFORDSHIRE AND HERTFORDSHIRE: Vic Lea
Thirty, compulsively retold historical incidents.

Further titles are in preparation.

All the above are available via any bookshop,
or from the publisher and bookseller
THE BOOK CASTLE,
12 Church Street, Dunstable, Bedfordshire LU5 4RU. Tel (0582) 605670